W9-CCH-467

ROBERT B. PARKER'S
DEBT TO PAY

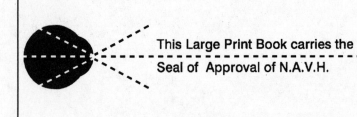

This Large Print Book carries the
Seal of Approval of N.A.V.H.

A JESSE STONE NOVEL

ROBERT B. PARKER'S DEBT TO PAY

REED FARREL COLEMAN

THORNDIKE PRESS
A part of Gale, Cengage Learning

GALE
CENGAGE Learning·

Farmington Hills, Mich • San Francisco • New York • Waterville, Maine
Meriden, Conn • Mason, Ohio • Chicago

GALE
CENGAGE Learning®

LIBRARY OF CONGRESS CATALOGING-IN-PUBLICATION DATA

Names: Coleman, Reed Farrel, 1956- author.
Title: Robert B. Parker's debt to pay : a Jesse Stone novel / Reed Farrel Coleman.
Other titles: Debt to pay
Description: Waterville, Maine : Thorndike Press Large Print, 2016. | Series: A Jesse Stone novel | Series: Thorndike press large print core
Identifiers: LCCN 2016029809 | ISBN 9781410492241 (hardback) | ISBN 1410492249 (hardcover)
Subjects: LCSH: Stone, Jesse (Fictitious character)—Fiction. | Police chiefs—Fiction. | Assassination—Fiction. | Mafia—Fiction. | Revenge—Fiction. | Large type books. | BISAC: FICTION / Mystery & Detective / General. | GSAFD: Mystery fiction. | Suspense fiction.
Classification: LCC PS3553.O47445 R634 2016b | DDC 813/.54—dc23
LC record available at https://lccn.loc.gov/2016029809

Published in 2016 by arrangement with G.P. Putnam's Sons, an imprint of Penguin Publishing Group, a division of Penguin Random House LLC

Printed in the United States of America
1 2 3 4 5 6 7 20 19 18 17 16

For Helen Brann

ONE

He didn't like exposing himself to video cameras when there were no crowds affording him his usual anonymity. His talent wasn't just for killing, but for blending in as well. He was like a khaki-colored pixel in a camouflage pattern. Stare at the pattern long enough and the individual pixels disappear. Today he meant to put the world on notice that he was back and the time had come to repay his creditors. He very much wanted to do both, and had waited more than a year for this opportunity. Still, he couldn't afford carelessness. He was seldom careless. He had taken precautions and the soaking rain was doing its part to cooperate. The gray was so heavy in the air that it seemed like its own weather condition separate from the rain and mist.

He parked the stolen Yaris out behind the building, because not even he could haul his intended cargo out the front door and hope to get very far. He went through his mental checklist, patted his pockets, and exited the car. He walked through the alleyway, turned right, and then right again. There were people on the street, many people, their heads down against the weather, too busy fussing with umbrellas to take notice of the little bearded man with the long gray hair and porkpie hat shuffling by them. Nor did they notice his large belly beneath the ill-fitting green mackintosh he'd bought at a church thrift shop outside Paradise. While he was unrecognizable, he made certain not to look directly into the security cameras as he entered the building.

He knocked at the office door, turned the handle, and let himself in. The young man sitting at the reception desk was really quite beautiful to look at. Dressed in an impeccably tailored designer suit of summerweight wool, he had fine features, long lashes, eyes that matched the deep blue of his suit fabric, and perfectly coiffed dark blond hair. The light stubble on his face was shaved and shaped in such a way as to enhance the power of his angular jawline. He had an ingratiating smile full of straight white teeth. He stood up from behind his desk outside Gino Fish's office to greet the odd-looking little man standing before him, water dripping off the hem of his coat and the brim of his silly hat. *Takes all sorts,* he thought, and Gino did do business with a lot of unsavory types. The little man took two steps toward the receptionist.

"How may I help —"

The beautiful young man never finished his sentence or took another breath. He had been so focused on the odd man's bad gray wig and fake beard that he hadn't seen the blade in the man's small hand. He'd felt it, though, if only very briefly, as the assassin thrust the knife forward. Using his legs like a boxer to supply the necessary power, the little man plunged the razor-sharp blade through the receptionist's tailored suit jacket, his shirt, his perfectly tanned skin, and his breastbone. The blade cut a fatal gash in the young man's heart. With incredible speed and surprising dexterity, the killer removed the blade and thrust it deeply into the receptionist's throat, making sure the mortally wounded man could not cry out. Careful to avoid getting bloody, the killer caught the body by the sleeve and eased it gently to the floor as if placing a sleeping baby in its cradle. There was blood, but not nearly as much as there would have been had the killer reversed the order of the wounds.

He knelt down beside the results of his handiwork, wiping the blade off on the wool suit before replacing the assault knife back in his pocket. He lingered, admiring the fine features and lovely blue eyes of his victim. He stroked the body's still warm cheeks with the back of his hand. Ran his fingers over his dark blond hair. Shook his head in regret. Just because he lived to destroy didn't mean he had no appreciation of beauty. On the contrary, he had an abiding appreciation for it, though he resented beauty far more deeply. To be human was to possess opposing feelings. In this instance, it wasn't so much that he minded having to kill the man, but more that circumstance dictated that he kill him quickly. How much more pleasure could he have derived from the experience had he been able to take his time? He took enormous delight in tearing beautiful things apart by the inch. *Quel dommage,* he thought. *What a pity.*

He stood; removed the beard, wig, and hat; and placed them all in a plastic bag, then tossed the bag in the trash. Law enforcement already had epithelial and hair samples from any number of his crime scenes. They had samples of his blood from the incidents with Stone's deputy and Joe

Breen, but it was of no consequence. They had no name, no face, no person to match them to, only a question mark and a despicable nickname. Sometimes he had to remind himself of his given name and to remember where he'd come from. But now was not the time to dwell on the past.

He removed the pillow from under his thrift-shop raincoat and, in a cruelly ironic gesture, placed the pillow beneath the murdered receptionist's head. Amused, he checked his watch and smiled. He was very good. Less than a minute had elapsed from the time he'd come into the office until he'd placed the pillow beneath the dead man's head. He retrieved his .22, stepped up to Gino Fish's office door, and knocked.

"Come on in, Drew," Gino said, his voice almost a purr.

The killer stepped into the office, closing the door behind him. The aging mobster's head was buried in the Friday edition of *The Globe.*

"We should be okay for our weekend on the Cape," Fish said, still not looking up. "Not supposed to rain again until late Sunday."

"Sorry to disappoint you, Mr. Fish," the killer said, gun hand raised. "I'm afraid Drew won't be accompanying you to the

Cape this weekend, but don't be sad. I have other more exciting plans for you for the weekend."

Although Gino Fish had never seen or spoken directly to the man standing before him, he knew immediately who he was.

"Mr. Peepers. Fuck!"

The killer was tempted to put a bullet in a very painful but nonlethal area of Fish's body, but he fought the impulse to do so.

"If you refer to me by that name again, Mr. Fish, I promise you your death will take even longer and be far more painful than you could possibly imagine."

The old mobster tried to remain calm, though his left hand was trembling. "Then what should I call you?"

He thought about it, smiled a smug, self-congratulatory smile. "Call me Mr. Mantis."

Gino didn't argue. "All right, Mr. Mantis. You killed the boy, huh? Did you have to do that?"

Mr. Mantis nodded. "A shame, I agree. Nice-looking man. My compliments on your taste."

"This about that thing with Stone that went south?"

"What else? I warned the people who contacted me for you that if anything went wrong, you would pay the price for interfering in my affairs."

"I don't suppose there's any bargaining room here?" Fish bowed his head at the gun in the killer's hand. "I can offer you a big sum of cash to put that thing down and walk out of here. I'll see to Drew."

Mr. Mantis shook his head, smiling all the while.

"And I don't figure telling you that Vinnie Morris won't let this stand will intimidate you?"

Mr. Mantis continued shaking his head and smiling.

"Yeah, I didn't think so."

The killer motioned with his .22 for Gino Fish to stand.

"Slowly, Mr. Fish. You and I are going to take a walk down the hall and out the back door of the building."

Gino Fish didn't move. He was well aware of Mr. Mantis's reputation for sadism. Fish had heard stories about how the man he knew as Mr. Peepers delighted in torturing his victims. He understood that if he left the office with this man, he would suffer a long and horrible death and that his body would probably never be found. For some reason that last part bothered him. Gino Fish was well past his prime, having grown too soft, too comfortable, and too careless, but he was no old fool. He hadn't made it to the top echelons of the Boston mob and stayed there as long as he had by blind luck. He always had a backup plan. Always.

Mr. Mantis motioned again for Gino to stand, only this time Fish did as instructed. But as he rose, he reached into the open top drawer of his desk, grabbing the old Colt snubnose .38 he'd kept there for many years, just in case. Just in case was now, though he knew better than to try to engage his captor in a shootout. Instead, in one swift motion, he pressed the revolver into the flesh beneath his chin and, without hesitation, pulled the trigger. He hung upright for what seemed a very long second, then collapsed into a lifeless pile of well-dressed skin and bones.

Mr. Mantis was impressed by the speed with which Fish had acted, but was furious at being robbed of his vengeance. He was also unnerved. Twice recently, he had let victims slip through his fingers, but he didn't have the luxury of time to dwell on it. He knew exactly what to do and how to do it. He removed the assault knife from his coat pocket and moved toward the lifeless body of Gino Fish. Afterward, he retrieved the plastic bag from the trash.

Less than five minutes later, the odd-looking little man with the long gray hair, ragged beard, and porkpie hat walked out the front door of the building and back into the rain.

TWO

After last year's spasm of blood, life in Paradise, Mass, had settled back into its predictable, small-town rhythms: steady as the tides, no waves cresting over the sea-walls. There hadn't been a single act of violence for months, the last one being a bar fight among four drunk musicians at the Gray Gull. Oh, there had been some snowfall, but nothing record-breaking, not even a hint of a nor'easter. The spring had passed as if following the script of old rhymes and adages. March had started out blustery and cold and ended on a week of sunny sixty-degree days. It had rained every two or three days in April, and by mid-May the gardens in town were so lush and colorful with early-spring blooms the place looked like . . . well, a paradise. What passed for a crime wave in Paradise these days was a spate of car vandalism. Somebody had lately taken to shooting out the rear tires of cars parked all over town.

"Anything?" Jesse asked Molly, coming through the station house door on Saturday morning.

"Nothing worth mentioning."

"Mention it anyway."

"No, really, Jesse, there's —"

"Crane, can't you ever make it easy?"

"Where's the fun in that?"

"Fun for who, exactly?"

"Whom," Molly corrected.

Jesse shook his head and laughed. "Are you sure it's 'whom'?"

"I'm not, but it's fun to think you're wrong. Did Diana come down from Boston last night in that rain?"

"Uh-huh. But don't change subjects. What's not worth mentioning?"

"Some water got into our basement and we had to turn on the pump."

"For crissakes, Molly, is that —"

"I told you it wasn't worth mentioning, didn't I?"

Jesse raised his hands above his head. "I surrender."

Molly frowned. "No fun in that, either."

"No new flat tires?"

"No."

Jesse turned and went into his office. He picked up his old baseball glove off the desk even before sitting down. He removed the hardball from the pocket of the glove where it resided, slid the glove over his left hand, and marveled that the glove was still in one piece after all this time. The glove had been his when he was a minor-league shortstop for the Dodgers, and he didn't like thinking about how many years ago that was. Nor did he like thinking about why it was sitting on his desk in Paradise instead of in a display case at Cooperstown. For the moment he wasn't worrying about his absence from the Hall of Fame, but rather about the big softball game tomorrow night against the fire department team.

He had other things on his mind, too. One, a fancy envelope inside the top drawer of his desk, and the recent rash of vandalism. For the moment, he was focused on the latter. Although Mayor Walker and her merry band of selectmen were all over him to do something about it, it was Jesse's experience that the perp was some stupid kid or a cranky old man with a grudge against the town or against Goodyear. He knew that this sort of thing would end soon enough, that the guy doing it would get bored or get sloppy and be caught. Of course there was always potential for things to turn bad. No good ever came of bullets

18

in a populated area. So as Jesse pounded the ball into his glove — it helped him concentrate — he considered ways of catching the shooter in the act.

He heard the phone ring and Molly answer it. A few seconds later, she was sticking her head through the doorway.

"It's Robbie Wilson. You want me to tell him you're not here?"

"No," he said, putting his glove and ball back down on his desk. "I'll take it."

Jesse generally didn't have much use for Wilson, the chief of the Paradise Fire Department, but he was happy for the distraction.

"Morning, Robbie."

"Morning, Chief Stone."

"So?"

"Fifty bucks on tomorrow's game?"

"Gambling's illegal, Robbie."

"Dinner, then?"

"Field might be too sloppy to play on," Jesse said.

"Don't you worry about that. My guys are over there now taking care of it. So, are we on? Dinner to the winner?"

"How can I turn down an offer from a man who can rhyme *dinner* and *winner*? We're on."

19

Jesse put down the phone and stared at the top drawer of his desk.

THREE

He sat very low in the front seat of the Yaris, not because he was worried he would be recognized, but because caution and invisibility were words he lived by. The stolen car . . . no problem. As was his style, he had removed the nondescript subcompact late at night, from the garage of an elderly person away on a long cruise. He laughed his gloating, superior laugh, thinking about the stupidity of the masses. At how key codes made them feel safe and secure. *How typical and how foolish.* All he ever needed to do was find his mark, sit on her house for a few days before her trip, and use a long lens to watch her punch in the garage code. He always chose elderly widows because they lived alone, put very low mileage on their cars, and kept their cars well maintained. If he didn't possess such a cautious nature, he believed he could simply trick most people into volunteering their key codes. *Morons!*

He knew he was in almost no danger of being recognized because there were only two men in all of Paradise and, quite possibly, the entire world, who might know his face. And those two were busy playing softball on the other side of town. He had made sure of that, as he had made sure that the mess he had left behind in Boston had yet to be discovered. That was what he did, he made sure of things, controlling as many factors in any given situation as he could. Until the unfortunate incidents in the wake of his crossing paths with Jesse Stone, his record of success had been impeccable. He had been able to kill with impunity, at will, and the way he most enjoyed it: slowly, torturously, and profitably. But the two men at the softball field had taught him a valuable lesson about the limits of control. For that lesson, the little man sitting low in the front seat of the stolen car felt he had a debt to pay. He meant to pay it on his own terms and in blood — their blood and that of their loved ones.

For now, he was playing a bit of cat-and-mouse with the Paradise PD by shooting out the tires of cars around town. Of course he could easily have killed the chief or that idiot deputy of his at a distance, but where was the sport in that? Where was the pleasure in killing anonymously? He wanted them to know, as Gino Fish had known, who was doing this to them and why. He shook his head, upset that Fish had robbed him of his enjoyment the way he had. He wanted to see them helpless and begging, powerless to stop him from grinding their loved ones into dust as they watched.

Although it was that moose Simpson who had shot him, he would take his greatest delight in paying his debt to Jesse Stone. Stone had lied to him and it was Stone who had toppled the first domino in his run of misfortune. If Stone hadn't stuck his nose in where it didn't belong, none of his other troubles would have followed. And Stone, like Fish, had called him Mr. Peepers, a name he detested beyond all reason. Only Stone had lived to tell the tale. Even now, long after his encounter with the chief, he felt fury welling inside him, his cheeks flushing with rage. Reaching up, he readjusted the rearview mirror to see his reflection. The ashen skin and unremarkable features of his face turned an ugly shade of red beneath his wire-rim glasses.

In spite of his rage, he had a measured respect for Stone. A host of agencies and organizations on both sides of the law had tried unsuccessfully to put an end to him. They might as well have tried to lasso a ghost or to capture shadows in a box. No one had ever seen him for who he was until it was too late. With Stone, it had been different. But some of the respect he had for the chief was diminishing by the day. He thought for sure that by now Stone would have figured out the admittedly subtle message he had been leaving for him in the rear driver's-side tires of used cars all over Paradise. He was about to leave another two hints.

The street was quiet. Not a single car had driven past his location in forty-five minutes and not a soul had strolled along Scrimshaw Street in twice that amount of time. Dusk was deepening, and there were dark, threatening clouds in the sky. He sat up as tall as he could in the driver's seat and reached over to the passenger seat. He lifted the edge of a plaid blanket and folded it over on itself. On the seat beneath the blanket sat a handsome .22 pistol, the one he had waved at Gino Fish. He laced his fingers around the custom wood grip of the Smith & Wesson Model 41 and thought what he always thought at moments like these: A great artist uses great tools. And this gun was a work of art itself. Then he felt a twinge of pain in his shoulder and the rage rose up in him again. There had been a time not too long ago he could have put a man's eye out from twice the distance he could now, but Luther Simpson had ruined that with a single lucky shot to his right shoulder.

Swiveling his head and using the car's mirrors, he took one last careful look at the street to make sure he wouldn't be spotted. It was safe. Turning in his seat, he raised his pistol and rested the bottom of the grip in the niche of his bent left arm atop the doorsill. He took aim and fired. The tire flattened in short order. He laid the pistol in his lap, started the car, and rolled farther up the street to repeat the process. With the last two hints left behind, he drove toward the turnpike. He made sure not to speed or do anything else that might bring undue attention to himself. If Stone didn't get the message by now, he would as soon as the bodies were discovered in Boston.

FOUR

Jesse Stone didn't strike out, not in softball, yet he was in danger of doing just that. He stepped out of the batter's box with a two-strike count against him. Resting the knob of the bat against his left thigh, he tugged at the left shoulder of his jersey, squeezed his shoulder blades together, stretched his neck, and closed his eyes. He took three deep breaths, trying to refocus his mind on the task at hand. Because Jesse had once been a phone call away from starting at shortstop for the L.A. Dodgers, he understood better than most that physical gifts were only part of the equation. Aside from talent, the other element separating highly skilled athletes from everyone else was the power of concentration.

Whether he was in the midst of a hostage crisis or standing in the middle of the infield during a Pacific Coast League champion-ship game, Jesse could shut out the rest of the world. Suit had once asked Jesse if the crowd noise ever bothered him during a big game. Jesse laughed. Not at Suit. At himself.

"You know, Suit," he'd said. "I never heard the crowd."

And as Jesse dug his back foot into the dirt of the batter's box, preparing to wait for the next pitch, he laughed at himself again. Many years and many miles separated Jesse from those big games. This was the Paradise slow-pitch beer league, and the crowd, if you could call it that, consisted of wives and kids and girlfriends and a few drunk guys whose games were already over. Still, try as he might to collect his thoughts, Jesse couldn't focus. He had his reasons.

One of them was the former FBI special agent sitting in the stands on the first-base side of the diamond. She was a stunning, sharp-witted blonde named Diana Evans. If Jesse had been given the power to create his perfect woman, he would have created Diana. They'd first met in New York City at the ill-fated reunion of Jesse's Triple-A baseball team. Although it had taken a long time for them to end up together, together they were . . . sort of. Diana wasn't the settling-down type, and even if she had been, small-town New England wasn't where she would have picked to do it. For the time being, she was working as a security consultant for a high-tech firm in Boston. She came up to Paradise most weekends and Jesse spent his free weeknights at her Cambridge apartment. The arrangement seemed to work for them both.

Then there was Jesse's drinking — or, rather, his lack of it. He had stopped for long periods in his life before now, but as Dix had said, those other times were like Jesse holding his breath. Sooner or later he was going to breathe again. *Not this time,* he thought. *Not this time.* He stopped drinking for himself and not to prove a point to someone else. Maybe because he had attached the notion of forever to his farewell to Johnnie Walker Black Label, stopping hadn't been as easy as during his earlier periods of sobriety. There were days his lack of alcohol really screwed with his usual calm demeanor. His patience was more easily worn thin and he snapped at Suit and Molly on occasion.

But Jesse had no illusions as to why he couldn't focus today. It was the fancy, embossed wedding invitation sitting on his desk back at the Paradise PD. Molly had whistled at the sight of it and told him that the gilding on the invitation was the real deal, twenty-four-karat gold leaf. The invitation was irksome enough by itself, but it was the RSVP card and the answer he would have to put on it that haunted his thoughts. That and the conversation he would need to have with Jenn about it.

"Play ball!" the ump said, jarring Jesse out of his trance. "Come on, Chief, sometime before midnight."

Jesse got back in the batter's box, gripped the bat, and took a few practice swings. Robbie Wilson, the squat fire chief and pitcher for the Paradise Pumpers, stared in at the catcher and went into his windup. Jesse locked eyes on the release point of Wilson's pitch, followed its high arc, waiting for the ball to come to him. He repeated to himself the mantra of every batting coach he'd ever had. *Let the pitch come to you. Let the pitch come to you.* Yet somewhere between the zenith of the pitch and its fall toward home plate, Jesse got lost in his own head again. Whether it was muscle memory or pure instinct, he swung the bat without actually seeing the ball.

Instead of the usual crisp ping of metal alloy making flush contact with the ball, there was a rubbery dull thud. And when Jesse snapped back into the moment, he was pumping his arms, running hard as he could toward first base. He caught sight of the ball centered between the pitcher's mound, the foul line, and first. The ball was spinning sideways like a cue ball, the way it does when hit off the very end of the bat. Robbie Wilson bent down to field it and, tripping over his own feet, collided with his first baseman. The first baseman swiped at the ball as he fell, knocking it away from both men and into foul territory. Jesse reached first safely and Suit Simpson scored from third.

Jesse hadn't struck out. The winning run had crossed home on what had been very generously scored an infield hit and RBI for the chief. Yet even as the team swarmed around him, slapping his back, hugging him, shaking his hand, the reality of what had happened wasn't lost on him. No, he hadn't struck out, but he'd come pretty damn close. And when he looked up into the stands for Diana, he noticed a roiling line of lead-gray clouds stretching across the horizon. The meaning of those clouds wasn't lost on him, either.

FIVE

Jesse skipped the customary postgame team trip to the Gull. Part of it was that he didn't want to be in a crowd of drinkers. He had never been a celebratory kind of drinker, anyway. For Jesse, imbibing was kind of like a boxer's roadwork: something to do every day whether he felt like it or not. It was part of him. Ritual. In this instance, Jesse's decision was less about the drinking than his recent distraction. That little squib he hit toward the pitcher's mound was bothering the hell out of him.

Jesse was a quietly confident man by nature, not a vain one. Though, like everyone else, he had his small vanities, and baseball was one. Playing ball, no matter that it was in a slow-pitch softball league, kept him connected to his glory days. Even at his age, he was by far the best player around. Reality had long ago forced him to accept that the shoulder injury he had suffered in Pueblo had finished his dreams of a major-league career, but his love of the game and the what-ifs stayed with him. Secretly he worried that whatever skills he still possessed might finally be fading. Now, pulling his old Explorer up to the station house, Jesse thought that fading skills might have been easier to deal with if he was still on friendly terms with Johnnie Walker. He didn't share that thought with Diana, sitting there right next to him.

"I'll be back in a few minutes," he said.

Molly was at the front desk. When she saw Jesse, she gave him a puzzled look.

"What are you doing here?"

Jesse pointed at his office door. "See, Crane, it says the words *Chief's Office* on the glass? Every now and then I like to pretend that means something."

She made a face. "But I heard you guys beat the fire department." She pumped her fist. "I bet Robbie Wilson is somewhere drowning his sorrows right about now."

In every city and town, large or small, there was a natural rivalry between the police department and the fire department. Usually it's as friendly a rivalry as that between lions and hyenas. And it was even less friendly in Paradise. Molly, in particular, despised Robbie Wilson.

Molly smiled. "And I heard you drove in the winning run. Sweet."

Those words stung Jesse more than Molly could know. "Uh-huh." He changed the subject. "Anything going on?"

He expected no for an answer. As to the general lack of crime, Jesse chalked that up to good fortune and an uptick in the economy. Manpower was also a factor. After several months on patrol, Molly was back in her old spot, working the desk. Suit had fully recovered from his gunshot wounds and had taken Molly's place on patrol. Gabe Weathers had finally returned after his long, painful rehab. And, most surprising of all, the town had let him take on a new officer.

"Yeah," Molly said. "We had some more vandalism along Scrimshaw."

"Tires again?"

Molly nodded. "Two cars parked a block apart."

"Anyone see anything?"

"Nothing."

"Who's over there?"

"Alisha."

"The new kid," Jesse said. "What do you think of her?"

"Hey, if you think I'm going to bad-mouth another female officer —"

He cut her off. "Come on, Molly."

33

"She's very good, Jesse. I hate to say it, but you've got the knack for spotting people cut out for this work."

"Thanks. Okay, I'm heading home. I'll be in early. Who's on the desk in the morning?"

"Alisha. I'm doing what you said, scheduling her so she learns the whole job."

He nodded his approval, then turned with a wave good night. As he headed out to the Explorer, he didn't like the feeling in his gut. Something about the vandalism was bothering him, something like the sight of those clouds at the softball field. Just as he reached his SUV, the sky opened up.

Six

Full control of her body still eluded Diana Evans, not that she was so anxious to have it back. The intensity and frequency of these tremors and aftershocks were one of the perks of loving Jesse Stone. She had always enjoyed sex. But it had been this way with Jesse ever since that first drunken encounter in New York. Now that she was with him, she had trouble believing she had been willing to risk losing him. For the moment, though, she was content to feel his strong arms around her, to feel his body pressed to her back, and to listen to the crackle of far-off thunder. Rain pelted the windows as her muscles began to finally relax. She watched the wind make the tree shadows dance against the bedroom walls.

When she felt Jesse stir, she said, "Could you get me a drink?"

"Sure."

He rolled out of bed and headed downstairs to the bar. There was no protest about how he wasn't drinking anymore. No complaints about how her drinking made it harder on him. That was one of the other things she loved about Jesse, his oneness. Molly called it his self-containment. But whatever you called it, Diana realized that some women would have been put off or intimidated by it. Not her. She wasn't looking for a man to complete her. She'd been looking for a complete man and she'd found him. And Jesse seemed as content with her as she was with him, seemed to love in her the same things she loved in him. Yet as she lay there in the dark, the room full of the raw scent of sex, of their sweat and her crushed herbs and cut-grass perfume, she worried about losing him. Losing him not to another woman, but to the memory of another woman. She wasn't afraid about competing with a real woman, but it's impossible to compete with a memory.

When Jesse walked back through the bedroom doorway, the ice rattling around in the glass, she sat up in bed. She shook out her hair, gathered it in her hand, and tossed it over one shoulder. He handed her the scotch.

"Don't lick your fingers," she said, a smile in her voice.

"No worries."

Diana took a sip, sighed. "Jesse . . . I . . ." Her voice faded into the noise of the rain.

She had tried to have this conversation with him a couple of times since the invitation had arrived a few weeks back, but whenever she tried to put words to her fears, she felt a fool. She had tried waiting Jesse out, hoping he would bring it up to her. That wasn't going to happen. If there was a negative to Jesse's oneness, it was his silence. He was a man who kept his cards close to his vest, a man who liked to work things out for himself. Still, Diana was a trained investigator and, in her own way, as competent as Jesse. She couldn't help but notice that Jesse had been different since he'd gotten the invitation to Jenn's wedding.

She'd never been married, so she could only imagine what Jesse was going through. It wasn't like Diana hadn't gotten offers. She'd been tempted by some of them. She'd been in love before, just not like this. At the Bureau she had struggled so hard to get ahead, to be noticed for something other than her looks. In the end she had thrown it all away, but not unhappily.

"Come on, Evans," Jesse said. "You want to say something. Say it."

"Jenn."

"Uh-huh."

"Uh-huh! What's that even mean?"

"Okay," he said. "What about Jenn?"

"Don't play dumb with me, Chief Stone. Ever since you got the invitation, you've been different."

He didn't answer right away because he didn't want to sound defensive and because she was right. He'd spoken to Diana about Jenn, but superficially. He never enjoyed being around people who went on about their exes. He certainly tried not to do it. And in spite of all the hard work he'd done with Dix on his relationship with Jenn, he was also unsure of how to explain the tangled, dysfunctional two-step they had done for so many years. He still wasn't completely sure he understood it himself.

"It's complicated."

She laughed. "No kidding. But you're going to have to do better than that."

"Not tonight," he said, cupping his hand behind her head and pulling her mouth to his.

But she pushed back. "The scotch," she said. "Don't."

He knew she was right. She guzzled her drink.

"Listen, Jesse, I'm going to use the facilities and brush my teeth. We don't have to talk about Jenn tonight, but you do have to talk to her and answer the invitation for my sake, if not for yours."

"How's that?"

"There's only room for two in my bed, Jesse: me and you. No room for memories and ghosts."

She put the empty glass on the nightstand and stepped out of bed.

SEVEN

Suit used the key Elena had given him. Elena, he thought, laughing to himself that he still sometimes caught himself thinking of her as Miss Wheatley. Miss Wheatley was pretty much all the eighteen-year-old senior and football star Luther Simpson could think about. She was certainly who he dreamed about. As an adult, he'd always had a weakness for older women — sometimes married, sometimes not. Stepping into the vestibule, he couldn't help but wonder if his high school crush on Elena had started him along that path. Not that there had been a huge age difference between them. She was a twenty-one-year-old student teacher in Suit's English class when they met.

Suit remembered the first day he saw her. She was pretty in a way he had never experienced before, her hair so black it almost shone purple in the sunlight spilling into the classroom through the high arched wood-framed windows at the old high school. She was what his mom used to call petite. He never knew exactly what that word meant until he'd laid eyes on her. Before that day, he'd thought it just meant small, but she wasn't just small. She was so delicate and her features were so fine that for the first time in his life he felt embarrassed by his hulking size. He didn't understand his embarrassment then, and he wasn't sure he did now. What he did understand was that he had fallen deeply, stupidly in love with her and that he was never going to be able to express the way he felt or have his feelings returned.

"Luther?" Elena asked, calling down again from the second floor of the house she'd inherited from her mom. "Did you guys win?"

"I scored the winning run."

She came downstairs dressed in a faded black tee and white satiny panties, the cranky old steps barely complaining under her weight. Although there were gray threads in Elena's hair now, they didn't register for Suit. Every time he saw her it was that first day all over again. Standing on the bottom step, she leaned over the rail and kissed him.

"I was kind of hoping you'd come straight from the bar and we'd shower together."

He smiled at her and at his good fortune. One night, three months earlier, Suit had been driving by the house on patrol and noticed the front door open. The house was dark, but he saw the telltale beam of a flashlight cutting through the living room. When he got out to investigate he found Elena Wheatley, sitting on the sofa, in tears. When Suit saw who it was, he couldn't believe it.

"Miss Wheatley?" he said, feeling like the lovesick high school senior he had been all those years ago.

"Luther Simpson! Is that really you?"

"Why is your front door open?"

"The electricity went out and it got really hot in here."

Ten minutes later, after Suit had found the electrical box and flipped the circuit breakers, they were seated at the kitchen table, sharing coffee. Elena was explaining how her mom had died a few months back and that she'd come home to sort through her mom's things.

"Then there's the house," she said. "It's mine, but I don't know what to do with it."

That was when Suit uttered the words he couldn't quite believe he had it in him to say. "There's at least one person in Paradise who wishes you would stay."

"Two," she said. "I find that now that I'm here, Boston seems like a lonely and faraway place."

Maybe it was that only several months before he had been close to death, or that he was tired of the life he had carved out for himself. Whatever it was, something made Suit say what had been in his heart to say for two decades.

"I was in love with you, Miss Wheatley."

"Elena. Call me Elena, Luther."

"Elena." He repeated her name, his face turning red with the realization of what he'd just confessed. "Call me Suit. Everybody does these days."

"Everybody but me," she said. "I'm hurt, you know?"

"I knew I shouldn't have said what I said about —"

"No, no, Luther, please, don't be embarrassed," she said, placing her right hand on his cheek. "It's just that you said you were in love with me. I have a confession to make to you. I used to wait for you to come into class. I used to look forward to seeing you. Whenever you were sick or you cut class, I missed you. I couldn't have said anything to you then, but now we're both adults."

43

He took her tiny hand off his cheek and kissed her palm. When he stood, he kissed her on the mouth. He remembered very little else of what happened during the remainder of his shift. What he did remember was that he had never been happier.

EIGHT

Diana was dead asleep. Jesse had showered, shaved, and crept quietly downstairs. He was dressed in a pair of raggedy athletic shorts and an old LAPD T-shirt so worn and faded that it was in danger of disintegrating into a memory at any second. The den was mostly dark and he spent a fair amount of time — more than he should have — staring at the bar. He poured himself a club soda, got a lime wedge out of the fridge, and squeezed it into the glass.

He walked back into the den, raised his glass to the poster of Ozzie Smith, and drank. Twisted up his lips. He liked soda and lime well enough, just not as much as good scotch or second-rate scotch or wine or beer.

"So, Wiz, what do you think about my swinging bunt today?" Jesse asked the man in the poster.

Suspended in time and captured by the

photographer in midair as he leapt to make a play, Ozzie kept his answer to himself.

"When did you know it was over, Oz? When did you know you were losing it?"

Same answer.

Resigned to Ozzie's silence, Jesse shook his head and said, "At least you're consistent."

He checked the time. *Ten-thirty-five. Nine-thirty-five in Dallas.* Jenn would probably still be up. Pacing, cell phone clutched in his hand, he knew Diana was right. He had to talk to Jenn before he answered her wedding invitation. He wanted to get some sense of her. Did she actually want him there? Was she playing with him? It wouldn't be the first time. Was this a last desperate attempt to get him to reconcile? Truth be told, he wasn't sure he wanted to know any of these answers. Although he had moved on and was in love, far more in love with Diana than he had ever really been with Jenn, there was a gnawing stubborn part of him that didn't want to let go. And what that piece of Jesse was shouting at him was "Jenn is mine. She always was and always will be."

He guessed he dreaded the notion that Jenn's little voice wasn't shouting the same thing to her about Jesse as Jesse's voice was screaming to him about her. He didn't know why it was so important to him, but it was. And if there was one thing in this world Jesse Stone wasn't, it was a liar. Did he tell lies? In the name of right or justice, definitely, but never to fool himself.

Good thing there was another voice in Jesse's head: Dix's voice. And though it spoke to him more calmly, it was equally insistent. "Therapy changes you, but the old you never disappears. You still carry all that old baggage — the bad patterns and self-destructive attachments — with you until the day you die. The difference is you keep it separate. You know it's there as a reminder of what not to do. How not to react."

He dialed the 214 number. It was answered on the second ring.

"Hell, if it isn't Jesse Stone. Not the way I thought we'd meet," a man said. He had a booming friendly voice. Then, "Hold on a second. Hey, Jenn, hon, it's Jesse on the phone. Gimme a second, then come and get it. Hey, Jesse, Hale Hunsicker here."

"Nice to meet you, Hale," Jesse said, trying to match the friendliness in his counterpart's voice. He was doomed to fail, because boisterousness and glad-handing weren't in his DNA.

"I hope you're gonna grace us all with your presence at the wedding, Jesse. It'll break Jenn's heart if you're not there. I don't mind telling you, your opinion still means an awful lot to our girl."

Our girl! This was getting strange and uncomfortable. This wasn't a phrase he had expected to hear when he called.

"That's exactly what I wanted to talk to Jenn about, Hale."

"Good man. Good man. Well, here she is. Like I said, nice meeting you. Come down a few days early and we'll do some shooting and riding together. You be well."

"Jesse . . . Jesse," Jenn said, her voice several decibels lower than Hale's and much more tentative. It sounded like maybe she had dreaded receiving this call as much as Jesse dreaded having to make it. "Is everything all right? It's an hour later there."

"Fine, and yes, it's around ten-forty."

"Are you sure you're all —"

"Hale sounds like a good man," he said, cutting her off.

Jesse had learned not to fall into the well of Jenn's neurosis and manipulations. He wasn't in the mood for her drama because, if he let the pattern play out, her drama would somehow become his, too. They needed to talk about the wedding, but that was it. Although in reality Dix rarely gave Jesse an "attaboy," he pictured his therapist standing in the corner, applauding.

"Jenn, I'm not coming. I'm sorry. I needed to tell you and not just mail you the RSVP."

Before the words came out of his mouth, he wasn't sure what his answer would be. But as soon as he heard the neediness in Jenn's voice, all sorts of alarms went off in his head. No, he had to move on once and for all. If he had any real hope with Diana, he had to leave Jenn in his rearview and then break the mirror. But if Jenn were the type to give up easily and let go, they wouldn't be having this conversation.

"Why not? Is it Hale? You don't have to worry about him. He's like you, Jesse. He's his own man. He's not intimidated by our past."

"It's not Hale, Jenn. He sounds like a good guy."

"He's a wonderful man. I want you to meet him."

"I will someday."

"Why not at the wedding?" she said.

"Because your ex-husband doesn't belong at your second wedding, and things in Paradise . . . well, you know how things come up."

"It's her, isn't it? It's Diana. She doesn't

want you to come."

That wasn't it at all. In fact, Jesse had hoped Diana would make this easy for him by saying just that, by expressing her desire for him not to go. But Diana treated Jesse as he deserved to be treated, as a man to be trusted, a man who knew his own mind, a man to make his own decisions.

Jenn didn't let him answer. "Bring her along, Jesse. It was stupid of me not to have invited you with a guest. That was just me being me. Please don't hold that against me, not now. Not when I'm on the verge of being happy for the first time in a long time."

There it was, Jenn trying to make Jesse responsible for her happiness. If he'd had any doubts at all about not going, he didn't have them any longer.

"Sorry, Jenn. I can't. And just so you know, my decision has nothing to do with Diana."

"Then who?"

"Me and you, Jenn. Same as always. I wish you all the best. Hale does really seem like a good guy."

Then he was off the phone. He was feeling a lot of things, but not the one thing he wanted to feel: relief. He looked up at Ozzie Smith and said, "Yeah, Oz, I know. What did I expect?"

NINE

The rain hadn't let up since it had begun, and it was causing a fair bit of flooding in low-lying sections of Paradise. For the first time in weeks there was some buzz at headquarters about something other than flat tires. Of course there wasn't much the police could do about floods except reroute traffic away from dangerous areas, but that didn't stop people from calling 911. The phone was ringing so often that Jesse was forced to help Alisha handle the calls. It was good experience for her, a way for her to listen to how Jesse dealt with folks panicked by rising waters or angry that their sewers hadn't been cleaned since the fall.

When the phones stopped, Jesse turned to look at his new hire to see how she was holding up. He was pleased to see she didn't look the worse for wear. The stress of dealing with people during heightened states of emotion could be withering for even the most experienced cops. It could be fatal to a rookie's career. Jesse had seen it in L.A., rookies melting down under the pressure of the moment. Some losing their cool, blowing up at citizens. Others reduced to tears. While others still just walked away. Takes a special kind of person to be a cop. It's not about the gun and the badge. What it is about is hard to define, hard to quantify, but whatever it is, Alisha seemed to have plenty of it.

"You hear that, Jesse?" she asked. She had taken to heart his admonition against calling him Chief.

"Hear what?"

"Rain stopped. Phones stopped ringing."

"Funny how that works. They'll start ringing again soon."

She asked, "You want some coffee?"

"No. Thanks."

He watched her as she made her way to the new coffeemaker. It was one of those one-cup-at-a-time machines with individual plastic containers. Jesse liked the coffee, but not much else about the machine. It wasn't that he missed day-old coffee grown thick and black at the bottom of the pot. No sane human being missed that. It was that he remembered a thousand conversations he'd had over the years, here and in L.A., beginning with complaints about bad coffee. Alisha Davis would never have that experience. He wondered if she would be better for it. There was a lot to like about technology, but Jesse saw the other side of it, too. Technology eroded shared experience, and that wasn't good for his cops.

He'd taken a big risk by hiring Alisha ahead of other candidates, men and women alike. Most of them with law-enforcement backgrounds. Then there was the fact that Alisha was African American. There wasn't much overt racism in Paradise, at least not since Jesse had cleared Hasty Hathaway and his militia types out of town soon after he took the job as chief. But Alisha's hiring had caused a stir. He had seen the looks she got when they went out on patrol together. Two selectmen had approached Jesse when he submitted her for the town's approval. They'd tied themselves up in knots as they'd tried to talk around what they really meant.

"Weren't there safer hires?"

"Weren't there more experienced candidates?"

"Isn't she too young?"

"Won't her youth be a problem with . . . you know, some of our . . . You understand."

Jesse understood, all right. Some codes were more easily broken than others. Good thing the mayor, a woman, had his back on Alisha or there might have been some real trouble. In the end, it didn't hurt that Alisha was attractive. Black or white, man or woman, good looks were an asset. It was unfair, but Jesse had stopped tilting at that windmill a long time ago. What was right and what was just, he'd fight for those, but unfairness was someone else's battle.

Just as Alisha got back to the front desk with her coffee, the phones started up again. They both took calls.

"Yes, Mrs. Hammond, the power company knows about it," Jesse said, his voice calm and reassuring. "I alerted them early this morning. They have a crew already working on it. The cable company, too."

Almost before he put the phone back in its cradle, it rang again, but Alisha grabbed Jesse's arm before he could pick up.

"I'll take that one, Jesse. I'm on with Captain Healy from the state police and he says it's urgent. I'll put him on hold and you can take it inside."

Jesse patted the rookie on her shoulder and headed into his office. He sat down at his desk and grabbed the phone.

"What's up, Healy?"

"Something come across my desk a half-hour ago I think you'll be interested in."

"Uh-huh."

"Gino Fish is dead," Healy said matter-of-factly. "I had no use for the man, myself, but I know you two were friends."

Jesse ignored that last part. "How?"

"Bullet through his brain."

"Mob hit?"

"My first thought, too," Healy said. "So I called my liaison over there at the Boston PD. Their working theory is murder-suicide. Looks like it happened Friday afternoon. His pretty-boy receptionist's dead also. Twenty-three-year-old white male named Drew Kaiser. Looks like Fish stabbed Kaiser twice, once through the heart and once almost clean through his neck. Fish posed the body postmortem, laid Kaiser's head on a pillow and crossed his hands on top of his chest. After that he went into his office and blew his brains out with a .38 he kept in his drawer."

"Gunshot definitely self-inflicted?" Jesse asked, disbelieving.

"No doubt about it. Anyways, I just thought you'd like to know."

"Thanks, Healy."

Jesse hung up the phone, but before he could gather his thoughts, Alisha appeared at his door.

"What's up?"

"There's a man on the line for you. He says his name is Vinnie Morris and that you'll want to speak to him."

Vinnie Morris had never been more right about anything in his life.

TEN

Vinnie Morris and Jesse Stone shared the kind of grudging mutual respect hardened combatants had for each other. Their relationship, if that's what you could call it, went back to Jesse's first months on the job. Vinnie had been Gino Fish's right hand back then. And a very dangerous right hand he had been, too. He had remained by Fish's side for many years, but had recently split off to run his own crew out of a bowling alley off the Concord Turnpike. Through the years, Jesse, Gino, and Vinnie had occasionally found common causes, working together toward a mutually beneficial end. Jesse would get his man. Gino and Vinnie might gain territory or profit financially. Cops have to be pragmatists because you don't get intel about bad guys from the church choirmaster.

Now they sat next to each other at Dennis's Place, a bar in Southie where Vinnie was a silent partner. The place was as local as local could get and no one in the neighborhood called it by its name. When they set up the meeting, Jesse had wondered why they were going to meet at a bar and not at the bowling alley. Vinnie said he had his reasons, and Jesse understood that Vinnie wasn't the type of man to explain himself beyond that.

The front door of the bar was temporarily closed and Morris's men made sure they weren't disturbed. At any other time it might have seemed unusual that neither man was drinking anything stronger than club soda, but the circumstances surrounding Gino Fish's death made the meeting unique. Jesse and Vinnie didn't look directly at each other, staring instead at the big mirror behind the bar. As Vinnie had requested, Jesse was dressed like a civilian: jeans, running shoes, blue golf shirt, a Dodgers cap in place of his usual PPD cap. Vinnie was dressed casually, which, for him, meant a beige Armani suit of some featherweight material, a white silk T-shirt, and canvas-topped shoes.

Each studied the other's expression. Vinnie had the unreadable blank face of a dangerous man. It kept people off guard because you never knew what he was thinking. Yet with a simple curl or drop of one corner of his mouth, he could say more than most men giving an annual report. He sat in his familiar pose: arms folded across his chest, heels of his shoes hooked on the bottom rung of the barstool.

He spoke first. "I don't like it."

"In general?"

"Gino meant a lot to me. Taught me everything. I had the skills, but all the skills in the world aren't worth a thing if you don't know how or when to use them."

"Uh-huh."

"I know you're not a talker, Stone, but give me something more than 'uh-huh.' "

"You've never been much for talking yourself, Vinnie. First you've got to tell me what you don't like."

"How about the Boston PD, for starters?"

Jesse laughed a quiet laugh. "That narrows things down." But Jesse sensed what Vinnie was talking about. "They were rough on Fish's memory, huh?"

"When they had me in this afternoon to ask if I knew what was going on with Gino, they were calling him queer and faggot and a hundred other things. It was all I could do not to pop one of them guys. Gino was what he was and who he was. No need to disrespect him in death. Cowards. None of those cops would have dared insult him to his face when he was alive. He made it pretty far up the ladder and he stayed there for a long time. Longer than most."

"I get that," Jesse said. "What else?"

"The whole murder-suicide thing. I don't buy it."

"Listen, Vinnie, after you called me, I spoke to a guy I know at the BPD. There's no doubt Gino killed himself. It wasn't a setup."

All Vinnie Morris did was shake his head. *Denial.* Jesse knew all about denial. Alcoholics are expert at it. So are the friends and family of murderers and suicide victims.

Vinnie turned to one of his guys and wiggled his finger. "Give me the pictures."

A big man came over to his boss and handed him a beige folder. Vinnie opened the folder and spread crime scene photos out on the bar. They were pretty gruesome, especially since the bodies hadn't been discovered for a few days. But both Vinnie and Jesse had seen their share of violence and bloodshed. Both had seen bodies in all states of disrepair. Even so, Jesse could tell it was difficult for Vinnie to stare at the bloody photos of his old boss. Jesse opened his mouth to ask about how Morris had come to possess these photos and then thought better of it. Men like Vinnie also had sources inside the police department.

"Look here, Stone," Vinnie said, pointing to the red spatter on the wall high above Fish's desk. "He killed himself standing up. I don't like it. And why kill this kid? He was new. Wasn't there a week. You knew Gino. He liked young, pretty men. Since you know him, how many different receptionists you seen outside his old and new offices? Five? Ten?"

"Probably closer to ten."

"Gino never got too attached to these guys. It was a vanity thing for him. I was by there last week and Gino confided in me that as good-looking as this guy was, he might have to fire him. The guy couldn't even alphabetize."

"One of the first things I learned as a homicide detective was that you can only think you know someone else, but you really can't know someone deep down. We tell ourselves otherwise, because how else could we live in a world with other people? The second thing I learned was that people lie even when they don't have to, and they lie to people they don't have to lie to."

Vinnie Morris kept shaking his head.

"Look, Vinnie, Gino was getting older. He already lost you. My source inside the BPD tells me Gino's position in the hierarchy was slipping. Maybe he fell in love with this guy. Or maybe he just lost it."

"Gino did violence when he had to, but not for himself and not for a long time. He wasn't a knife man. And look at that pillow under the kid's head. It's all filthy. Gino would never have anything like that in his home or office. Where did it come from? Out of thin air? I'm telling you, Stone, there's something all wrong about this. Something else is going on here."

Now it was Jesse shaking his head. "You're grabbing at straws. Listen to yourself, Vinnie. You're talking about dirty pillows, but there's no doubt Gino killed himself and his prints are all over the knife. The cops tell me the dead man's blood is all over Gino's hand. I'm sorry. I liked Gino in spite of my better judgment and he always kept his word to me."

"How about you keeping your word to him?"

"How's that?" Jesse asked, his voice and expression hardening.

"Gino told me you owed him a big favor. That you agreed if he stuck his neck out for you with that Mr. Peepers thing a while back, you would do anything he asked. Anything."

"That's right, Vinnie. I did."

"Well, now I'm asking for him. I'm collecting his favor. You look into this. You owe him that much, no?"

Jesse thought about it and then offered his right hand to Morris. "Okay, but if I don't find what you're hoping for, that's it."

Vinnie Morris took Jesse's hand. "Deal."

ELEVEN

Diana was surprised to find Jesse waiting in his Explorer downstairs from her apartment. She rapped her knuckles against his car window to get his attention.

"Spying on me, Stone?" she said, unable to keep a straight face. "If you are, I can see that surveillance isn't your strong suit."

"Business in town. Thought I'd surprise you."

"Mission accomplished. Come on up."

When Jesse got out of his old SUV, Diana threaded her arms around him, holding him tight to her. The gun on her hip beneath her blazer dug into Jesse's side. He didn't seem to care. When he was with her, he was happy in a way he couldn't put into words. He'd once told Diana that she freed him from his own head. And that was as close as he'd come to explaining her effect on him. He'd since given up trying. Jenn always had the opposite effect on him. Her insecurities were contagious and had a way of focusing Jesse's attention on the things that had gone wrong between them and in his own life even before they'd met.

"Business?" she asked, pushing back from him to find her keys.

"Gino Fish."

"What about him?"

"Murdered his receptionist and then put one through his brain."

Diana, who knew a little something about the workings of the Boston mob from her FBI days and who had heard Jesse's stories of Gino and Vinnie, made a face. "Doesn't sound like the kind of thing a man like Gino Fish would do."

"That's what Vinnie Morris said."

He could tell she was going to keep the conversation going, so he held his palm up to stop her. "Let's continue this upstairs."

"When we get upstairs, I won't feel like talking anymore."

He smiled. "I was hoping you'd say that."

Ninety minutes later, Jesse was sitting at the kitchen table while Diana worked on a spinach, pancetta, and cheddar omelet.

"Okay, Jesse, to continue that discussion we were having downstairs . . ."

He played dumb. "What discussion was that?"

"Gino Fish. You said Vinnie Morris doesn't believe Gino would commit suicide."

"He doesn't buy either part of it: the murder or the suicide."

"What about you?" she asked.

He didn't answer right away. While he believed everything he said to Vinnie Morris about how one person can never really know another person and about how the Boston PD was sure they had the scenario right, Jesse also had his doubts. It wasn't as if he hadn't known Gino Fish for many years. He agreed with Vinnie that this wasn't the type of scenario he would have ever envisioned Gino being a part of. It was too operatic for a man like Fish. But Jesse believed just as strongly that a good cop followed the evidence.

"The evidence, *all* the evidence, points to murder-suicide. The receptionist was stabbed through the heart and posed in an affectionate manner afterward. And there's no doubt Gino killed himself."

She put a dish up to the edge of the pan, slid half the omelet onto the plate, and then, with a flick of her wrist, flopped the other half atop the omelet already on the plate. It formed a perfect half-moon, wilted spinach leaves and orange cheese oozing out the sides. The steam rising off the omelet smelled of the crisp, savory Italian bacon. Diana cut the omelet in two and used a spatula to place Jesse's portion on another plate beside a small mixed green salad. Diana was a woman possessed of many skills. Chief among them was her keen power of observation.

"I didn't ask you what the evidence pointed to," she said, sitting down across from Jesse. "I asked you what you thought."

"I have my doubts."

"Are you going to leave it, Jesse?"

He ignored the question and took a mouthful of the omelet. "This is great. Is there anything you can't do?"

"The cha-cha. I'm hopeless at it. Oh, and I can't forget an unanswered question."

He smiled. She did that to him a lot.

"No, I'm not going to leave it. I owed Gino a last favor and Vinnie called in the marker."

She screwed up her face. "But you owed the favor to Gino, not Vinnie."

"Not the way these guys operate. My debt didn't die with Gino. Truth is, I would have looked into it whether Vinnie called in the marker or not."

She dropped it, and he was happy to let her. They ate the rest of their omelet and salads in silence. When they were done, Jesse cleaned up.

"I called Jenn," he said, scraping off the dishes into the garbage. "I told her I wasn't coming."

"And . . ."

"And nothing. I wished her luck and success and said it would be odd for both of us if I was there. Then I got off the phone. Even spoke to her fiancé, Hale. Sounded like a nice man."

Diana stood up, came around the table, kissed Jesse's neck, and threw her arms around him.

TWELVE

Jesse got up early and drove straight from Diana's apartment to the Paradise police station. Molly was at the desk and gave Jesse the once-over.

"Rough night, Jesse?" she said, unsmiling.

Rough nights didn't mean what they used to for him now that he had given up drinking for good. Molly was skeptical, and with good reason. She had gone through dry periods with Jesse before and, in the end, he'd always dive back into the bottle. Jesse wasn't a man to care much about people judging him, but Molly's opinion mattered. It mattered a lot. He also wasn't a man to embarrass easily, but there had been a few times over the years since his arrival in Paradise that he'd embarrassed himself with his drinking. And on those occasions, Molly had saved his ass. She'd covered for him, making excuses and deflecting attention away from him.

"I was in Boston."

Molly smiled at that. "Diana's good for you."

"That settles it, then."

"You're a funny man, Jesse."

"Anything going on?"

"Not really," she said, a bit of hesitation in her voice. "Power's been restored all over town. Cable is back up. No one was injured during the flooding, and none of the damage is serious."

The hesitation in her voice did not go unnoticed, but Jesse was in desperate need of some coffee.

"Okay."

He turned to go to the coffee machine.

Molly called after him. "How did Alisha do at the desk yesterday?"

"Better watch it, Crane. The rookie handled it like a pro."

"I'm not worried." She smiled, but it didn't last. "I read about Gino Fish. What do you think?"

Jesse wasn't in the mood for this discussion again. "I think I need coffee."

When he got inside his office, he called Healy and asked him to stop by if he had time. Healy agreed, saying he'd be by in an hour and that he had something to run by Jesse anyway. Jesse got a few swallows of

70

coffee down before Molly stuck her head in his office.

"You got a minute, Jesse?"

"If I didn't, would it stop you?"

She laughed. "No."

He waved for her to come in and sit. She sat across from Jesse but seemed out of sorts. She was rubbing her palms together and squirming in her chair. Molly rarely seemed uncomfortable in her own skin, which is why her obvious distress surprised Jesse.

"What's wrong? Is everything all right at home with —"

"Jenn called me last night."

"My ex?"

"No, Jennifer Aniston!" she said, the sarcasm thick in her voice. "Of course your ex."

"Since when are you two close?"

"Since never. We had our issues with each other, but we were never enemies or anything."

"Then what was the call about?" he asked.

"Don't be dense, Jesse."

"The wedding."

"She's hurt that you're not going."

"I know that, but what are you supposed to do, talk me into going?"

Molly said, "That's about the size of it."

71

He shook his head. "She doesn't get it."

"Get what?"

"That it's just this sort of thing that drove us apart in the first place."

"I thought it was that she was cheating on you with a smarmy movie producer."

"There was that, too. Thanks for reminding me, Crane."

They both laughed at that.

He asked, "Would you want your ex at your wedding?"

"I think it's weird, but I'm not surprised. Jenn always wants your approval or forgiveness."

"Uh-huh. So what did you say to her?"

"I told her what she already knew. That once you make up your mind, no one is going to change it for you."

"But she pleaded for you to. She said something like 'Jesse listens to you.' Right?"

"Verbatim."

"Consider yourself off the hook. You tried. I didn't listen. Go back to work."

But Molly didn't move. "Are you going to call her?"

He shook his head. "I already called her and explained. And no, I'm not going to call her again."

Molly stood, sighed in relief, and left the office. Jesse held his anger until she was gone. Then he picked up his old baseball glove and began pounding the ball into its pocket. Pounding the ball into the glove was a kind of physical mantra for him. It helped him focus his thoughts. What he was trying to figure out was whether he was angrier at Jenn for trying to manipulate him or at himself for still caring. As far as he was concerned, her wedding couldn't happen soon enough.

THIRTEEN

There was something different about Healy. Jesse noticed it the second the state police's chief homicide investigator walked into his office. The obvious thing was that the captain was dressed in a way that Jesse had never seen the man dress before. Healy had always been old-school. More often than not he was done up in the same brown suit, a white shirt, often a less-than-fashionable tie, and ugly cop shoes. Yet the man who stood before him looked like a senior tour golfer straight from a fitting with his clothing sponsor.

"Wife burn your clothes or did you rob a Golfsmith?" Jesse asked.

"It's my day off. I get those every now and then. Going straight from here to my lesson."

That comment set off all kinds of alarms in Jesse's head. He asked, "You putting in your papers?"

Healy made a face. "That obvious, huh?"

"A lifer like you starts taking golf lessons and dressing like Tiger Woods, usually means only one thing."

"I was always more of a Phil Mickelson guy myself."

"Your retirement. Is that what you wanted to run by me?"

"You first, Jesse. You called me, remember?"

"Okay." Jesse nodded. "Gino Fish."

"That again." Healy grunted. "I knew it. You're not going to let it be."

"Can't."

"Bullshit. With all due respect to the recently deceased Mr. Fish, I don't see anyone holding a gun to your head."

"I really can't let it be. Vinnie Morris is calling in a marker on me."

Healy raised his eyebrows and gave Jesse a harsh look. "How did a mobbed-up shark like Vinnie Morris come to hold a marker on you?"

"He inherited the marker from Gino Fish," Jesse said.

"Same question, only substitute Fish for Morris." Healy sat down across from Jesse where Molly had sat an hour earlier. "And if I'm going to have to listen to this, can I get a drink?"

Jesse shook his head. "Sorry."

"Drying out for a while?"

"Forever."

Healy considered saying something and thought better of it. Besides, that wasn't what he wanted to hear about.

"We've been friends a long time now, Stone. I'd like to think I know the man you are, but —"

Jesse held up his palm as if stopping traffic. "Remember that whole mess when Suit got shot?"

Healy nodded. "Mr. Peepers."

"Exactly. To get a line on Peepers, I made a deal with Gino Fish. If he could put me in touch with Peepers, I would owe him a favor, no questions asked."

Healy shook his head in disbelief. "How could you do that with a man like Fish? Who knows what he would've asked you to do?"

"A woman I once loved was facing a slow, painful death at Peepers's hand and Fish was the only person I knew who could put me in a room with Peepers. My blank check to Gino was the only chip I had to bargain with. I'd do it again to save her life."

"Then I guess it's a good thing we'll never find out what he would've asked for," Healy said. "You sure you don't have a bottle hiding out in here somewhere?"

"Hundred percent sure."

"So why'd you want to see me?"

"I need everything there is to see on the Fish case. Everything," Jesse repeated.

"That the marker Morris is calling in?"

"Uh-huh. I've got some contacts at the BPD, but not like yours."

"Okay, I'll see what I can do."

"Now what's this about you putting in your papers?"

"It's time, Jesse," Healy said, strain in his voice.

"Why is it time?"

"The wife," Healy said, his voice cracking. "She's sick and I owe it to her and to me."

Now Jesse understood Healy's needing a drink.

"How sick?"

"Her heart. Could need major surgery. Maybe not. Anyway, it's time."

Jesse didn't push for more details. He didn't have to. Healy looked at his watch and stood to go.

"The driving range and my instructor await. I'll get you everything I can from Boston PD," Healy said. "They owe me about a million favors. Shouldn't be any trouble."

Jesse shook Healy's hand and held on to

it a beat or two longer than normal. That said more than Jesse could have expressed in words. Healy nodded and turned quickly away.

FOURTEEN

Everyone needs some luck, even assassins.
It wasn't luck that had helped him turn the
mess of Gino Fish's unexpected bullet to
the brain into a neat package of murder-
suicide. That was skill, experience, and a
chameleon's ability to adapt to its surround-
ings. He was rather proud of himself for
how he'd handled that, in spite of the
bother, particularly the little touch of pos-
ing the receptionist's body. How sweet. He
laughed to himself, though Fish's suicide
was yet another reminder of the limits of
control. He would have to keep that in mind
when the time came to pay his debt to
Stone. If a wretched old crook like Gino
Fish could surprise him, there was no
predicting what a capable adversary like
Stone could do.

With that in mind, he had reconsidered
his approach, hoping the chief would miss
the bread crumbs he had left behind in

Paradise. He would let Stone know he was coming when he was good and ready. And it was to that end he was now in Salem at two-thirty a.m., returning the Yaris to the garage from which he'd taken it. The stolen car, that's where luck had entered into it. On his way out of Boston he'd heard a news story about a cruise ship whose crew and passengers had been overcome by one of those fast-spreading viruses. The ship had been ordered back to port. The woman who owned the Yaris was on that ship. And if Peepers's calculations were correct, the owner of the Yaris would be home later that morning. No doubt she would report her car stolen shortly thereafter. With his change in strategy, the last thing he needed was a report on the police wire that might remind Jesse Stone of their previous encounter. Better a report of a murder, he thought, than of a widow's stolen car in a nearby town.

He wasn't a superstitious man by nature — no spilled salt over his little sloped shoulders — but when he heard the panting of a dog and human footsteps on the pavement behind him, he wished he hadn't had that thought about murder. If he hadn't already hit the close-door button on the garage keypad, he was certain he could have just stood in the shadows and the dog walker would have passed on by. But lately, nothing was easy. No matter. As the rubber gasket at the bottom of the door kissed the concrete garage slab, he carefully screwed his sound suppressor onto the barrel of his .22. He stood in the shadows, waiting for the inevitable.

"Connie, is that you?" An elderly woman's voice cut through the early-morning air. "I thought you were —"

"No, ma'am," Peepers said, stepping out of the shadows, one arm behind his back. "I'm Connie's nephew, Paul. Aunt Connie gave me permission to use her car while she was on her cruise. I was just returning it."

"You a nephew on her late husband's side of the family?"

"Hers."

The old woman was about twenty feet in front of him. She was a small target, thin and hunched, with a tangle of steel-colored hair on her head. And even at this distance he caught wind of her sickly-sweet old-lady perfume. The stuff made him gag. Why did they wear that stuff? Why at this hour? The dog was one of those yappy, shaggy, nervous little things that paced around the old lady's feet.

"Odd hour to be returning a car," the

woman said, a skeptical look on her wizened face.

"Odd hour to be walking your dog."

"Don't get old, son. I can't sleep worth a damn anymore." She nodded at the dog circling her feet. "And he likes the walk."

He hoped this would be the end of their conversation and that she would move on. His cab would be here any minute and he couldn't afford their conversation attracting any attention from the neighbors.

"Okay, then, son. Be safe. Come on, Rags," she said to the dog, tugging his leash.

He breathed a sigh of relief. As the old woman moved on, his cab turned onto the street. Then the old lady stopped in her tracks. She turned back toward him.

"Wait a second," she said. "Connie was an only child. How —"

The headlights at his back helped illuminate his targets. He raised the .22. It flashed four times in an instant, coughing wisps of acrid smoke. The old lady went down without much of a sound and the dog barely had any distance to fall. When the cab pulled to a stop behind him, he spun and shot directly through the windshield. Fortunately, the driver did not slump forward against the horn, but fell against the door.

He did not believe in God. How could he? He had killed more people than he cared to count, most in far more painful ways than he had just used to dispatch the old woman, the cabdriver, and the dog. He had listened to men and women alike plead and bargain with a deaf God, a God who abandoned them as he tortured them, killing them inch by excruciating inch. Only once had he been thwarted, and that time it wasn't God who had interceded. No, that time it was Jesse Stone. Still, Peepers was tempted to shake his fist at the sky and curse. Instead, he drove out of Salem in the cab as quickly as he dared.

FIFTEEN

Jesse had barely settled into his desk chair after lunch when Healy came into his office. This time he was dressed in his familiar brown suit and not done up like a country-club gigolo. Not only was the captain's attire back to normal, but so too was his cop face. Jesse was glad to see this version of his old friend and colleague. He hadn't dwelled on Healy's news about retirement, though seeing him again today in his usual getup made Jesse realize just how much he would miss having Healy around. In spite of the gap in their ages, they had a lot in common. Healy, like Jesse, had been a minor-league baseball player: a pitcher in the Phillies system. Both men were good detectives blessed with the skills for finding killers. Both had a powerful sense of right and wrong. And, until very recently, both were more than fond of blended whiskey. With that in mind, Jesse had made sure to make a special purchase on his way home from work the night before.

"Two days in a row," Jesse said. "But I can see by that look on your face that this is business."

Healy plopped a file onto Stone's desk. "That's the preliminary report on Gino Fish. I don't think you're going to like what it has to say."

"You could have faxed it to me or mailed it."

Healy shook his head. "Since I had to go over to Salem, I figured it was just as easy to drop it off."

"Salem? What happened in Salem?"

"Double homicide. Locals wanted some help."

"You look like you could use a drink. Something else going on?"

"The wife," Healy said, burying his face in his hands. "It's not great news. They're going to try meds first."

Jesse pulled a bottle of Tullamore Dew, Healy's favorite Irish whiskey, out of his bottom drawer and put it up on his desk. He placed a single red plastic cup by its side.

He said, "You look like you could use a drink."

"Even if I didn't, I'd have a drink of that. But I thought you said —"

"I can't have you putting in your papers and remembering me badly."

He poured a finger of the light amber liquid into the cup and handed it to the captain. Healy held the rim of the cup up to his nose and breathed in.

"Are you sure you don't want to join me, Jesse?"

"I'm sure I won't. I'm not sure I don't want to."

"*Sláinte.* To your health."

Jesse raised his empty hand and said, "To your wife."

"To the old gal."

Healy raised the cup and sipped. When he lowered the cup, he stared into it as if into an abyss. A tear formed in the corner of his right eye, which he wiped immediately away. He put the cup back down on the desk and Jesse refilled it, putting the bottle back in his drawer afterward. He waited for Healy to regain his composure and said, "So tell me about Salem."

Healy looked up. "A woman came home early this morning from a cruise. You know, the cruise that's been all over the papers. The ship where everyone on board got one of them viruses and had to come back to port."

"Paradise doesn't have a newspaper anymore. Remember?"

"Boston does, and there are these new things called TVs, radios, and computers, you know? Even your damn phone will read you the news."

"I've been a little preoccupied lately." He considered explaining about Jenn's wedding, but decided not to.

"Anyway, this woman returns home and sacks out for an hour or two. Wakes up and realizes she doesn't have anything to eat in the house because the cruise was supposed to last for six weeks. When she goes to the detached garage for her car, she notices drag marks in her gravel driveway. She opens the garage door and finds the bodies of an elderly neighbor woman, her dog, and an African American man in his forties she has never seen before. All three with two bullets in them. Turns out the black guy is a cabdriver for a local company who was called to the address at around two-fifteen in the morning."

"Cab gone?"

Healy nodded.

Jesse asked, "Robbery gone wrong?"

"Don't think so. Nothing missing. No forced entry."

"Professional hit?"

Healy shook his head. "We're talking an

eighty-two-year-old woman and her shih tzu, Rags."

"The cabdriver, then?"

"No way the killer could have known who'd be picking him up. And it's Salem, Mass, for crissakes! If the killer wanted to rob a cabbie to make some money, he should've gone to Boston. None of it makes any kind of sense. Especially the murder weapon. Looks like a .22. And this guy could shoot. The old lady got one to the head, one in the pump. Driver got two in the head. Forensics guy thinks one of the shots was through the windshield. Glass fragments on the body." Healy made a pistol of his right thumb and forefinger and shot it. "The second bullet through the back of the head. Contact wound. Guy even got the dog in the noggin. Like I said, it makes no sense."

"Sometimes things don't."

Healy stood. "Good point. You might want to remember that when you read through Fish's case file. Now I got to get back to the office."

"How was the golf lesson?"

"Instructor says I'm a natural."

"You think he's said that to a new student once or twice before?"

Healy laughed. "Maybe once or twice."

When Healy left, Jesse flipped open the file on Gino Fish's murder-suicide, but he couldn't concentrate. The murders in Salem were gnawing at him, only he couldn't put his finger on why.

Sixteen

Jesse made a face, and not a happy one, as he drove past the *For Sale* sign at the edge of his property. For the most part he had enjoyed living on the outskirts of town. The quiet, the water views, the woods were all good for his head, but the isolation was getting to him. Even a man like him, a man apart, can have too much of a good thing. And he supposed that he was partially motivated by his relationship with Diana. There was no way she would ever be happy living out in the woods, listening to the grass grow and having cicadas sing her lullabies, though he doubted there was any place in Paradise that could hold her attention. Good thing he could. The plan was for him to begin shopping for a condo when someone put a serious bid on his house. As yet it had been slow going. There had been a few nibbles, but mostly lowball bids to see if he would bite.

This part of the day had become his toughest hurdle in his effort to give up alcohol for good. The part of the day he used to look forward to more than any other. When he'd get home from work and fix himself a tall Johnnie Walker Black Label with soda, stir it with his index finger, and lick his finger like a kid with Mom's chocolate cake batter. Then he'd sit in his recliner and discuss his day with Ozzie Smith. It was easier on the weekends with Diana in town to focus on, to come home to. The lack of action on the house sale didn't make this part of the day any easier. Still, he went through the ritual, using club soda and lime. Only today he plopped down in his recliner and opened the file Healy had given him from the Boston PD. He'd already gone over it once at the station. He hoped a second look, away from work, might help him find something new.

But Healy had been right; Jesse wasn't happy with what was in the file, not earlier and not now. So far everything confirmed the original theory in the case. Although the DNA results weren't back yet and wouldn't be for several weeks, the initial blood-type results showed only two contributors, both consistent with each victim's blood type. The only fingerprints on the knife belonged to Gino Fish. The blood on the knife was consistent with the receptionist's blood type. The autopsy showed that the knife wounds matched the knife found on the scene. The fingerprints on the .38 belonged to Gino Fish and no less a source than Vinnie Morris had confirmed that Gino kept the .38 in his top drawer.

He called Tamara Elkin, the local ME. They'd become close friends over the last year or so, though Tamara never made it a secret that she would have preferred the bounds of their friendship extend into the bedroom. But Jesse had held fast to his devotion to Diana even when she was still down in D.C., putting her life back in order and ending her career at the Bureau.

"Hey, cowboy," she said when she heard Jesse's voice. Tamara had spent years in Texas and liked to tease Jesse that he was the embodiment of the cowboy myth. "To what do I owe the pleasure of your call?"

"A favor."

"Do I get to call in a favor in return?" she asked, her voice suddenly deeper and raspy.

"Depends on the favor."

"I've seen Diana," she said, her voice back to normal. "I've got no shot. I wish I didn't like her so much. Makes it hard to be as jealous as I want to be."

"Don't sell yourself short, Doc."

She ignored that. "So what's the favor?"

"I need you to go over a file for me, including an autopsy report and crime scene photos."

"Sure. Just bring it by whenever. What is it I'm looking for, exactly?"

"Inconsistencies."

"That all?" she asked, skeptical.

"I don't want to prejudice you. See what you see and we'll talk."

"Okay. So, Jesse . . . how's the not drinking coming along?"

He could hear the ice in her drink rattling around in the background. Their mutual love of Johnnie Walker Black was one of the things that had helped cement their friendship. Sometimes when she asked him questions about his drinking, he could swear she was rooting against his success. He guessed he understood her point of view.

"Some days are rougher than others," he said.

"Like tonight?"

"Uh-huh."

"Okay, Jesse, I'll see you when you drop the file by."

"Tomorrow."

"Until tomorrow," she said, and then clicked off.

He closed the file, got up off the recliner, and ambled into the kitchen to whip up some eggs for dinner. His cell phone buzzed in his pocket. When he fished it out and looked at the screen, he saw that the call was from a strange number with a 214 area code. Dallas. He recalled what he had said a few minutes before to Tamara Elkin. Some nights truly were rougher than others.

Seventeen

The mystery was short-lived. He didn't have to be a police chief or an ex–homicide detective to work out who was on the other end of the line. It wasn't Jenn. Jenn had retained her old cell number with the Boston area code. He stared at the screen for a long moment, thinking about letting it go to voice mail. He weighed the value in postponing the inevitable. Though he didn't know much about Hale Hunsicker beyond his home state, his college football career, wealth, and taste in women, Jesse got the sense that Hunsicker wasn't the type of man to surrender easily. And phone tag was one of Jesse's least favorite games.

"Hale," Jesse said, picking up.

"Jesse."

In just the way he said his name, Jesse could tell this wasn't the same version of Hale Hunsicker he'd gotten the other night. The other night he'd gotten the happy, friendly, good-ole-boy version. He supposed part of that was performance for Jenn's sake.

"What's up, Hale?"

"From everything Jenn tells me about you, I figure you to know exactly what's up."

This was definitely a different Hale Hunsicker on the phone. No "our girl" references, no offers to go shooting and riding out at the ranch. But Jesse didn't necessarily hold Hunsicker's more businesslike tone against him. Jesse had been in this man's shoes and had many more years' experience of dealing with Jenn's whims and quirks. He could very easily imagine the fallout this man had been forced to endure after Jesse had told Jenn he wasn't coming to the wedding.

"She's upset I'm not coming to the wedding."

"Jenn always says you are an understated kind of man. *Upset* doesn't begin to do it justice."

Jesse laughed in spite of himself. And when he heard Jesse laugh, Hale Hunsicker laughed, too. Jesse liked that. He liked it a lot. It told him that Hunsicker knew Jenn for who she was and loved her just the same. For some reason that mattered to Jesse. He wanted Jenn to be happy just so long as the equation didn't include him.

"Look, Jesse, I've got nothing against you, but I thought it was strange that she invited you to the wedding. She said it was important to her, so I went along with it. I'm not threatened by you being there. I know you two have a connection that will always be there, but I also know it's not what it was. So if that's why you're not —"

"It isn't, Hale. You sound like a man who wouldn't be easily threatened by me or much else."

"Kind of you to say."

"I'm not blowing smoke. I wish you both the best. I really do. You sound like a good man and I want Jenn to be happy. You *do* make her happy?" Jesse said with a slight edge to his voice.

Hunsicker laughed. "Yeah, Jesse, I believe I do make her very happy. And as neurotic as she can sometimes be, she makes me happier than I've ever been. It's not just her looks, either. Believe me, down here in Dallas beautiful blondes of all ages are plentiful. There's just something about Jenn. But you know her. She craves approval. Yours most of all."

"I approve."

"Are you sure there's nothing I can do or say to get you to change your mind and to come to the wedding?" Hunsicker asked, his tone sincere. "You can skip all the pre-ceremony stuff."

"Sorry."

"Yeah, me too, Jesse, but I had to try."

"Understood."

"Well," Hunsicker said, "you've still got a few days to change your mind. I know the chances are you won't, but please don't send the card back just yet. Will you do that for me?"

"Least I can do."

"Much appreciated, Jesse. Shame I won't get to meet you. My guess is we'd get along fine."

"When the time comes, tell her I really do wish her all the happiness. She deserves it."

"Will do."

That was that, though Jesse felt much better about Jenn's future without him than he ever had before. And suddenly he wasn't dying to have a drink quite as bad as he was before.

EIGHTEEN

Time was up. Those days Hale Hunsicker had talked about had come and gone. There hadn't been any further attempts to induce him into heading down to Dallas for the September nuptials and the five days of parties in advance of the main event. Though the night after he'd spoken to Hale, he'd gotten a hang-up call from Jenn's number. He gave her credit for hanging up. But the response card wasn't the most pressing matter on his desk. His attention was focused on the report Tamara Elkin had handed to him.

The ME sat across from him, her finely tooled kangaroo-leather boots up on the edge of Jesse's desk. She was sipping her coffee, patiently waiting for Jesse to read her notes. The pointy-toed, slope-heeled boots were a Texas habit she'd never wanted to lose when she'd moved back north. After a few minutes, her coffee and her patience came to an end and she strolled around the office, looking at the photos of the past chiefs, of Jesse in a Dodgers uniform at his only major-league spring training.

Jesse looked up to refocus his eyes and found himself watching her move. She was tall and lean and moved with a big cat's grace. Her wild tangle of hair only enhanced that comparison. Tamara came by her grace naturally. She had once been a world-class long-distance runner, one ruined knee away from the Olympics. She and Jesse had a lot in common. He went back to the notes. She went back to strolling.

Molly Crane came into the office with some paperwork she left on Jesse's desk. Tamara waved Molly over to where she was standing.

"What's with your boss?" she asked Molly, her voice low.

"The Gino Fish thing," she said in a whisper. "That and the wedding."

"Wedding. What wedding?"

"His ex."

"The infamous Jenn?"

Molly nodded.

"How's he taking it?"

"You two do realize I'm sitting right here?" Jesse said, then pointed at the door. "You want to talk about me, take it outside."

100

Molly rolled her eyes. "No, thanks."

"What did you just put on my desk, Crane?"

"Ballistics report on the last shot-out tires. Same as the others, a .22, but I think our shooter's moved on. Been the longest period between incidents since they began."

"I agree," he said.

"Good. Now I'll be able to sleep tonight."

"Very funny, Molly. I think I hear your phone ringing."

"That's my cue to leave," Molly said to Tamara and slipped out of the office.

Tamara Elkin turned to Jesse, who had put her notes down. "You didn't tell me about Jenn getting married."

"I didn't know I was supposed to."

"Where's the wedding?"

"Dallas."

She laughed. "Great town if you like blondes, makeup, and barbecue."

Jesse made a face.

"Oh, shit! Sorry, Jesse. Diana's blond, isn't she?"

"So is my ex and I love good barbecue, but I'm not going, so let's move on."

"Okay," she said. "First just let me remove my foot from my mouth."

"Forget it." He changed subjects. "Says in your notes that you have some issues with

101

the angle of the stab wound to the victim's chest."

"Nothing outrageous, but by my calculations, the person who stabbed the receptionist was shorter than Gino Fish by at least a few inches. Here, stand up," she said, waving Jesse to come over by her. When he got to within a few feet of her, she signaled for him to stop. "The chest wound to the victim was an ascending wound and very deep. The murder weapon was a sharp knife, but the blade was broad and it would require a lot of force to penetrate as deeply into the victim's heart as it did, especially as it clipped the sternum. Unless the person making the wound was very strong, it would be a difficult wound to produce with a bent arm jabbing in an upward motion, like so." She pantomimed stabbing Jesse in the chest. "And even if Mr. Fish had been strong enough to do that damage and given the length of his arm, I would have expected the angle of the wound to have been steeper. I think the blow was more of a thrust, like this," she said, straightening her arm as she took a long stride toward Jesse. "If that's the case and the measurements in the file are correct, the wound should not have been ascending at all, possibly even slightly descending."

Jesse didn't react right away. He knew that real police work wasn't like police work on TV, that different MEs could reach different conclusions based on the same evidence. And there was also the element of human error. But he knew the Boston Homicide detectives were likely to accept their own theory of the case and overlook any minor discrepancies. It was human nature and it was the nature of the Homicide bureau. He'd been there himself. Clearing cases, that's what it was all about.

"Thanks, Doc."

"Was I any help?"

He shrugged.

"Remember," she said, leaning forward and kissing him on the cheek, "you owe me a favor."

"I'm sure you'll remind me if I do forget."

She laughed, shook her head at him, and turned to leave. She stopped at the door and called back to him, "Diana's lucky to have you, you know?"

"You got a funny definition of luck, Doc."

NINETEEN

Jesse was just dialing the Boston detective in charge of Gino Fish's case when he gave a cursory glance at the ballistics report Molly had left on his desk. He didn't pay it much attention, as he was more focused on what he was going to say if the detective picked up the phone. Cops, especially detectives, can be very territorial, and Jesse was about to intrude on turf that was most definitely not his. Not only was he about to step on the Boston PD's turf, he was probably going to ruffle some feathers. It wasn't difficult to anticipate the chilly response he was bound to get after mentioning the discrepancies Tamara Elkin had noted.

It was one thing to point out differences between conclusions drawn by different MEs. Cops accepted that stuff like that happened. It was something else to question how detectives were handling their cases. That was the stuff feuds were made of and no department as close to Boston as Paradise could afford getting frozen out by the BPD. The Boston Police Department had resources a small-town department couldn't touch. If he pissed the wrong people off, Jesse's contacts at the BPD would dry up. And with Healy putting in his papers, the state police might not be as helpful, either. Jesse's title or his past in Robbery-Homicide in the LAPD wouldn't matter. He was taking a calculated risk, but given the marker Gino or Vinnie could have called in on him, Jesse felt it was a risk he was duty-bound to take. Honor and keeping one's word might not be fashionable in today's world, but they still meant a lot to Jesse Stone.

Jesse went utterly still for a second even as he heard a voice in his ear. He slammed the phone back down in its cradle.

"Molly!" He screamed, loudly enough to be heard on the street, never mind beyond the walls of his office.

"What is it, Jesse?" she asked, poking her head into his office. "Is everything all right?"

"Have all the reports on the tire shootings been logged in to the system yet?"

"Just the preliminaries, but I was going to get to that later to —"

Jesse shook his head violently. "Never mind that. Get all the files and bring them in here. Now!"

"What is it, Jesse?"

"Now."

Molly didn't hesitate. When Jesse issued orders to her this way, which was infrequently, she knew something was up. Something big. She came back into his office without knocking and placed the folders in a neat stack on his desk.

"Here they are, Jesse. What is it? What's going on?"

"Sit," he said. "Take half the files. Tell me the make and model of car in each incident."

"I don't have to sit for that and I don't have to open the files."

Jesse looked up at her, the corners of his mouth turned down. The sickly feeling he got in his belly when he first noticed the caliber of bullet used in the last incident was now full-blown.

"All Honda Civics more than five years old," he said, not an ounce of joy in his voice.

Molly glared at him. "For goodness' sakes, Jesse, if you already knew that, why all the shouting and —"

He raised his palms to her. "I'm sorry, Molly. Do me a favor and get Healy on the phone for me. I've got to think."

"Don't worry about raising your voice at me. Not the first time and I'll live, but what is it?"

Jesse pulled open his desk's right-hand drawer. He searched through some papers piled up inside and came out with a brown envelope. He handed it to Molly. "Go ahead, open it."

Inside was an 8×10 color photograph of Jenn. It was a candid shot of her in the sun at an outdoor café.

Molly was confused. "It's not Jenn at her best, but so what?"

"Flip it over."

On the back was a handwritten note, the lettering neat and square. The note read:

Do you ask a praying mantis why?

Now Molly got that same sickly feeling in her belly and said, "Oh my God, Jesse. It's him."

Jesse nodded. "Uh-huh. Mr. Peepers."

"You still want me to get Healy on the phone?"

"I do . . . and get Suit in off patrol. Get him in here right now. He's got to be alerted."

Molly was gone. Jesse picked his old glove off his desk and pounded the ball into the pocket so hard it might have shaken the windows.

TWENTY

Suit wasn't having any luck with his concentration that morning. Patrol was going smoothly enough, like it almost always did. He supposed he had liked his life well enough, but it had been pretty boring. Being a cop in Paradise wasn't exactly life on the mean streets. It was mostly parking tickets, the occasional bar fight, and traffic control when the town filled up during the annual regatta. He thought about how different it had been for Jesse. Jesse had done things, big things, in his life. Besides being one step away from Dodger Stadium, Jesse had been out there in the world. He'd kicked ass and solved murders. He'd been married to a newscaster, for crissakes. The glory in Suit's life had come and gone with his high school graduation. Suit knew that his constantly comparing himself to Jesse was unhealthy. It had nearly gotten him killed. But it wasn't Jesse or the scars on his abdomen that were ruining his concentration, not today.

"Car four to base," Suit said into his car mic.

"What's up, Suit?"

"What's up with you? You sound out of breath."

"Jesse's got me running around looking for reports."

"It's quiet out here. I'm going ten-sixty-three."

"Little early for lunch," she said.

"Never too early for lunch," he said, letting Molly believe it was food he was stopping for.

"Roger that."

Suit pulled the car up in front of Elena's house, but he didn't get out. He sat there for a few minutes, frozen with panic over what he was about to do. He wasn't given to profound thoughts, not that he wasn't smart. It was just that he tried not to dwell on things. Yet after reconnecting with Elena, it had occurred to him that he had been lonely for too long. He had never lacked for friends. Suit knew he was a likeable guy. Imposing as his size made him, people felt comfortable around him. Nor had he lacked for the company of women. The problem was his relationships with women were usually short-lived and often carried out under cover of darkness. There was never any future in them, just temporary comfort. But nothing focuses a man's mind like facing his own mortality. As hard as he tried not to think about getting shot, it was impossible to escape.

He took three deep breaths and got out of the cruiser. He stuck his hand in his pocket, got panicky again when he couldn't find the ring. Then relaxed a little bit when he found it. He had thought about doing this in some romantic way like they did it in the movies. He'd meet her down in Boston or even New York for a weekend, making dinner reservations at a fancy restaurant, and then having the ring delivered to the table as part of her dessert. He'd considered taking her to a Sox game and having a plane fly overhead, trailing a banner with his proposal on it. But he realized that he loved her too much for that stuff and that Elena would be embarrassed by it. She was too private a person. And they had both agreed to keep their relationship to themselves until they had a sense of where it would go.

Luther "Suitcase" Simpson had a sense of where he wanted it to go from the first time he had seen Elena Wheatley all those years ago. Now he was sure of where it was going and he was sure life was too short to spend another minute apart from her if he didn't have to. He wanted to share his joy with the world and the rest of his life with Elena.

He stepped around the cruiser and up the walk. The beads of sweat on his brow had nothing to do with the heat of the day. He knocked at her door, not wanting to let himself in. He hadn't let her know he was coming. He was about to knock again when the door pulled back. Suit beamed at the sight of her in a bathrobe, her wet hair dripping onto her shoulders.

"Luther . . . this is a happy surprise," she said, smiling, waving him inside. She stood on her tiptoes and kissed him. "Is everything okay?"

"Fine, good. Everything's good." His voice was brittle.

Elena threaded herself between his big arms and pressed her body close to his. The light coconut-and-floral scent of her conditioner filled up Suit's head and he was lost for a second. Then Elena tilted her head back and said, "So what's up, Officer Simpson?"

He didn't speak, plunging his right hand into his pocket, fishing for the ring. Then, just as he was about to pull it out of his pocket, the radio crackled.

"Suit." It was Molly. "Get back in here. Now."

He dropped the ring into his pocket, raised his right arm, and pressed the talk button on the mic on his shoulder. "But I'm —"

"Right now, Suit. Jesse wants you in immediately."

"Roger that."

"What's that about?" Elena asked.

Suit shrugged and kissed her hard on the mouth. "I've got to go."

"I love you, Luther."

He smiled at her, kissed her on the top of her head. "Me, too. Very much."

Back in the cruiser, he patted his pocket and hoped it would go easier the next time he tried to propose.

Twenty-One

He had called Healy, but hadn't explained why he'd asked him to come to the station house. After talking to Healy, he'd called back the Boston Homicide detective to apologize for hanging up on him. Jesse made a perfectly reasonable excuse about an emergency situation popping up just as he'd called. The detective seemed only too willing to accept the little-town chief's excuse and rushed him off the phone without bothering to ask why he'd called in the first place. That suited Jesse fine. The bigger issue was that Jesse suddenly knew things that other cops would want to know, but he wasn't sure he could risk telling them . . . at least not yet. That was where Healy would come into it.

Suit, still wound up over having nearly proposed marriage, was annoying Molly, eating donuts, and drinking coffee. Suit was basically his old self now that he was back on patrol again, but Jesse worried about him. He had always worried a little more about Suit than he did about his other cops, even before the shooting. Suit was a living example of the adage that men grow old, but never grow up, and his still-boyish face only served to drive the point home. He was a kid in a big man's body. The question in Jesse's head was, What would happen if Suit ever had to pull his weapon again? Would he hesitate? Worse, would he be too quick to shoot? The department shrink had given Suit a clean bill of health, but Jesse worried just the same. Back in L.A. he had seen what violent encounters could do to even the most experienced cops. Shooting another human being, even one as detestable as Mr. Peepers, comes at a price. Getting shot yourself comes with an even bigger price.

When Healy showed up, Molly called in to Jesse to let him know.

"You and Suit come in, too. Tell Suit to bring in two extra chairs."

Healy was in golfing mode today but had already managed to make his attire look well lived-in. The worry over his wife was evident in his eyes. Molly was concerned. You could read it on her face like a bold headline. Suit was Suit. He would take things as they came and deal with them then. Jesse took the bottle of Tullamore Dew out of his drawer and waved it at Healy. Healy nodded his approval.

"Molly? Suit?" Jesse asked.

Molly nodded, too. Suit looked at Molly like she'd sprouted a second head. For Molly to drink on duty, things had to be seriously wrong.

"You better have one, too, Suit," Jesse said, pouring three shots into the red plastic cups.

"What's going on, Jesse?" Suit asked, taking the cup off the chief's desk.

Jesse said, "I'll get to that in a second, Suit. First I need to talk to Captain Healy, but you two should stay."

"You got my attention," Healy said, sipping at the fine Irish whiskey.

Jesse stood, turned his back to the others in the room, and stared out his window at Stiles Island beyond.

"Healy, what if I told you that I'm sure Gino Fish didn't kill his receptionist and that he only killed himself to save himself from an even more painful death?"

The captain laughed a strange, strangled kind of a laugh, but stopped when he noticed no one else was laughing with him. "I'd say you should start drinking again, because being sober isn't doing a damned thing to make you more clearheaded."

"And what if I could tell you who killed the old woman, the cabbie, and the dog in Salem?"

Healy didn't laugh this time. "Yeah, who?"

Jesse didn't answer, not directly, this time turning to look at his old friend. "And what if I told you that the same person was responsible for both crimes and for all the tires getting shot out in Paradise over the last few weeks?"

"I'd say I'm getting tired of you asking me questions and that I'm ready to hear your answer."

"Fair enough," Jesse said. Then he turned to Molly. "Go to the evidence locker and get out any two of the bullets recovered from the car tires."

Molly did as she was asked.

"What's going on, Jesse?" Healy asked the same question both Molly and Suit had asked before him.

Jesse didn't answer, choosing to wait until Molly returned. When she did, she handed two plastic evidence bags to Jesse, who in turn put them in front of Healy.

"You have your ballistics guys run those with the bullets the ME pulled out of the Salem vics and they'll match."

Healy held the bags up to the light. "Yeah, they look like .22s, but even in Massachusetts, there are a lot of .22 handguns floating around."

"Same gun," Jesse said. "Same ammo. I'd bet on it."

"Okay, so let's say what you claim checks out. Then what? I still need a name. Do you have a name for me?"

"Sort of."

Healy banged his empty cup on Jesse's desk. " 'Sort of'?"

"Sort of."

"Are you going to share with the class, Jesse, or do you expect me to guess? You know I got a lot going on in my life right now and I don't have a lot of patience for this stuff."

"Here's my problem, Healy," he said, pouring a second shot into the captain's cup. "If I tell you the name, I need you to sit on the information. Lives depend on it. Probably the lives of the people in this room and their families."

Healy didn't flinch. "I can do that for a few days, sure. Wouldn't be the first time I sat on things."

Jesse shook his head slowly. "Not a couple of days, Healy. A month, maybe a little more."

Healy looked sick, as if the whiskey had turned to battery acid in his belly. "I can't do —"

Jesse took the brown envelope back out of his desk and pushed it over to Healy. And when the captain saw the writing on the back of Jenn's photo, he knew as Molly knew before him.

"Jesus!" he said. "Not him again."

Suit had had enough. "Not who again? C'mon, guys. I'm tired of being the only one in here who doesn't know the secret. Who are we talking about?"

Molly, Healy, and Jesse looked at one another, then all turned to look at Suit.

"Mr. Peepers," they said, as if in a single voice.

And for the first time in all the years they had worked together, Jesse saw real fear on Suit's face.

TWENTY-TWO

Healy stood up from his chair and poured himself double the amount of whiskey Jesse had already poured in his cup.

"How much more than a month?"

"Five weeks total," Jesse said.

"You know what you're asking me to do?"

"I know."

Healy took half the whiskey in a single swallow and made a face. "Why five weeks? Why not three or six or three months?"

Molly answered for her boss. "Because of Jenn's wedding."

Healy tilted his head at Jesse like a confused puppy. "Your ex?"

"Jenn's getting married to a rich real-estate guy in Dallas in five weeks. And as a run-up to the wedding, they're having a week's worth of events. That's when he'll try to kill her," Jesse said.

Healy shook his head. "And what, you're going to be Captain America and stop him?"

"Hopefully, I'll have Diana with me and I'll alert the people who need to know."

"That's big of you, Jesse. You're a good cop, maybe the best cop I ever met, but this sounds crazy. First off, I need more than the bullets to prove we're talking about the same guy who did the Salem vics and the vandalism here. And you've got to do better than your word to prove that Fish didn't kill his boy toy and then himself of his own accord. And even then, even if you convince me you're right, you're putting me in a bad spot."

"Uh-huh."

"Give me something, Jesse. Make the case."

"Right now we know his target. We know approximately when and where he's going to strike, but if we blow the whistle and let him know we're onto him, we give up any edge we've got. He may come after me through Molly or through Diana. Maybe Sunny Randall or even you, Healy. And I can tell you right now, he's coming after Suit one way or the other. Suit may have been the one to shoot him, but he blames me for going back on my word. This is all payback for what went down during the thing with Vic Prado. That's why Gino Fish is dead. It was Fish who put me in touch with Mr. Peepers. Fish warned me that if things went sideways, Peepers would come after us both. And you know his rep. He even scares Vinnie Morris, and no one scares him. Peepers enjoys his work. Fish killed himself to save himself."

Healy drank the rest of his Dew. "Okay, so let's say you prove all this to my satisfaction. Why not go wide with it? Put every law enforcement agency on earth onto this guy? We'll have everybody from the top folks at Interpol to the lowliest square badge at Shop-Mart on the hunt for Peepers."

Jesse shook his head. "C'mon, Healy, you know why."

"He'll go to ground," Suit said in an uncharacteristic monotone. "And he'll come after us another way and when he feels like it."

Molly took up where Suit left off. "Look, Captain, this man waited over a year to make his move after sending that photo to Jesse to let him know he was coming. He likes torturing people physically and psychologically. If we drive him into hiding now, we may never get a chance at him again."

"She's right," Jesse said. "We won't see him coming next time. Besides, according to the research I've done, law enforcement has cast a wide net for him for two decades and they've never gotten close. Suit and I came as close as anyone's ever come and that was mostly luck. Suit winged him and was nearly killed himself. We have an idea of what he looks like, which is added incentive for him to kill us. Right now, he wants to hurt me first by getting Jenn. He wants maximum effect, but if we screw up his plans, who knows what he'll do? Who knows how he'll react?"

Healy pounded his fist on Jesse's desk, "Damn it, Stone! Fuck!"

"I know I'm asking a lot."

"I'll put a rush on the ballistics comparison," Healy said, putting the two evidence bags in his pants pocket. "If the slugs match, you've got two days to make the case to me that what you said about Peepers and Gino Fish is fact. Then, and only then, I'll put in my papers and take all my vacation time. That will give you what you've asked for. It'll make my wife and my damned golf instructor happy. But Christ help you if something goes wrong or if somebody else is killed. We're friends, Jesse. I don't suppose I've gotten as close to another cop since my first partner. No shame in admitting it to you, but like I say, Christ help you." He walked to the office door and about-faced. "I'll call you as soon as I get

122

the ballistics. Then you've got forty hours. Not a second more."

"Understood."

Healy slammed the door shut.

Molly, Suit, and Jesse stared at one another in silence for the longest moments of their lives.

TWENTY-THREE

The world was back on his schedule.

He had just put in his application at Big Dee Caterers and had no doubt he would be getting the call to come in for his orientation any day now. He was best at killing, but he had other skills, too. Lying, for instance. He was a good liar. He knew how to fill out a job application so that he would look good for a job without looking too good for it. You never want to be perfect. You want to be just good enough. It was harder for some jobs than others. For a catering job, you basically needed to have a pulse and the ability to lift a heavy tray. He'd passed that test easily enough in spite of his now balky arm and shoulder, though the hard-faced woman who'd put him through his paces had been skeptical. He knew she would be. They always were, women especially. Perhaps that was why he enjoyed hurting them the way he did.

He turned his attention away from that preoccupation to the barbecue on the brown-papered metal tray before him. He pinched off a bark-covered chunk of beef rib. As advertised, it fairly melted in his mouth. After that, he sliced off a piece of hot link. The unexpected smokiness of it was almost as welcome as the taste of the meat itself. He washed that down with a too-dainty sip of his Shiner Bock and then went for a forkful of coleslaw.

He had been in Texas before, had killed in Texas before. A drug dealer's mistress in El Paso — *El Asshole,* he thought and laughed to himself — had to be dealt with because the dealer was getting paranoid about her going to the DEA. He had enjoyed that aspect of his visit, leaving parts of his victim out in the scrub for the coyotes after he was done with her. The food sucked. Everything but the killing sucked. Then there was the time in Houston he'd been hired to make an heir to an oil fortune look like he'd committed suicide by taking a dive out the window of his hotel suite. The food was an improvement. The work was not.

He had two other places at which to put in applications, but he was enjoying his food far too much to rush back out into the midday heat and baking sun. Dallas was like an inferno. He'd heard someone at the train station call it a dry heat. *Yeah, so is sticking your head in an oven.* People were such morons. He smiled his smile. His smug, superior smile. The one dripping with self-congratulation and contempt and loathing for everyone else. He liked the way that smile felt on his unremarkable face and the way it made him feel inside.

He was luxuriating in the taste of his food, the pleasing cold tang of his beer, and the feel of his smile when an impatient-looking blonde pulled out the chair across from him at the two-top table. She was pretty enough, he guessed, if you liked your blue-eyed women in gray business suits and white silk blouses, with too much makeup and too much hair spray.

"Do you mind?" she asked without a hint of sincerity in her voice, and sat without bothering to wait for his answer. "The place is so damn crowded today and I've got to get back to the office in fifteen minutes."

Of course he minded. He minded every-thing about her, from her looks to her man-ner. He minded her presence. The smile disappeared from his face. He knew her, all right. Or, rather, he knew her type. The pretty girls who took one look at him and thought he'd get excited just to have a woman like her sit in close proximity. She probably thought he'd ask her permission to take a selfie with her.

He grunted at her, not wanting to draw attention to himself. He had to keep his focus on his reason for being in Dallas in the first place: that other blonde. But when she pushed her tray into his and his tray knocked the remainder of his Shiner Bock onto his lap, it was difficult to just grunt and ignore it.

"Damn it!" He jumped out of his seat, pressing a wad of paper towel onto the spreading wet spot covering his crotch.

"Oh, I'm so sorry," she said with that same lack of sincerity. She almost sounded annoyed at him.

"Look what you did."

Then she got indignant. "I said I was sorry, didn't I?"

He opened his mouth to say something threatening, but realized that about half the restaurant was now turned his way. Many of the women were pointing at his wet pants, giggling, covering their mouths. Men shook their heads at him. *Poor ugly little fella.*

"Never mind," he said to the blonde. "That's all right. It'll dry off outside in a few minutes."

But instead of smiling at him or nodding

her pretty head or apologizing again, she pulled out her cell phone and began tapping away.

He picked up his beer bottle, placed it on the tray, threw the wad of paper towels onto the wet floor, and took his tray over to the garbage. He turned back to look at her, but she had already forgotten he existed. She had probably forgotten the second she laid eyes on him.

He stepped through the doors of the barbecue joint and back onto the furnace-like streets of Deep Ellum. Walking back to his stolen Civic, he tried desperately to forget the blonde and the quickly drying spot on the front of his pants. He couldn't forget, though. He just couldn't. So when he got into the sweltering Honda, he drove over to the barbecue restaurant and parked where he could see the entrance. He parked and he waited. He would make her remember him. He would make it so that he was the only thing she would remember. Him and the pain.

TWENTY-FOUR

Jesse had driven down to Boston and arranged to take Diana to a hot new Malaysian restaurant in the Back Bay, a restaurant she had mentioned wanting to try after reading a review in the Sunday paper. *Hot, new,* and *Malaysian* were not adjectives usually associated with Jesse's idea of great food. These days his tastes ran more to donuts and sandwiches from Daisy's, but he had to ask some things of Diana that were going to be hard for her to swallow. He hoped that if the food pleased her, it might make his requests easier to digest.

Diana, dressed in a simple white summer dress and heels, met him downstairs and hopped into his old Explorer. She was already suspicious of this hastily arranged date and when she saw Jesse was wearing a freshly ironed button-down shirt, his blue blazer, and gray dress pants, her suspicions grew stronger. But it wasn't until she noticed his shined shoes that she knew something was definitely up. When it occurred to her what that something might be, Diana Evans got slightly nauseated and asked Jesse to crank the AC. Looking out of the corner of her eye, she searched for a ring box–shaped bulge in his jacket pocket. Just because she couldn't see one didn't mean he might not have the ring somewhere else on his person.

He turned to stare at her. "You okay?"

She lied. "Fine."

"You look beautiful and smell even better."

She smiled her neon-white smile at him. She knew she was pleasing to look at. She always found false modesty nonsensical, but that didn't mean she wasn't conflicted about her beauty. Being taken seriously had been a struggle for her since she turned thirteen. It was never worse than at the Bureau. Still, when Jesse complimented her appearance, it was different somehow. Maybe because she knew he loved her or because he had consulted with her on cases. Maybe it was because he had forgiven her for the lies she'd told him when they first met. No man she'd ever encountered had taken her as seriously as Jesse Stone did. Even so, she dreaded the idea of him popping the question. She loved him something awful, but she wasn't sure marriage to Jesse or any man was for her. Monogamy suited her. Marriage was a different animal altogether. And even if she could bring herself to get married, she didn't want to put down roots in a place like Paradise. Pretty as it was, she just couldn't picture herself locked into small-town life.

Jesse could see Diana was squirming a bit in her seat and that this whole last-minute deal was making her curious and uncomfortable. He laughed at himself for trying to go about things this way. The grand gesture had never been his style, but he supposed it was a measure of his love for her that he was willing to try things this way. Either that or a measure of his concern. As he had suspected, the bullets matched. Healy had called to confirm that the .22s dug out of the rear tires of the cars in Paradise were twins to those removed from the bodies in Salem. Now he had to prove that the shooter was Mr. Peepers. For that he would need Diana's help.

"You still pals with Abe Rosen at the Bureau?" he asked.

"That's a weird question."

"But are you?"

"Sure," she said, wondering where Jesse

was headed with this.

"You think he would do you a favor?"

"Depends on the favor. Last time he did one for me, he put his own neck in a noose to cover for me. If things had gone a little bit differently, he would have been shown the door and not quietly, the way I was asked to leave."

"He was in love with you. He probably still is."

"Jesse!"

"I don't blame him. You're pretty easy to love," Jesse said, a slight smile at the corners of his mouth. "And Abe came out of it all right."

"All right, but not unscathed. So what's the favor I'm asking him?"

Jesse reached into his jacket pocket and handed her a slip of paper. "I need all the street surveillance footage, Federal and BPD, for those streets on the day Gino Fish killed himself."

She squinted, pursed her lips, and tilted her head at him. "Can't you just ask your contacts at the Boston PD?"

He shook his head. "I can't let them know I'm looking at it this closely."

"Why not?"

"Long story."

She pointed at the car in front of them.

"We've moved twenty feet in five minutes, so we've got plenty of time." But now Diana was gesturing to her right. "Holy crap! Did you see that? That asshole just knocked the woman over and stole her bag."

Before Jesse could answer or move, Diana was out of the car. She shed her heels and took off down the street after the man. Jesse pulled his Explorer to the curb, dialed 911, and went to see how the woman knocked to the ground was doing. When he saw that she was just stunned and that other people were tending to her, Jesse took off after Diana and the mugger. He was about twenty yards behind them when Diana leapt forward, tackling the mugger. They went down hard, the mugger face-first into the sidewalk. His nose broke; the sidewalk didn't. There was blood everywhere, some of it on the front of Diana's dress. But by the time Jesse got there, Diana had the perp in an armbar and was threatening to rip the guy's lungs out if he tried to run.

"Too bad I already hired Alisha," Jesse said to Diana as he slapped handcuffs on the mugger. "That was pretty amazing."

Diana caught her breath and asked, "This surprises you?"

"I guess it shouldn't."

"Don't ever underestimate me, Stone, or

I'll do to you what I just did to this clown."

"I don't doubt it. Your dress is ruined."

She shrugged. "I guess I can't show up at a restaurant looking like this. After the cops come, let's go back to my apartment. I want to clean up."

An hour later, Diana freshly showered, her scrapes washed and treated, a scotch in her hand, she asked Jesse to finish the explanation that had been so rudely interrupted.

"What's up? Why the sudden date? Why do you need Abe to get this surveillance video? What the hell is going on?"

When Jesse explained about the bodies in Salem, the .22 bullets in the tires of the cars in Paradise, and about Mr. Peepers, it got very quiet in Diana's apartment. Diana suddenly didn't feel much like eating, whether it was Malaysian food or at Burger King. Instead she guzzled her drink and poured herself another.

"I have another favor to ask," he said.

Before Jesse could get the question out of his mouth, Diana thought she heard herself say yes.

"But you don't know what I'm asking."

"I do, though. You're going to ask me if I'd go to Jenn's wedding with you."

He smiled at her. Diana continued to surprise him at every turn: first the mugger and now this. What Jesse couldn't have known was how conflicted Diana felt. She felt an immense sense of relief that there would be no kneeling, no ring box, and no proposal of marriage. She also felt equally hurt and disappointed. She wasn't sure Jesse would understand it if she were to explain it to him. Never mind him. She wasn't sure she understood it.

TWENTY-FIVE

Jesse watched the street camera footage over and over and over again until it felt like his eyes were going to fall out of his head. A few men on the footage were about the correct height for Mr. Peepers, but none of them was right. There was a delivery man who matched Peepers's size perfectly, and if he wasn't African American, Jesse might have felt encouraged. Then there was the bearded little man in a raincoat, but he was far too stout to have been Peepers.

He looked over his left shoulder at the wall clock. Healy would be by in less than an hour, and if Jesse couldn't find Peepers on the surveillance footage, he was screwed. He wasn't so much worried for himself. He had always believed that if your number was up, your number was up, and that worrying about it was a waste of time and energy. The uncertainty of police work fosters a belief in fate. No, he was worried for Suit,

Molly, Diana, even Healy. The only one likely to come out better for Healy going public with his suspicions was Jenn. Jesse doubted Peepers would go after her once the drama of the wedding was past. Once she was Mrs. Hale Hunsicker more than she was the former Mrs. Jesse Stone, Peepers would have less incentive.

"Alisha," he said, sticking his head through the office doorway. "Get Suit in here, pronto. Lights and siren."

Confused, she stared at her boss. Jesse had a strict rule against using the light bar and siren in town unless it was absolutely necessary. And even then, as she had heard from everybody else on the force, from Molly to Peter Perkins, you better not do it. But she didn't say a word to Jesse and got right on the radio to Suit.

Less than two minutes later, Jesse heard Suit's siren cutting through the late-morning quiet. Thirty seconds after that, Luther "Suitcase" Simpson came rushing into Jesse's office, a semipanicked look on his boyish face. He was breathing heavily. His attempts to slow his breathing were futile.

"What . . . is it . . . Jesse?"

Jesse crooked his finger at Suit. "Come sit in my chair. Healy is going to be here soon and I need your help."

Suit tried to squelch a smile. He was as unsuccessful at it as he was at slowing his breathing. Suit lived for Jesse's approval. Jesse knew it. Suit knew Jesse knew it. Suit's need for Jesse's approval was what had gotten him shot by Mr. Peepers and what had started this whole mess to begin with. Both men understood as much, but neither talked about it. Jesse supposed he was as responsible as Suit because he had always been on Suit about taking the initiative, about doing for himself, about acting on his cop instincts instead of waiting for orders. And when he finally did what Jesse had urged him to do, it blew up in both of their faces.

Suit sat in Jesse's chair and stared at the frozen image of the entrance to the building that had housed Gino Fish's offices. He showed Suit how to operate the video equipment.

"I can't find him, Suit," Jesse said. "I know he's in here somewhere, but I didn't get as good a look at him as you did. You got a clearer view of him when you exchanged gunfire. I only saw a flash of his face and a few bad photos of him."

"I'm not sure I'd recognize him, Jesse. It all happened so fast, and then when I was hit . . ."

"I'm counting on you."

"But what if I can't find him? What if he's not there to be found?"

"He's there. You know it and I know it. He has to be there."

"But what if we can't prove it, Jesse?"

"You know what will happen if Healy goes public and other agencies start hunting for a gunman like Peepers."

"He'll do what I said the other day. He'll disappear and then he'll come for all of us. He'll come for me and Molly and Diana and you."

Suit got a sick look on his face.

Jesse nodded. "You and me, Suit. That's who he wants to hurt most of all."

Suit hung his head, fear welling up inside him. Fear not for himself, but for Elena. It occurred to him that he was vulnerable to Peepers in a way he hadn't been before. "I won't see him coming, will I, Jesse?"

"None of us will."

"Then I better find him," Suit said, his voice strained.

Jesse put his hand on Suit's big shoulder. "You will. I have confidence in you."

As Suit began searching through the surveillance footage, Jesse stepped out of his office and made some coffee for himself. Alisha was handling a lot of radio chatter, everyone calling in to see what the emergency was. Alisha, as she had done the other day during the storm, handled it like a pro.

Jesse needed to see Suit . . . No, he's my boss, he doesn't need to tell me why . . . Molly has the desk next shift . . .

Jesse smiled to himself. Alisha was going to make a hell of a cop. He hoped that small-town policing would be enough to keep her interest and that she could resist the siren's song of big-city police work. Suddenly his mind drifted away from Alisha to thoughts of Diana. He didn't sweat the future very much, but he couldn't help wondering what their future held in store if he stayed chief in Paradise. Diana made no bones about her distaste for small-town life. None of it would matter if they didn't stop Peepers. Several people, including himself, wouldn't have a future if he slipped through Jesse's fingers this time.

"Jesse! Jesse! I think I got him!" It was Suit, barreling down the hallway toward the conference room. "I got him."

TWENTY-SIX

Jesse frowned when he saw the man Suit was pointing to on the screen. It was the little potbellied man with the shaggy beard, wearing a raincoat and hat and seeming to look directly into the camera, then turning away just as quickly.

"Yeah, Suit, he caught my eye, too. He's the right height and he's got the narrow sloped shoulders, but he's too heavy."

Suit smiled that loose-mouthed smile of his. "Jesse, wait. Look at this."

The images flashed by on the screen until the time stamp at the bottom right-hand corner indicated twenty-three minutes had passed since the little man appeared on-screen. And there coming out of the building that housed Gino Fish's offices was that same man. But Jesse was unconvinced.

"I've done this already, Suit. Given the time frame set by the ME for times of death, forty-two people enter and leave the building through the front entrance. None of them is a perfect match for Peepers."

But Suit was still smiling. "You never had to diet to lose weight, did you, Jesse?"

"What are you getting at? Healy's going to be here in a few minutes."

"C'mon, Jesse, go with me on this, okay?"

"No, I never really had to diet."

Suit slapped his once sizable belly, smaller now since the shooting. "I've had to diet a few times, like in high school when I wrestled my junior year. And I've been on a few diets since. It ain't easy losing weight."

"I've heard."

"Well, this guy in the raincoat, he's got a diet secret that could make him millions," Suit said. "Watch."

Suit advanced the footage frame by frame until the man on the screen was no longer obscured by passersby, light poles, or parking meters and they could see his entire body. Jesse felt a jolt as he finally saw what he had missed before. He clapped Suit hard on his shoulder.

"Now I know where that pillow came from."

"What pillow?"

Jesse said, "Under the receptionist's head, there was a ratty, stained pillow. Vinnie Morris swore up and down to me that Gino Fish would never have anything like that in his office. I guess he was right."

"So wait a second, Jesse. There's some stuff I don't get. Why would Peepers come to Paradise and risk shooting out tires like he was doing? You would have put it together. It was almost like he was hoping you would."

"Why? For the same reason he sent me the photo of Jenn: to let me know he could hurt me and how he could hurt me. He's a twisted little man who enjoys killing and inflicting pain. I think he wanted me to know he had decided the time was right for his revenge. It isn't enough for him to just kill."

"But then he just stopped."

"Uh-huh."

"Why? And why kill those people and the dog in Salem? They didn't do anything to him."

"Collateral damage," Jesse said. "For him it was like swatting flies. They got in his way. Both of us know what happens when you get in his way."

Unconsciously, Suit rubbed his abdomen above where he was shot. "See, this is where I get confused. If he wanted you to know he was coming for his revenge, then why go back to Salem to return the stolen car?"

"My guess? Things didn't go the way he planned in Boston with Gino Fish, so he had a change of strategy."

Suit laughed without joy.

"What is it?"

"For a second there, Jesse, I thought you were going to say he had a change of heart. But he'd need a heart in the first place."

Jesse nodded, the smile on his face as empty as Suit's laughter. That was when there was a knock on the pebbled glass of the office door and Captain Healy stepped in. He was dressed for business in his favorite jacket.

"Well . . ." Healy said, walking toward the desk to peer over Suit's shoulder.

"Suit, get the bottle and a cup out of my drawer for the captain."

"Why am I drinking, exactly?"

"To celebrate your retirement," Jesse said. "Time to put in your papers."

"So you found the little bastard?"

"Not me. Suit. He'll show you when you're ready."

Suit wasn't smiling now as he put the bottle of Tullamore Dew and the red plastic cup on Jesse's desk. None of them were smiling, each for his own reasons. But the moment weighed most heavily on Healy. No detective who had the job in his blood the way he did was ever really ready to put in his papers. He'd always figured the job would kill him before he had a chance to walk away from it. Yet here he was, bound by his promise, about to make it official. He supposed today was as good a day as any, and if it helped put an end to Mr. Peepers, he was good with it.

He poured himself a drink, took it in a single swallow, and said, "Show me."

TWENTY-SEVEN

The brushed-steel doors parted and she strolled out of the elevator car and into the underground garage. She was prettier than he had given her credit for. Maybe it was that she had exchanged that gray business suit she had worn the other day for a form-fitting black dress and heels. Or was it that she had washed all that silly lacquer out of her highlighted blond hair and let it fall over her bare brown shoulders and spaghetti straps? Her skin was indeed very brown and her legs were so perfectly hairless and smooth that they practically reflected the dull, ambient lighting. A small, silky black bag dangled off her left shoulder, swaying as she moved. The only sounds in the cavernous car park were the muffled whirring of exhaust fans and the echoes of her pointed heels clickety-clacking on the concrete slab. Her calf muscles pulsed as she walked.

This was perfect, he thought, something to keep him occupied while he marked off the days until he paid off the first installment of his debt to Jesse Stone. Frankly, the very thought of spending weeks on end in Dallas with nothing to do except working part-time at three dead-end jobs nearly bored him to tears. Revenge was worth a lot to him, everything, but boredom could be pure hell. He had no choice, though, because there were so many contingencies to plan for, so many moving parts to attend to.

Having a Plan B wouldn't be sufficient with a man like Stone, especially after how things had gone so wrong back up north. It was, he knew, his own fault. He had let hubris get the better of him. That silliness with the car tires. He shouldn't have done that. He shook his head even as he thought of it. It was a severe miscalculation and had led to the messes in Boston and Salem. But payback was so much sweeter when they knew he was coming for them and they were powerless to stop him. The notion of the condemned waiting for him to pay them a call excited him. Daydreaming of them searching for him under every rock, peeking around every corner, seeing him in every shadow, looking for him everywhere but where they should look, was almost as powerful as the kill itself. Almost.

Now, though, he had to anticipate Stone's moves. *What if he had finally figured out who'd put the bullets in all those tires? What if he had warned his ex? What if the cops knew he was in Dallas? What if . . . What if . . . What if . . .* Uncertainty was usually to his advantage, because it was his victims who suffered from its corrosive effects. When he took a job, he worked hard to figure out the best way to come at his target, how to maximize results and minimize the chances of his capture. Contingencies? He always had contingencies, but because of his own foolishness, he had made his task exponentially more difficult. Yet he found he could not focus on Stone or contingencies. Since getting into town, he had been preoccupied by one thing and one thing only: the discourtesy of the woman at the barbecue restaurant. Dealing with the latter, he reasoned, would help him with the former. It was one of life's great contradictions that distraction could sometimes help you concentrate.

As she approached her red Audi convertible, the sound of her heels made his heart beat that much faster. He wondered how she would die: easy or hard. He liked it better when they died hard, clinging to, clutching at the tiniest specks of hope or stubbornly clawing to hang on to whatever time they had left, no matter the pain. Pain so intense that not even unconsciousness provided an escape. He smiled that smug smile to himself as he lowered his head below the dashboard. Then the clacking of her heels came to an abrupt halt. He peeked up above the dashboard to see why she had stopped.

There she was, twenty feet in front of her car, cell phone in hand.

"No, Jordan, honey, I'm leaving now," she said, her voice bouncing off the concrete. "I'll call you back when I get out of the garage and on the road. Okay, see you in a bit."

He lowered his head back down and listened as her heels got louder and louder. He ran the tips of his fingers along the length of the syringe. In the syringe was his own proprietary little cocktail of drugs. All they ever felt was a pinch, and before they had any idea of what was happening to them they were in another world. Many of his victims had told him that the cocktail induced gloriously vivid dreams. Dreams that were wildly random but often hyperreal. They often begged for him to dose them with those same drugs once he began working on them. Sometimes, when it suited his state of mind, he did as they asked. And he always enjoyed watching the horror on their faces when they came out of it and realized where they were and whom they were with.

Now that she was so close to him, he imagined he could almost smell her perfume. He waited until she had settled into the camel-colored leather seat of her Audi. Then he got out of his car and came up from behind her.

"Hi, there," he said, friendly as could be.

Startled, she whipped her head around. At first the only thing that registered on her lovely face was confusion. There was no hint of recognition. Just as he thought she would, she'd forgotten he even existed.

He screwed his face up into a frown. "Oh, you don't remember me."

Confusion changed quickly to anger. "Listen, ass—"

But she didn't finish the thought, distracted by the sharp pinch in her neck. When she went lax, he pushed her back in her seat to make sure she didn't fall against the horn. He pulled the Honda up in front of her Audi and popped the Civic's rear lid. After folding her neatly into the trunk, he stroked her hair, ran the back of his hand

150

along the smooth, brown skin of her cheek, and slammed the lid shut. Almost immediately, his mind turned to thoughts of Jesse Stone and Jenn.

TWENTY-EIGHT

Jesse Stone stopped and stared into a men's clothing store window as if he was actually interested in the preppy summer closeout clothing displayed on the frozen-smile mannequins. He never understood the appeal of seersucker, never thought it looked anything other than ridiculous. Nor did he get the appeal of most of the clothing in the shop window on Fifth Avenue. Some of the shoes, he supposed, were okay. He liked some of them. The rest of it . . . you wouldn't catch him dead in any of it. And that was why he had stopped. Not to check out the clothing, but rather not to be caught dead. It was an old trick, using a plate-glass window as a mirror to see who walked past you or to see who had stopped behind you. An old trick, yet still an effective one. As best as he could tell, he wasn't being tailed.

He turned away from the seersucker-clad mannequin and headed back up Fifth to the building that housed the offices of Pervil, Kennedy, Neer, the law firm that represented the East Coast interests of Hunsicker & Hunsicker Development LLC. Jesse hadn't made it ten steps when he felt a hand clutch his forearm. His body clenched, his mind racing. *Was this when Peepers would come at him? Was this where? Was this how? Had he overthought it?* He had no time to react. Jesse Stone was not a man to feel vulnerable, but he felt awfully vulnerable right at that moment. As Jesse shifted his free hand toward his holstered nine-millimeter, the already noisy street was overwhelmed by the shrill siren, the electronic whoops and barks of a passing ambulance. If this was Peepers, if he was going to use that .22, no one would hear the shots above the din and street commotion. His execution would go unseen. In that mass of bodies, even the street cameras would have trouble picking up what was happening. By the time anyone noticed him slumping to the ground, Peepers would be half a block away.

"*Perdón, señor,*" a man's voice said to him as the ambulance wailed its way downtown.

Jesse looked first to the hand on his forearm and then to the face of the man to whom it belonged. And when he saw the reddish skin of the hand, the thick wrist and ugly fingers, Jesse breathed again and moved his own hand away from the nine-millimeter. The man peering up at him had a familiar face. It wasn't a face he recognized, per se, but it was familiar nonetheless. He had seen many such faces in L.A., faces that spoke of invading conquistadors and native peoples. The man had jet-black hair, deep brown eyes, high cheekbones, a crooked smile, and a beak of a nose. Jesse noticed, too, that the man wasn't alone. Alongside him was a woman about his age and a teenage boy and girl. The teenagers were too busy with their tablets to pay the rest of the world any mind. Jesse smiled back at the man as if he were an old friend and asked, in Spanish, how he could help. Although Jesse wasn't exactly fluent in Spanish, he managed directions to the United Nations easily enough. The man thanked him. The wife, too. The teenagers looked like they would have rather gone anywhere else.

As the family disappeared into the crowd behind him, so too did Jesse's smile. This innocent encounter was a cruel reminder that Peepers had, in his way, already won. As certain as he was ten minutes ago of how, when, and where the killer would come at him, that was how unsure he was now. And it was a bad day to be unsure. The worst day, because now more than ever, he knew that convincing Hale Hunsicker to go along with his plan would be perhaps the most important thing he'd ever had to do. If he couldn't convince Hunsicker to agree, it would be as good as handing down death sentences to most of the people he loved on this earth. And they likely wouldn't be quick deaths, either.

Jesse got that sick feeling in his gut again, remembering how he'd found Suit all shot up. How he'd had to practically hold Suit's abdomen together until help came. Jesse recalled the state Kayla and Vic Prado were in when they were rescued from the basement of an abandoned house that Peepers had used as his own temporary house of horrors. Vic's teeth had been yanked out of his mouth, one at a time, and many of his bones systematically broken. Vic still wasn't right and never would be. Fortunately, Jesse had gotten to them before Peepers had lost full interest in Vic. Although he'd burned the inside of one of Kayla's thighs to make a point, he'd yet to start on her in earnest. Jesse didn't like thinking about what might have been.

As he passed by the front entrance of the

building that housed the offices of the law firm, Jesse was thinking deeper thoughts than he usually troubled himself with. He was thinking about what one of his high school science teachers had said a long, long time ago about how the universe was a mechanism of balance and how it strove for that balance at all costs. *A mechanism of balance.* Jesse hadn't thought about that phrase or old Mr. Farman for years. It was no mystery why it had come back to him now. By asking Gino Fish to intercede on his behalf in order to save Kayla and what was left of Vic, Jesse had set things in motion that had already condemned Gino Fish and his receptionist to death. As he doubled back to the building entrance, sure again that he wasn't being followed, Jesse wondered what it would take to have balance restored.

TWENTY-NINE

Pervil, Kennedy, Neer was an established firm in a solid old building, so their offices lacked flash and glitz. That worked for Jesse. He didn't have much use for flash and glitz. He'd had his fill of both in L.A. and there was little chance of encountering either in Paradise. Paradise was definitely more seersucker than gold lamé, more boats than feather boas. The reception and waiting area décor of brown leather, brass-tacked chairs, of dark wood and green glass, recalled an old-fashioned bank or a country-club card room. Jesse imagined he could smell the lingering scents of cigars and cherry pipe tobacco. Given all that, it surprised him when the person who came to greet him was a rangy kid who looked like he'd started shaving last week.

"Follow me, Chief Stone. The other party is waiting for you in our conference room."

Jesse followed him down a hallway of

closed office doors and walls lined with portraits. The portraits were of stern-looking white men, old white men, with white hair. Some were portraits of yachts and golf holes.

"Here we are, sir," said the kid, putting his hand on the oval-shaped doorknob to the conference room. "Would you care for coffee, tea, or bottled water? A Coke or Diet Coke?"

Jesse shook his head, then asked, "Summer associate?"

He smiled at Jesse as he opened the door. "Something like that. Go on in."

The conference room was a large, windowless space that only enhanced the country-club feel of the office. The walls were paneled in walnut and the forest-green carpeting was springy under Jesse's shoes. The huge rectangular table that dominated the room had twelve black leather swivel chairs around it, but could have easily accommodated a further six. Spaced evenly along the centerline of the table were six banker's lamps, their dark green shades aglow.

"Well, how do, Jesse Stone?" Hale Hunsicker said, all six-foot-five of him rising up out of the big leather chair at the head of the table. Hunsicker offered Jesse his right hand. It was nearly the size of Jesse's old baseball mitt. "I've been waiting to meet you for a long time. Yes, sir, a long time."

Jesse let the Texan's hand swallow his and waited for Hunsicker's to spit it back out. He'd Googled Hunsicker the day he got the invitation to the wedding, but he was still taken aback by the man's physical presence. Hunsicker had played defensive tackle in the burnt-orange uniform of the Texas Longhorns back in the day, but after making second team all-American, he'd chosen Wharton and the family business over the NFL. He was still a specimen. His body tapered from his broad shoulders to a waist that was probably an inch or two smaller than Jesse's. And his hand-tailored suit made sure to emphasize his build. But size and build weren't even the man's most impressive features. He was a handsome SOB with a square cleft chin, an angular jawline, and a loose mane of prematurely silver hair. He looked like a cross between the damned Marlboro man and a Greek sculpture.

"So, Jesse, what's all the cloak-and-dagger for?" Hunsicker asked, some of the good-ole-boy charm disappearing from his voice. "We could have just gone out for a friendly meal."

"Jenn."

"I kinda figured it was about her. That's why I agreed to go along with all this secrecy hoo-ha. I may be just an ole Texas shitkicker, but —"

Jesse laughed, shaking his head. "Hale, we need to be straight with each other. How many ole Texas shitkickers are Wharton MBAs?"

Now it was Hunsicker laughing. "Probably more than you'd think." He stopped laughing or smiling. "Listen, Jesse, you're not thinking of trying to put a stop to the wedding, are you? Because if you are, don't waste your breath, son. I know who Jenn is. I know about her vanity and neediness. I knew about them in the first five minutes I spent talking to her. And unlike you, I'm the man for that. I'm the man to feed her vanity and take care of her needs. I also know about how you two are connected. There's nothing I can do about that. Don't want to, but don't tell me you're here to proclaim your everlasting love for her or anything like that. I've got no room for that, son. Not an inch of room for that."

Jesse waited a few seconds to make sure Hunsicker had said his piece. He'd kept Hunsicker in the dark about the exact nature of their meeting, so it was no surprise to Jesse that the man had prepared some comments just in case.

"Hale, it's not like that. I want Jenn to be happy and everything I see and hear from you says you are what you claim: the man for the job."

"Then what's going on?"

"For Jenn to be happy, we have to keep her alive."

All the charm and friendly veneer slid right off Hunsicker's handsome face and in its place was the cold, angry stare opposing offensive linemen must have looked at across the line of scrimmage.

"What the fuck is that supposed to mean?" Hale's voice was an icy growl.

"It means I think someone is going to try to kill or abduct Jenn at your wedding."

Hale tilted his head. "Someone?"

"Mr. Peepers," Jesse said, feeling ridiculous.

Hunsicker's stare grew icier and meaner. He took a step toward Jesse. "Is this some kind of sick joke? 'Cause if it is, I'm severely unamused."

"No joke, Hale." Jesse reached into his sport jacket pocket and retrieved a photocopy of the picture Peepers had sent him. "Here."

Hunsicker was confused. "This thing

about a praying mantis, what's it mean?"

"That's why we're here, so I can explain."

Hale held up his huge right palm. "Wait a second." The big man strolled to the door, stuck his head out, and said, "Scott, come on in here a second."

The kid who'd greeted Jesse in the reception area stepped into the office, a sly smile on his face.

"I don't think we need a lawyer in here," Jesse said.

Hunsicker nodded. "Far as I'm concerned, I'd be happier without lawyers altogether, but Scott's no lawyer."

Jesse frowned. "I thought you said you were a summer associate."

"Sorry, sir," the kid said, "but that was you."

Hunsicker broke up the stalemate. "Jesse Stone, chief of the Paradise Police Department, meet Scott Kahan, my head of security."

"Head of security? He looks about fifteen years old."

Hale Hunsicker was laughing in spite of himself. Kahan stood ramrod straight, his hands clasped behind him. And in that instant, seeing the kid's pose, remembering the inflection in Kahan's voice when he'd called him *sir,* Jesse thought there was something vaguely military about Kahan . . . but only vaguely. There was something else about him Jesse hadn't seen before, something like what you see when you look into the eyes of a shark.

THIRTY

When he rented the small corrugated-steel building in West Dallas, Jenn Stone was the only woman he had on his mind. Only Jenn. Jenn and how she would help him pay his debt to her ex-husband. That smile spread across his face again as he thought of the photo of Jenn he had sent to Chief Stone and the surprises he had in store for them both. If Jesse Stone only knew how close he had gotten to Jenn, how on any number of occasions he could have taken her or simply snuffed the life out of her. Yet he had developed an odd sort of affection for her.

It wasn't that unusual to know your targets in ways that even their lovers, priests, or parents never could or would want to, but he had never experienced "feelings" for any of his intended prey before this. He knew all sorts of things about Jenn, things he had learned when studying her in L.A. before she met Hunsicker and moved to

Dallas. He knew the makeup she wore, the spa she went to for waxing, the dermatologist she used for her Botox treatments, the motels she used for trysts with her Pilates instructor.

He shook his head, thinking about Jenn's foolish insecurities. He knew all about those, too. She didn't love the Pilates instructor. He was certain, in fact, she didn't even like him, but he was younger, much younger, and very good-looking. Good-looking in the way Jesse Stone was good-looking: dark, athletic, a little sullen. He was fascinated by Jenn's contradictions. She had been dating a wealthy TV producer at the time, not an unattractive man himself. Why, he wondered, would she risk everything for a man she could barely tolerate? She never looked pleased when she left Mr. Pilates and she always left the motel first. He was struck by the expression on her face as she made her way back to her car. He had taken many pictures of that expression, had stared at it for hours, contemplating the feelings behind it. And still, he could never work out its meaning. Was it boredom, guilt, or nausea? Was it all three? He found himself wondering about Jenn quite often.

He went to his duffel bag and fished out some of the photos he'd taken of her. He had hundreds of them. All sorts of photos featuring Jenn in all states of dress and undress, but he wasn't looking for the ones of her nude sunbathing or the ones of her and the TV producer making love poolside at his house in Benedict Canyon. No, he was looking for the motel shots, the ones where she had that jumbled expression on her face. But as he pulled out the stacks of neatly organized photos, there was a noise, a stirring from behind the temporary wall in the old factory building. He shoved the photos back into the duffel bag and went to see about the noise.

When he stepped around the wall, he remembered the other reason this building was perfect. He had rented it mostly to ensure his privacy and anonymity, but now he had even greater motivation to be left alone: the rude blonde. Before going out to apply for those other jobs and to further scout out the locations where Jenn's pre-wedding parties were being held, he'd dosed his victim with more of his special drug cocktail. Nude and gagged, she was strapped down to an old workbench that had once been used for building furniture. He checked his watch and did the math. She'd be coming out of it soon. Not just yet, though.

He stood over her, watching her. She was perspiring heavily, and he wiped her down with some shop rags he found in a forgotten storage room. The perspiration was one of the side effects of the drugs. He'd seen it many, many times before and had to be alert to keep her hydrated if he wanted to keep her alive long enough to teach her about rudeness. But for now, he stood watching. Her eyeballs were moving furiously behind their lids, rolling, darting from side to side. Muscles twitching, her arms and legs straining against the straps. She was having one of those vivid dreams. What, he wondered, was she dreaming about? No matter what the dreams were inside their heads, their bodies all reacted this way, men and women alike. Some shared their dreams with him in hope of establishing a human bond. *As if.* Some held stubbornly on to their dreams, foolishly thinking that it gave them dignity and a small victory over him. In the end victory was always his. How many had died bargaining with him, offering up their false dignity as barter?

"I'll tell you now. I'll tell you my dreams."

He wondered if anyone who contemplated their final utterances predicted their last words would be *I'll tell you my dreams.*

He sometimes toyed with the idea of

injecting himself to see what those dreams were like. He never did. How much more vivid could a dream be than this? The rude blonde's body went slack, her eyes no longer moving beneath their lids, her arms and legs no longer straining against the leather straps. This was the calm before the storm. They went limp for a few minutes before coming out of it. He enjoyed this aspect of things. When their eyes would flutter open and they began to drift away from the dream that had just seemed so real to them into the reality of their situation. When the horror would come rushing back to them all at once and they would strain furiously against their straps.

He went back into the other room and got a water bottle from the little fridge he'd bought at a secondhand store in West Dallas. But as he headed back to the rude blonde, his eyes drifted over to the duffel bag and he thought of Jenn. He put the water down and retrieved those photos of her. He stared at her face. It was surely a less beautiful face than it had once been, but it had character like the faces of women in French paintings. He could hear the blonde coming out of it. Hear her writhing on the workbench, straining fiercely against her bindings. He heard her muffled screams for help mutate into sobbing. Yet he did not move, pinned in place by Jenn's expression, as the woman in the next room was by leather straps.

THIRTY-ONE

Without warning, Hale Hunsicker spun on his heel and threw a big fist aimed directly at Scott Kahan's youthful good looks. It was a punch meant to do some serious damage, but the only damage done was to Hunsicker's pride. In a blur of arms, legs, and torsos, Hunsicker was facedown on the plush carpeting, his arm bent behind his back. Kahan's legs were on either side of the big man and he was holding his employer by nothing more than his thumb.

"All right, son, I think we've made the point to Chief Stone."

Kahan released Hunsicker's hand, stepped aside, and assumed the military stance he'd been in a few seconds ago. Hunsicker did a push-up, got to his knees, and stood. He replaced his pants over the tops of his pointy-toed ostrich-skin boots, then brushed off his suit jacket. He shook the pain out of his right wrist.

Jesse said, "Very impressive." But he wasn't impressed. "Problem is, the man we're up against isn't going to throw an unexpected punch in anybody's face."

"With all due respect, sir, my team is prepared to deal with any sort of threat," Kahan answered. His lips bent up in a sly, arrogant manner.

Hunsicker laughed. "You have your SEAL Team Six types, Jesse, then you have people like Scott. People governments don't go on TV to brag about. People who do the jobs that don't involve helicopter assaults, night-vision goggles, grenades, and the like."

"CIA?" Jesse asked.

Kahan did that thing with the corners of his mouth. "Something like that, sir."

"Uh-huh."

Hunsicker wasn't laughing anymore. "So now why don't you tell me why you had me fly up to New York and pretend like I had business here this week? What's this stuff about somebody trying to hurt Jenn?"

Jesse reached into his inner jacket pocket and removed a second piece of paper. He unfolded it and stretched it out on the conference room table, a table for which many trees had made the ultimate sacrifice. It was a sketch of Mr. Peepers culled from Suit's and Jesse's recollections of the man and from whatever they could glean off the video. Kahan stared at it, studied it. His expression was basically blank. Not a hint of arrogance to be seen. On the other hand, Hunsicker was laughing again.

"Scott, you're too young, but Jesse's old enough to remember him. Guy kinda reminds me of the old-time actor Wally Cox."

Jesse nodded. "Exactly. That's why they call him Mr. Peepers."

Kahan did the talking. " 'They'?"

"He is a contract killer known to about every law enforcement agency in the world."

"Name?"

"No identity other than Mr. Peepers. And if you cross his path, don't call him that."

Kahan's expression changed, the corners of his lips turning down, so Jesse kept at him. Jesse could see that it was Kahan he had to convince.

"No one even knew what he looked like until one of my officers and I had a confrontation with him. Shot my officer in the gut below his vest, but my guy wounded him in the right shoulder."

"Hold on one second, you two," Hunsicker said. "Before you go all covert ops on me here, I need to know what the hell is going on. What's this about him wanting to hurt Jenn? Why would he want to hurt Jenn?

172

She hasn't been married to you for a far bit longer than you two were married in the first place."

Jesse wasn't anxious to tell the story, because no matter how he related it, the bottom line was an unpleasant one for all sorts of reasons. And there was no way around the fact that all roads led back to Jesse himself. Peepers might have been the bad guy in this, but it was Jesse who had set the chain of events in motion. He told them straight out, no excuses, no explanations of why he'd done what he'd done. He'd had to save an innocent woman's life, so he did what he had to do. Hunsicker's expression displayed a full range of emotions as Jesse spoke. Kahan kept that blank, dispassionate look on his face as he listened. When he finished, Hale Hunsicker looked more worried than angry. Like earlier, Kahan spoke first, and to his boss's ears it was a peculiar question.

"You say in Salem he killed the dog, too?"

Jesse nodded, but unlike Hunsicker, he understood the question.

Hale had had enough. "All due respect, who gives a good goddamn if he killed the dog?"

"It speaks to a lack of compassion," Kahan said. "He killed the dog in Salem

173

because it was efficient to do so. He didn't think twice about it."

Hunsicker plopped himself hard in a chair. "I must be losing my mind. You two are talking about a lack of compassion because he killed a dog when he had just killed two complete strangers, an old woman and a cabdriver, for no good reason."

Putting his hand into the side pocket of his jacket, Jesse said, "I've shown up at many brutal murder scenes where bodies were everywhere, bodies that were barely even human anymore. But the killer or killers couldn't bring themselves to hurt the pets. There were a few instances when the perps had risked capture to feed the dogs or cats before leaving the scene. Killing the dog says something about who we're dealing with." Jesse pulled his hand out of his pocket and arrayed nine small color photos on the table. "These say much more."

Hunsicker's eyes got big, though he said nothing. Kahan looked distressed and also kept silent.

Jesse pointed at some of the photos. "That's what he did to Gino Fish's receptionist. Those are the victims from Salem. That's what Vic Prado looked like before I stopped Peepers from finishing him." Next Jesse pointed at what was left of some of

Peepers's female victims. "He likes hurting people when he has the chance, women most of all."

Hunsicker said, "Okay, Jesse, you've made your point. We'll call out the National Guard and the Texas Rangers. We'll round up every law enforcement type and ex–Blackwater employee we can find and we'll —"

But Kahan shook his head and said, "I would advise against it. We'll drive him underground, then he'll come at Mrs. Hunsicker when she's more vulnerable. You can't protect anyone twenty-four/seven. If you can kill a president or a man in prison in solitary, you can kill anyone, sir. I've had occasion to carry out missions against targets who considered themselves invulnerable. No one is invulnerable. No one."

"Okay, then we'll move the wedding venue and —"

"Same answer, Hale," Jesse said.

"He's right, sir."

"Then what, I'm supposed to let the woman I love be the bait?"

Neither Jesse nor Kahan spoke, but their message was clear enough.

Hale Hunsicker stood and kicked over the chair he'd been sitting in. He walked up to Jesse and stuck a finger in his face. "All right, Stone. If Scott says this is what's got to be, then it's got to be. But if Jenn is injured in any way, this Peepers a-hole will be the least of your worries. I will make it my mission to fuck up your life and then kill you." He pointed at Kahan. "And it won't be him doin' the killin'. We understand each other?"

When Jesse nodded, Hunsicker stormed out.

Kahan looked Jesse in the eye. "He means it, Stone."

"I know he does," he said. "I know."

THIRTY-TWO

The rude blonde's voice was almost gone. She had been screaming through her gag from the moment she came out of her dream-filled stupor. You can scream for just so long. Only one other person was in earshot: the plain-faced man who'd stood over her, watching her, soaking up her panic like a lizard warming its cold blood on a rock in the sun. He seemed to enjoy the screaming, enjoyed her straining so hard against the straps that held her tight to the table. Eventually, she had nothing left in her to scream with and her panic dissolved into sobbing.

When the tears came, he gently stroked her sweat-soaked hair, smiling that smile of his. That frightened her most of all, his smile. His eyes went opaque and he seemed to go into a place in his head. She didn't want to think about what went on in that place. During her lucid moments, she had tried desperately to remember where she recognized him from, but it was always just beyond her grasp, like an itch too far down her back to reach.

"Shhh . . . shhh," he said in a nasal whisper, putting his index finger across her dry, cracked lips. "I haven't even hurt you . . . yet. If you stop crying, I'll remove the gag for a while and give you something to drink. If you misbehave, though, I promise you you will regret it." He put his lips so close to her right ear that they brushed against it. She could hear his excited breathing. He said, "I would like that very much. I would like it if you misbehaved."

That stopped the crying, but only induced another round of screaming into her gag. There was profound panic in her eyes and she struggled mightily against the restraints. Then suddenly there was a popping sound and her body went stiff with pain. Following the stiffness came her clenching in pain. But her left arm hung oddly off her shoulder.

He laughed at her, shaking his head. He'd seen this before. Sometimes when they fought too hard against the straps and twisted in just the wrong way, they would dislocate a shoulder or an ankle.

"You've dislocated your shoulder," he

said. "Immensely painful, isn't it? If you keep this up, I won't have to lift a finger to hurt you. Live with the pain for a while. Let it be your teacher. Maybe, if you behave, I'll reset it for you. Are you going to behave?"

She nodded furiously.

"Are you sure?"

She was nodding even more intensely now. Anything to make the pain stop. Anything. She'd never felt anything like it before. She was dizzy and nauseated from it.

"Please! Please!" she shouted through the gag.

He smiled at her. "Not so rude now, are you?"

She didn't understand, but shook her head. "Please! Please!" she screamed again.

"You did this to yourself, you know?" he said. "All I wanted to do was to have lunch in peace, but you just couldn't leave me alone. You just couldn't sit at another table."

Then she knew. The itch was scratched. He was the guy from the barbecue joint, the one who got the beer spilled on him. Maybe it was the aftereffects of the drugs or the intensity of the pain, but suddenly the absurdity of her situation struck her as funny. And instead of screaming or sobbing into her gag, she laughed.

He'd seen this, too. It was a kind of pain-induced madness. He didn't like it very much, even if he understood it. He laughed with her for a few seconds, then his eyes went opaque, his laugh morphing into a mocking imitation of her laugh. He put his face very close to hers.

"I'm glad you think it's funny, because laughing is misbehaving."

With that he stood and pushed hard on her dislocated shoulder. The laughter came to an abrupt halt. Again, her body went stiff with pain. When her body went limp, he began to stroke her hair again.

"Don't worry, I'll reset your shoulder. You and I are going to get to be good friends over the next several weeks. Good friends. I'm going to teach you things about yourself that you never knew you were capable of. But for right now, I have some calls to make and other business to attend to. When I come back, I'll do as I promised. While I'm gone, while you learn to live with pain, think about your rudeness. Make it the only thing you think about."

When he left the room, he took out his throwaway cell phone and dialed a Boston area number.

THIRTY-THREE

Scott Kahan and Jesse Stone sat across from each other at the Italian restaurant on Fifty-third Street, alternating their gazes between the menu and the man on the opposite side of the table. Hale Hunsicker had wanted to be a part of their conversation, but Kahan advised against it, saying that it wasn't a good idea for him and Jesse to be seen together in public before the week of the wedding. Hunsicker didn't like it but had agreed not to come if it helped keep Jenn safe. Jesse got the sense that Hunsicker was a man who usually got his way, through charm or money or sheer force. He gave Kahan props for both his willingness to say no to his boss and for having enough credibility with the man for Hunsicker to back down.

Jesse knew that the system was rigged for the rich and powerful to get their way. He'd learned that lesson as a cop and detective in

L.A., a town that churned out rich and powerful people by the dozen. And it wasn't any easier in Paradise, where the old money and town elders constantly held the loss of his job over his head. Not that he was given to buckling under the pressure. Buckling wasn't in his DNA.

"I noticed you didn't order a drink," Kahan said.

"Uh-huh."

"What's up? Not in the mood for Black Label today?"

Jesse didn't look up from the menu. "Don't need sources in the intelligence community to find out about my drinking. I'm sure Jenn's recited chapter and verse about my problems to your boss."

Kahan laughed. "Actually, Mr. Hunsicker's intended basically sings your praises. I think it annoys the piss out of him."

"Jenn is good at that."

"I spoke with several of your former LAPD Robbery-Homicide colleagues."

Now it was Jesse's turn to laugh. "I'm sure they gave you an earful."

"To a man they said you were the best until you self-destructed. They said they couldn't trust you to have their backs anymore."

"I'm surprised you didn't just break into

my shrink's office. It would have saved you a lot of bother and money."

"Dix? I tried scamming him into releasing your files to me. He didn't buy it and told me to go fuck myself."

"He can be a pain, but he just scored big points in my book. Look, you want to know something about me, ask me."

"Okay. You still a drunk?" Kahan was goading as much as he was asking.

Jesse nodded. "Technically, I guess so. You never stop being one, even if you stop drinking."

"But you're not drinking today. Trying to impress me?"

"Nope. The last time I did something to purposely impress anyone was in A ball."

"And what was that?"

"I bet the other shortstop on the team I could hit the first baseman in the glove with the ball three times in a row with my eyes closed."

"What happened?"

"The other shortstop bought my meals for a week." Jesse smiled. He hadn't thought about that in years. Maybe not since it happened. Now it seemed as if it was almost someone else's memory.

Kahan looked away from Jesse and back at the menu. "We have a common purpose, but I need to know whether I can depend on you, whether you'll have my back. You would have the same concerns in my shoes."

Jesse didn't like Kahan's tone, but he had a point. They did need to trust each other.

"Fair enough."

After the waiter came and took their orders, Kahan asked, "So, you're a hundred percent sure Peepers is our target?"

"Hundred percent. We've got him on surveillance leaving Gino Fish's office right after the murders."

"Then why the sketch? Why not bring me a photo of him?"

Jesse said, "He was disguised."

"Then you're not a hundred percent sure."

"I'm sure."

Kahan opened his mouth to argue, but thought better of it.

"Does Peepers know you know about him?"

The million-dollar question. Jesse wasn't sure of the answer. That was the thing with Peepers: You could never be sure what he wanted you to know. Jesse was going to keep that to himself, but he needed this guy, for better or worse.

"I don't think so. My guess is he wanted me to know, but then changed his mind when things went wrong in Boston. He's a planner, but he's also quick on his feet. He can improvise and he's not afraid to take big risks."

"How big?"

"First time we crossed paths, he set off a smoke grenade in another town's police headquarters, waited until the building was evacuated, and then broke into their property room in order to locate a camera that might've had his photo on its chip."

"We might be able to use that," Kahan said.

Jesse was skeptical. "Maybe." Then he shifted gears. "We both told your boss not to call out the cavalry, but I'm uncomfortable operating on someone else's patch without giving them a heads-up, especially if we have to call on them."

"Agreed. The wedding and most of the pre-wedding events are taking place in Vineland Park Village. I know the chief there, Jeb Lockett. We can trust him to be discreet."

"Can you arrange a meeting between us before the wedding?"

"But —"

Jesse put his right palm up. "You know your world. I know mine. Lockett will want to speak to me. How about next week?"

"It's a big risk, you coming to Dallas

before the wedding week."

"A risk worth taking. Besides, Peepers can't be everywhere at once. He won't be watching the cops. He'll be looking for a change in Jenn's routine or an obvious change in your procedures. That's why you can't do obvious security checks on employees of the caterers, the valets, the country-club employees, or —"

"You think?" Kahan made an angry face. "Give me credit for knowing my job, too."

"Sorry."

"One last question, Stone."

"Shoot."

"Mr. Hunsicker was too preoccupied by all this for it to register. Maybe it will occur to him later or maybe not. But how long have you had the photo of your ex with the message about the praying mantis?"

"More than a year."

"And this is the first anyone's hearing about it. Why?"

"If you don't already know the answer to that," Jesse said, "then I shouldn't give you credit for knowing your job."

Kahan smiled, looked over Jesse's shoulder, and said, "Food's here."

THIRTY-FOUR

As Jesse drove along the Concord Turnpike, his thoughts drifted back to earlier in the day. He didn't know how to feel about what had gone down in New York. He'd had to tell Hale Hunsicker. The man had a right to know Jenn was in danger. And if Jesse wanted to protect Jenn, he needed Hunsicker's help. But now he wasn't so sure he'd made the right move. Jesse didn't usually second-guess his decisions, but this wasn't usually. By his telling Hunsicker, things had suddenly gotten exponentially more complicated. He had ceded that much more control of the situation, whatever little real control he had of it to begin with. Jesse remembered something he'd heard a long time ago. So long ago that he'd forgotten who'd said it, yet the words stuck in his head. *There's no such thing as a secret when more than one person knows it.*

Telling Hunsicker wasn't like telling most

people. People with money are trouble because money gives people power and a sense of entitlement. They also think having money means they're smarter than everyone else in the room, that they always know better even when there's no evidence to support that belief. And most people can't afford or don't need a head of security. As unsure as he was about giving Hunsicker a heads-up, he was even less sure of Kahan. Jesse disdained arrogance. Arrogance was the emotional equivalent of wealth. It gave you a false sense of superiority, a sense of invincibility. Jesse had seen it as a ballplayer. He played with guys who thought great talent made them invulnerable, but as Kahan himself had said, no one was invulnerable. He didn't need Kahan to tell him that. The aching in his wrecked right shoulder reminded him of that lesson every day of his life.

For all of his worries about loss of control, Jesse was now about to cede more of it by letting someone else in on the secret. He clicked his turn signal and pulled into the bowling alley's lot. There were only a few other cars in the lot, but the one he was looking for was there. Like its owner, it was expensively appointed, perfectly detailed, and painted a vaguely threatening flat black.

Getting out of his Explorer, Jesse noticed it was cooler here than it had been in New York. Then he turned and went inside.

Bowling alleys were mournful when they were silent, but he wasn't here to bowl or play candlepin. He was here to see Vinnie Morris. Jesse had needed to get Healy on board and to alert Hunsicker before telling Vinnie. Strangely, it was Morris he trusted most of all not to do anything to screw things up. Vinnie was a lot of things. A cool customer above all else, not a man given to acting on his first impulse. Unlike those of Healy, Hunsicker, or Kahan, Morris's loyalties weren't divided. He was deadly, a shark, but a thinking man's shark.

Jesse stopped at the counter and asked for Morris. The fat guy behind the counter was wearing a Red Sox jersey that fit him a few lifetimes ago. The top of his head featured lots of skin and a few lonely gray hairs. He was too busy reading the *Globe* to look up from the paper.

"Fresh outta Vinnies here," the fat man said, looking up, his eyelids as droopy as his belly. "You want bowling shoes? We got plenty of them. Vinnies we ain't got."

Jesse wasn't in the mood and stuck his shield in front of the guy's face.

He was unimpressed. "Paradise, huh?

Where's that at? I been searching for it my whole stinkin' life."

"Get on the phone and tell Vinnie Morris Jesse Stone is here to see him. And don't say there's no Vinnie here."

"There's no Vinnie here."

Jesse grabbed a handful of the fat man's jersey and yanked his head down onto the counter so that his fleshy left cheek spread out across the sports pages.

"Last chance," Jesse said.

"Stone, Stone, take it easy," Vinnie Morris called out from behind him. "The man's only doing his job."

Jesse let the man go and smoothed out the top of his Sox jersey. "Sorry."

Fat man shrugged and made a face, jerking up one corner of his mouth. He went back to the paper.

"What is it, Stone?" Morris asked.

"Can we talk . . . alone?" Jesse said, pointing at the two big men flanking Morris.

Morris jerked his head and his bookends stepped back.

"This way," he said to Jesse, pointing toward the game room.

The game room was fairly dark but for all the colored lights on the row of unused pinball machines. Every few seconds one of the pinball machines would flash, bells would ring. Vinnie stopped by the air-hockey table, wiped an area along one of its rails with a handkerchief, and then sat back against the table.

"So, you got my attention, Stone."

"You were right about Gino, but you were wrong, too."

"I already have enough headaches and I don't like riddles."

"Gino didn't kill the boy, but he did kill himself."

Vinnie shook his head. "Then it don't figure."

"It does if Gino was saving himself from a long and painful death."

"Like I said, Stone, I don't like riddles."

"It was Peepers."

"Fuck." Vinnie Morris didn't usually show emotion, and Jesse had never seen Morris afraid. Not until that moment. "You sure?"

Jesse nodded.

"I told Gino not to do that thing for you. So, what are you going to do to make it right?"

"That's why I'm here, Vinnie," Jesse said, "to try and make it right."

THIRTY-FIVE

It was past one a.m. when he reentered the corrugated steel building in West Dallas. He was carrying a copy of *The Dallas Morning News* under his left arm and a large coffee in his right hand. After closing the door behind him, he stood very still, listening for signs of life from the rude blonde. Not that he had done much to her beyond toying with her head. Hell, he'd even reset her dislocated shoulder and bathed her a few times. He'd fed her, too. In her way, she was very lucky. Under nearly any other set of circumstances, she would be begging him to kill her to stop the pain. But no, he had other plans for her. Big plans.

Hearing nothing but the buzz of traffic from the highway, he put the coffee and the paper down. He stripped out of his sweat-dampened waiter clothing: clip-on bow tie, the white tuxedo shirt, black polyester pants, black socks, and ugly gum-soled black shoes. Perfect camouflage for an invisible man doing an invisible job. He sniffed the shirt and gagged. It stank of sautéed shrimp in sriracha sauce. He hated seafood, shrimp most of all, and the Asian pepper sauce had burned his eyes. Yet he had had to stand at the shrimp station for three hours in the main hall of the Perot Museum as wealthy Texans got progressively drunker, sloppier, and more inane. He wondered who had first said that thing about there being no dumb questions. Whoever said it, he thought, had never worked in catering.

At least eleven times during the evening, party guests had approached him and asked if those were shrimp he was serving. Eleven. Exactly eleven. He had counted. And each time it was all he could do not to scream at them, "What else do you think they are, wood grubs with tails?" People were such fools, but he'd just smiled his smile at them, placing a tablespoon of oil, twelve shrimp, and a ladle of the red pepper sauce in the hot pan. His shoulder ached from having to deal with that heavy pan, but he did enjoy watching the heat turn the shrimp's sickly gray flesh white and pink. He liked what fire did to flesh.

He thought about sponge-bathing himself, but realized that he had work to do. He had to start working on Jenn's wedding gift. After that, he would clean himself up and get some rest. He had another job for a different catering company later that afternoon. At least he wouldn't have to wear the same outfit. The other catering company was all about casual. Golf shirt, jeans, and running shoes were all they required. And mercifully, they didn't usually do shrimp. *Mercifully.* He laughed at himself for even thinking of that word. More than knives or fire or pliers, mercy and hope were his greatest devices for the delivery of pain. Then his contemplation of pain was disturbed by the sound of the rude blonde stirring.

He picked up the paper and the coffee and went into the workshop area, where she was tied down to the bench. He flicked on the light. She turned her head to look at him and when she saw he was mostly undressed, she began screaming into her gag and pulling on her restraints. He hadn't realized, and placed the paper and coffee down.

"Shhh," he said, stroking her hair. "I don't do that. I never do that. If I'd wanted to do that to you, I would have done it before now. It was just a long, miserable day at work and I had to get out of those clothes. I'm sorry. See, if you had only said sorry to me, you wouldn't be here."

She had a brief crying jag. When she calmed, he showed her the paper.

"You're famous," he said, pointing to the large photo of her adorning the front page. "This picture doesn't do you justice, though."

Her eyes got wide at the sight of her photo and the headline about her having gone missing days ago. He laughed at her when he saw a glimmer of hope in her red-rimmed blue eyes. She had hope and, if things progressed as he planned, hers might actually not go unfulfilled. But there was a lot of work to be done before he determined her fate. First, he grabbed a chair, sipped his coffee, and opened the paper.

"Says your name is Belinda June Yankton and that you're twenty-nine. They got that much right, at least according to your driver's license. You'd be amazed at the details newspapers get wrong."

She didn't move, didn't make a sound, for fear of angering him.

"A cheerleader at the University of North Texas. Yes, I can see that. I can only imagine how rude you were to the ugly boys and the fat girls at school."

He felt the heat rising in him as he remembered how she'd treated him at the barbecue joint, but he needed her in spite of a suddenly acute desire to hurt her.

"Divorced already . . . from one of Dallas's leading young attorneys," he said, going back to the paper. "I can see that, too. It would account for your fancy address and that car of yours. I bet your ex's rooting against you. Bet you he'd like to have some time with you trussed up this way. What do you think, Belinda June? Maybe I'll seek him out and ask him."

She shook her head violently and the crying started all over again.

He took a long sip of coffee and folded the paper. He walked over to her and said, "I have a lot of work to do and I need quiet. Would you like to go to sleep and dream again?"

She nodded, straining to say a gag-muffled "yes."

"First you need to drink. And remember, no talking when I remove the gag. I have need of you, but don't misbehave. I don't need you that much that I can't find a substitute."

Ten minutes and two bottles of cold Gatorade later, Belinda June Yankton was unconscious and well on her way to some vivid dreams. Peepers was drilling a fuse hole into a length of pipe.

THIRTY-SIX

Jesse was looking at the L.A. Dodgers Classics calendar on the wall to the right of the window behind his desk. The photo for the month of September was of Sandy Koufax, hands above his head in the midst of his windup, Willie Mays at the plate, awaiting the pitch. Jesse paid no mind to the photo. Instead he counted the days until he and Diana had to leave for Dallas. Only two to go.

Nearly a month had passed since his meeting with Hunsicker and Kahan in New York. Labor Day had come and gone. The kids in town were back at school and life in Paradise had settled into a familiar pre-autumn rhythm. The trees were hinting at their coming turn. Daylight hours were being gently squeezed out by invading darkness and the wind that blew a tad chillier than it had the day before or the day before that. Healy had stopped by the office a few times to check on progress in the case and just to talk. Retirement was going to be hard on a lifer like Healy, but at least his wife was responding well to the treatment and medication the cardiologist had prescribed.

"How's the golf game?" Jesse asked the last time Healy had come in.

"Hopeless. Fall can't get here too soon, so I can give it up."

Otherwise it had been a quiet month. Very quiet. Too quiet for Jesse's liking. He trusted calm up to a point, but that point had come and gone. Mostly it was the waiting that was getting to him. There'd been some news from Dallas. Kahan had found a few men fitting Peepers's general description who had worked or were working for the companies scheduled to do catering for the wedding week events. He'd had them followed at safe distances, had looked into their backgrounds. So far, they had all checked out. Jesse hoped like hell that none of Kahan's prying had tipped Peepers off to the fact that they were onto him.

"Two of these catering employees were fired or quit. One left town. Not uncommon with these types of jobs," Kahan said. "Lots of turnover. I don't think that's how he's coming at her."

"However he comes at her, he'll do it in

front of me. That's the point. He'll want me to watch."

"Then why come and give him the satisfaction?"

"You know the answer to that. If I don't come, no one will be safe, Jenn and your boss included, no matter how good you are at your job."

"Are you sure he knows you're coming?"

That was a good question. Frankly, Jesse had expected to hear from Peepers by now. Where, he wondered, was the taunting letter or photo? Just as Jenn had sent him an invitation, Jesse was sure that Peepers would have sent one of his own by now. It worried Jesse that maybe Peepers was already one step ahead of them all. That Peepers somehow knew Jesse had pieced together the carnage at Gino Fish's office, the vandalism in Paradise, and the murders in Salem. Or maybe Hunsicker's head of security wasn't as slick as he believed himself to be. The fact was that Peepers had lived one step ahead of everyone for many years. Jesse really had no way of knowing if he was right about Peepers. It was guesswork. Educated guesswork, but guesswork nonetheless.

Jesse was still staring at the calendar when his phone buzzed. He pulled the phone out of his pocket and was confused to see it was

Suit calling.

"Aren't you on patrol?" Jesse asked.

"You saw me head out an hour ago."

"Then why are you calling me on the phone."

"I didn't want this on the radio, Jesse. I'm over on the two-hundred block of Lexington Road."

"Uh-huh."

"I think you better get over here. Quick. There's something you need to see."

Jesse hung up.

"Where you headed, Jesse?" Alisha asked as Jesse passed her.

He didn't answer.

Less than five minutes later, Jesse and Suit were kneeling by the flat rear tire of a 2009 Honda Civic. It was obvious to anyone who looked at the tire what had caused the flat. There was about a dime-sized hole in the sidewall of the tire, about six inches above the pavement.

"I was driving by when I noticed it. Do you think it's a coincidence, Jesse, or maybe a copycat?"

"I don't believe in coincidences."

"I know you don't. I guess I was just hoping."

Jesse reached across and put his hand on Suit's shoulder. "I understand. Let's get someone over here to dig the slug out. Use your cell phone. I don't want this on the police radio, in case he's using a scanner."

"It's him, isn't it, Jesse? He's here, not in Texas."

Jesse shrugged. "Maybe, or maybe that's what he wants us to think. He's playing with us. It's what he does."

Suit stood up and paced while Jesse looked to see if there were any differences he could spot between this blown-out tire and the others before it. When he turned to look up at Suit, he saw the fear in the big man's face.

"Suit, c'mon, get Peter over here."

Jesse listened carefully to Suit's voice as he spoke to Perkins. He didn't like what he heard. Suit kept clearing his throat as he spoke, almost as if he was holding back tears. The fear in his officer's eyes, the pacing about, and the strain in his voice were all bad signs. It was the thing Jesse had worried about since Suit had returned to duty after he'd been shot by Peepers. Jesse couldn't afford to give Suit time off, not with leaving for Jenn's wedding, nor could he afford to have Suit fall apart on duty.

"Suit, are you all right?" Jesse asked, standing to face him.

"Sure, Jesse." His answer was firm, too firm.

"Everyone in your family's moved out of town, right? Your mom's down in Florida."

Suit nodded, plunging his hand into his pocket to feel for the engagement ring he'd moved from one pair of uniform pants to the other for weeks. After the day he was called back to the station, he hadn't been able to muster up the nerve to propose. At least that's what he'd told himself, but now he knew the truth. He knew that as long as he was a target and Peepers was out there, Elena was in terrible danger. He couldn't let anything happen to her, not on his account. His hand found the ring at the bottom of his pocket.

"Suit! Suit! What's up? Are you listening to me?"

"Sorry, Jesse, yeah. You're right," he said, running the ridges of his fingertip along a facet of the perfect cut diamond. "My family's safe. I've only got to watch out for myself."

"Luther, if you can't handle this, I'll understand, but you need to tell me the truth."

Suit laughed almost involuntarily. "Luther. You never call me Luther. I'll be fine. I swear. I know how to handle this."

Before the discussion went any further, Peter Perkins rolled up in his cruiser. Never in the history of the Paradise PD had a flat tire received the attention of the chief and two senior officers.

THIRTY-SEVEN

Belinda June Yankton's blue eyes snapped wide open, but she knew where she was. She was long over wishing or hoping that the next time would be different, that she would wake up in her bed, the sheets cool against her brown skin, happily sore from sex, the smell of eggs, frying bacon, and fresh-ground coffee beans filling up her head. She did sometimes find herself hoping her dreams would never end. Her dreams had never meant so much to her before, nor had they seemed so very real. Dreams had come to be where she did her real living these days.

Just before opening her eyes, she had been snorkeling above a coral reef. The water was so clear that if she turned to look up at the surface she could make out individual flames on the face of the sun. Its warmth reached through the light teal tint of the world, surrounding her like her daddy's arms. But it had been the fishes that captured her attention. There were thousands of them, millions of them in all shapes and sizes. And their eyes were not passive fish eyes, cold and unfeeling. Some of them, the little silvery ones with the iridescent skins and rainbow speckles, had black eyelashes, long and fluttery. Some, the big blue-skinned tunas, had lips and spoke to her, not in words but in thoughts. They asked a lot of questions, tunas did. She had answered them as best she could. Then she was out of the teal water and in the world of her own foul-smelling sweat.

She had come to accept that whatever remained of her life would be lived out strapped to a workbench, suffering through bouts of the chills as she came out of her dreams. The first few weeks when she'd awaken like this, the horror of her situation would come rushing back in so that it took her breath away and she'd break down. That had passed: the crying and choking into her gag, the begging and bargaining. He had told her he would teach her things about herself that she didn't know she was capable of. He was right about that. About a week ago, after he'd washed her down and loosened her gag, she had offered herself to him.

He just snickered and said, "They always

do that, offer themselves to me."

He said that phrase a lot, not the last part. The first part. *They always say that. They always do that.* She didn't like thinking about how many times he had done this sort of thing before.

Then he re-fixed her gag and stroked her hair. She hated herself for it, but she had come to like it when he stroked her hair. It made her feel human. It was something to hang on to. It gave her hope that he connected to her somehow. She might as well have wished for the talking tuna to be real. The only time he seemed even vaguely human was when she'd said she was sorry for spilling his beer in his lap. That opaque look in his eyes cleared and the perpetual smirk vanished from his face.

"You know," he said, "I think you actually mean it."

She did.

That was last week. Maybe not. It might've been yesterday. She had lost track of time. When you're strapped to a table like she was and likely to be tortured to death, losing time is a way to keep the little bits of sanity left to you. She knew she had been there for many weeks, at least. That was all she was sure of. He had been drugging her constantly of late, which was fine with her, but it completely discombobulated her and sometimes she felt she had lost whole days to unconsciousness.

She lifted her head off the table and reflexively tried to stretch the weariness out of her arms. It was ridiculous, of course, restrained as she was. But it was easier for her to accept her plight than for her reflexes. Only this time there was some give when she pulled her right arm toward her chest. At first, after feeling the give in the strap, she lay absolutely still, listening for signs of him. Nothing. Only the buzz of traffic, which had become the droning soundtrack to her captivity. Then she yanked her right arm again. More give. She girded herself, focused every ounce of strength and energy she had left into her right hand and arm. She counted to herself. *One. Two. Three.*

Her right arm was free, snapping forward so hard her hand slammed into her chest. She held her hand up and studied the frayed end of the leather strap. It must have torn from her weeks and weeks of pulling against it and it rubbing against a sharp edge. She gathered herself, then twisted her body so she could use her right hand to undo the left-hand restraint. After about an hour, she was free, but spent. He had kept her hydrated and fed her a protein bar or two a day, but she was weak and she collapsed to the concrete floor when she tried standing. She could not afford to wait and gather herself again. She had to get out of there before he got back.

By the time she rolled out the front door, her knees, forearms, shins, and elbows were raw and bloodied, but she barely felt the pain. It was bright and kiln-hot. The street she was on was deserted and dimly lit. She crawled across the burning-hot pavement to the opposite side of the street, then pulled herself to her feet. She needed to get her bearings, to get some sense of where she was and where she could go. And when she steadied herself as best she could on legs wobbly as a newborn calf's, she recognized a landmark in the near distance. It was hard to miss its huge, white tubular arch jutting up four hundred feet into the pale blue Texas sky and its splayed mass of taut cables giving the impression of an otherworldly stringed instrument. The Margaret Hunt Hill Bridge or, as everyone in town called it, Large Marge. It was no more than a mile away. She'd always thought it a hideous-looking thing, but at just that moment it was the most beautiful thing she had ever seen. She fell to her knees and wept.

THIRTY-EIGHT

When Jesse Stone got back to the station, he stopped at the desk to ask Alisha if he'd missed anything. As she opened her mouth to answer, Jesse interrupted, pointing at the large brown envelope in front of her.

"Is that for me?"

"It is. How did you —"

"Who delivered it?"

She shrugged. "A messenger."

"Did he make you sign something? Did he give you a receipt?"

"No. He just said this was for you and to make sure you got it."

"What did he look like?"

"I'm sorry, Jesse, I was taking a call and I really wasn't paying attention."

"White, African American, Asian, Hisp—"

"White," she said, "late thirties, I think. On the small side, but I couldn't swear to it. Glasses, maybe. That's all I can remember. I was paying more attention to the woman on the phone. I guess he was kind of nondescript."

Jesse's throat went dry. "That's okay. Did you hear a car pull up in front before he came in?"

"Come to think of it, I did. I heard brakes squeal, like they needed new pads. He left it running."

"Could you tell anything about it, from the sound of the engine?"

"Small car. A Honda, maybe." She shrugged again. "I don't know. I can't be sure."

"How long ago?"

"I'm surprised you didn't run into him outside."

"Okay," Jesse said, about-facing, "get on the horn to everyone on patrol and give them as much of a description of him and the car as you can. I want him picked up for questioning. He may be armed and dangerous, but maybe not. He may be what you said he was, a messenger. Emphasize nonlethal force and firing only if fired upon. I want to know if anyone spots him. And treat that envelope like evidence. Bag it and put it in the locker until I get back."

Jesse was out of the station and in his Explorer. He wasn't sure where he was going, but at least he had some idea of who and what he was looking for. This was all so reminiscent of how Peepers had had the photo of Jenn delivered after their first confrontation. That time Molly was at the desk when the messenger delivered the envelope and it was Molly who'd handed it to Jesse. He remembered going cold inside when he saw the message written on the back: *Do you ask a praying mantis why?* It was a reference to the one conversation Jesse had had with Peepers. It was just before Suit got shot. Jesse had asked Peepers why he enjoyed inflicting pain.

"Do you ask a praying mantis why?" was what he'd said.

That response alone was enough to put a scare into most people. It had certainly given Jesse pause. And when Jesse saw it written on the back of the photo of Jenn, he didn't hesitate before calling Jenn's phone. But when she picked up, he hadn't known what to say. *Watch out, there's a psycho killer following you around and it's my fault. Lock yourself in a room and don't come out until I tell you. Hire a bodyguard.* In the end, he figured the best way to keep his ex-wife safe was to keep his distance from her.

Since Jesse assumed the messenger, whether it was really Peepers or not, wanted to get out of town as fast as he could, he drove the most direct route away from the station to the highway. He didn't speed more than a little and didn't use his portable cherry top. He couldn't afford to spook the man he was looking for. He didn't want to give him a reason to run. After he listened to Alisha alert the patrol cars as he'd ordered her to, he got on the mic and told them to ride along the most traveled routes out of town.

"No lights and sirens unless he runs," he said. "We don't want any citizens caught up in this. First thing you do if he runs is get on the horn and report your position and where he's headed."

It didn't take long before someone was on the radio. It was Suit.

"I've got eyes on," he said. "White, 1991 Nissan Sentra, Mass tag number: four two one, X-ray one tango. He's proceeding north along Old Main Street, turning west onto Dock Road. I'm far enough back that I don't think he sees me."

"I'm close," Jesse said. "He's heading to the Swap and then —"

Then Suit shouted, "He's running. Just hit his gas and turned the wrong way north on Amherst."

Jesse heard Suit's siren pierce the late-morning quiet.

"Stay in pursuit, but don't try to overtake him," Jesse said. "I will head him off at Whaler and force him down Trench Alley. All other cars, block off access to the highway."

Jesse reached around behind him to the backseat and retrieved his seldom-used cherry top. He stuck it on the roof of his Explorer and hit the siren. With the tourists gone and the kids back in school, traffic was light. He floored the SUV and raced up past where Suit was chasing the suspect. Jesse wasn't sure whether his engine was revving higher than his heart rate. All he could think about was putting an end to it here, stopping Peepers before he got a chance to get at Jenn. If they could capture him now, everyone would be safe: Suit, Healy, Molly, Diana. They would all be able to breathe again. The last several weeks had been a hellish limbo for them all.

"Where is he now, Suit?"

"On Welby, heading toward Millstone."

Jesse swung a hard left onto Millstone. Just as he hit the intersection of Welby and Millstone, he saw the white Sentra heading right at his driver's-side door, Suit's cruiser four car lengths behind it. The little Nissan swerved left into Trench Alley, its tires smoking and rear end fishtailing as it went.

The acrid stink of burning rubber came up through the Explorer's air vents, but Jesse smiled. They had him penned in now. Trench Alley dead-ended at Sawtooth Creek. Jesse looked in his rearview, and when he saw Suit fall in behind him, he gave the thumbs-up sign in the rearview. Then things went sideways.

THIRTY-NINE

While Jesse was still looking in his rearview mirror, something hit his front windshield and sent bits of safety glass flying into the cabin. After reflexively turning away, Jesse saw the hole in the glass and the spiderweb of cracks spreading out from it.

"Suit," he said into his mic, "he just fired at me. He put one through my windshield, but we want him alive."

"Are you sure about that, Jesse?"

"No, but it's what we're going to —"

Jesse didn't finish the sentence because a second bullet went through his sideview mirror. He was tempted to return fire, but he knew that it was much easier in the movies than it was in real life. It was difficult enough to hit a stationary target when you yourself were stationary. Hitting a moving target from a moving vehicle while your arm was bouncing and you were full of adrenaline was a scenario unlikely to produce the desired result. Jesse didn't want bullets ricocheting off brick or concrete. He didn't want stray bullets going through windows or doors or through the bodies of innocent pedestrians.

Instead of returning fire, Jesse hit the gas pedal harder, surging forward, coming right up on the Sentra's bumper and ramming it. But if Jesse thought the Sentra would slow up or that the guy behind the wheel would stop shooting and surrender, he was wrong. The Sentra's back window blew out and a storm of buckshot pellets tore into the Explorer's front grille. Steam poured out of the front of the old SUV. The Sentra sped up, the driver yanking left on his steering wheel, trying to make an impossible turn into a narrow alley between a body shop and the two gas pumps used by the local cab companies and limo services to fuel up their fleets. The Sentra didn't make it.

When the front driver's-side tire hit the curb, the little Nissan wobbled, tipped onto two wheels, then flipped over, skidding on its roof toward the gas pumps. Jesse jammed on his brakes. Suit jammed on his in turn. They both watched helplessly as the Sentra slammed into the pumps, one of which was being used to fill up an airport shuttle van. When the van driver saw what was happening he took off, just clearing the pumps when the Sentra hit. At first the fire was small, but intense. Jesse and Suit were out of their vehicles, running, their sidearms drawn.

"I called it in," Suit said.

"You get everybody out of there and then the body shop. I'll get the suspect."

"But it's —"

"That's an order! And don't approach the car unless I give you the go-ahead. He's heavily armed. Fired a handgun and a shotgun at me."

Suit did as he was told and detoured into the garage area. Jesse went straight to the Sentra. He put his nine-millimeter at his side, because even at thirty feet, he could see this would end badly for whoever was at the wheel of the Sentra. How badly depended on how quickly the fire spread. The roof of the car had withstood the impact pretty well, crushing down only slightly after flipping over. The driver was a bloody, twisted mess. He hadn't worn his seat belt and the airbag hadn't deployed. And because the car was upside down, the driver's body slumped on top of his head, his neck at an angle that most living humans could never have achieved.

Jesse had seen a lot of dead bodies in his

time, enough to know that the driver was no longer among the living. It was still important to get to his body, to retrieve as much evidence as possible, and to discover who this guy was. Jesse wasn't big on prayer, but as he approached the car he found himself quietly muttering the outlines of a deal between himself and the Almighty. The heat was already nearly unbearable. Jesse tugged on the door handle, to no avail. He tried it again, harder, with the same result. Then he got as firm a grip on the door as he could, pressed his feet against the rear door, and pulled with all of his might. No good. With the weight of the car pressing down on the door, it was locked in place. He tried the back door. Same thing.

He became aware that his lungs were burning and that the air surrounding him was oven hot. The chemical stench of burning synthetics, melting plastic, and spilled gasoline filled his nose. Sirens, which only a second before seemed as distant as his ruined baseball career, now screamed in his ears so that he could hear nothing else. He became aware of people streaming out of the garage, running for cover. He turned toward the body shop and saw a blur of blue-coveralled men spilling out onto the street, one of them tripping as he went. Jesse stood and ran, too.

As he did, he spotted something on the ground near where the Sentra had hit the curb by the body shop. It had a familiar shape, the shape of a gun, an automatic. Jesse didn't want to pick it up with an ungloved hand, but there weren't many options and there was even less time. He kicked it forward, hopefully not hard enough to flip over. He needed to keep at least one side of the grip unscratched. It slid beneath the rear end of his Explorer just as a fire truck screeched to a halt behind it. Even as he ran he cringed at the thought of the pistol crushed under the weight of the fire truck.

Then there was a second of stillness and quiet the likes of which Jesse had never experienced before. It wasn't that the world slowed down or turned on its side, not exactly. It was more like a brief moment of clarity. There was the chaos before him, the fire behind him, and a piece of the world that was his and his alone. Suddenly, that piece of the world exploded in a roar and blast of heat that blew his blue PPD baseball cap off his head and knocked him completely off his feet.

The next thing he knew, Suit and Robbie Wilson were dragging him by the arms, the toes of his shoes and the knees of his pants scraping along the pavement. Then he was sitting on the back bumper of an ambulance, an oxygen mask on his face. Robbie Wilson was gone, but Suit was there, as was an EMT. He was a big kid, Tommy Simonetti, whom Jesse had known since he was in junior high.

"You'll be all right, Chief," Tommy said. "You're not burned and you don't check out as having a concussion."

But Jesse was barely paying attention to Simonetti. He was paying far more attention to the question in Suit Simpson's eyes. It was the same question going round and round in his own head: Was that Peepers in there? He hoped for everyone's sake that it was and that there'd be enough of him left so they could be sure.

FORTY

Simonetti tried to get Jesse to go to the hospital to have a doctor check him out. Jesse thanked Tommy but refused to go. Being police chief had its privileges. The mayor was the only one who could give him direct orders, but she was out of town and the deputy mayor would have all he could handle for the time being.

"Suit," Jesse said, pulling him aside, "give me the keys to your cruiser. You're in charge of the scene until the ME and the state forensics team show up. Don't mention Peepers or the shot-out tire. Tell the deputy mayor that you spotted a car driving recklessly. That when you followed, he ran. You called it in. I heard the call and joined the pursuit. When I joined the pursuit, the driver fired on me. The rest is straightforward. No need to fudge or sugarcoat. He just needs a reasonable story to tell the media. I'll handle it from there."

"But when he asks where you are, what —"

"Tell him I'm dealing with the staties. That a complicated investigation like this one is way above our pay grades."

Jesse took Suit's keys and turned to go.

"Jesse," Suit called after him.

He turned back. "Uh-huh."

"What do you think? Is it him?"

"I don't know, Suit. I just don't know."

He didn't get ten feet before someone else was calling after him.

"Where the fuck are you going, Chief?" It was Robbie Wilson, displaying his natural lack of charm.

Jesse had learned not to react to the Napoleonic Wilson. Nor did he answer the fire chief's question.

"What's your assessment of the situation, Robbie?" Jesse asked. Wilson hated to be called Robbie.

"We've poured tons of foam on the fire and we think we've got it under control, but that was a hell of an explosion and there's a gas tank buried down there full to the brim. They got a delivery last night. It'll be hours until we know anything for sure. I've been after the town for years to make these company-owned pumps meet gas-station fire standards, but no. Goddamned politi-

222

cians. We're lucky we only have one fatality, because —"

"Okay, Robbie," Jesse said. "Next time you bring it up, I'll back you."

Wilson smiled at that. Like Suit, Wilson yearned for Jesse's approval. "Good. One thing I can tell you about this mess."

"What's that, Chief?" Jesse asked.

"That there's not much left of that car or the guy driving it. Between the explosion and the intensity of the fire . . . The explosion alone probably blew a ton of debris into Sawtooth Creek."

Jesse shook Wilson's hand and thanked him. "When you know more, I would appreciate a call."

Wilson could be unpleasant, but he was good at his job, and Jesse was anxious to hear anything about the explosion and fire Wilson might discover. As soon as the fire chief was gone, Jesse headed for Suit's cruiser. He popped the trunk, put on a pair of blue latex gloves, and fished out an evidence bag. He walked back to where the first fire truck on the scene had parked near the back bumper of his Explorer. Jesse got down on his hands and knees, knees sore and scraped from being dragged along the pavement. There it was: the gun he had kicked as he ran. He reached as far as his arm would stretch, gently picked the weapon up by the tip of its barrel, and dropped it into the evidence bag.

He placed the bag beside him on the cruiser's front seat and backed the vehicle slowly out of Trench Alley. When he was far enough away from the excitement of the crime scene, he pulled over and reached for the bag. He inspected the weapon through the clear plastic. It was a Smith & Wesson .22 automatic with a long barrel. He didn't recognize this model, per se, but it had the look and feel of a target pistol. Just the type of weapon a professional like Peepers would carry to shoot out tires or to extinguish the lives of people and their dogs who had the misfortune of getting in his way.

Using a pen Suit had left on the seat, Jesse lifted the gun out of the bag and sniffed the end of the barrel. Although Jesse's nostrils were black with smoke from the fire, he thought he could smell the telltale odor of burnt gunpowder. He might not be able to swear to it in court, but he felt pretty confident the .22 had been recently fired. He slid the pen out from between the loop of the trigger guard and the gun fell into the evidence bag. After sealing it, he put the car in drive and headed back to the station.

FORTY-ONE

Jesse sat at his desk, head aching, exhausted, and sore. The things a rush of adrenaline could do to the human body were pretty amazing, not all of them positive. He recalled how the hardest thing he'd had to do as a minor-leaguer was not learning to hit a curveball or to lay off a slider at the knees. It was learning to control his emotions. Jesse understood how people perceived him: cool under pressure, self-contained. That was true enough now, but as a kid in A ball he was just as vulnerable to his hormones as the next guy. He had told Suit that he never heard the fans when he was playing ball. By the time he'd gotten promoted to Double A, he didn't. When he started, though, it was a struggle to focus for the roar of the crowd — even the small crowds — the pounding of his heart, and his nerves.

"Helluva thing, ain't it, son? Feels like your whole damn body's full of bees. Got to figure out how to trick yourself into believing it don't mean a thing when it's the thing you want most of all," said his first minor-league manager after he'd seen Jesse boot two routine grounders to short. "All the talent in the world won't do you no kinda good you don't learn to relax out there."

Jesse wondered why those words should come back to him now, but he didn't waste time delving too deeply into it. He wasn't in the right frame of mind for introspection, never his favorite activity to begin with. That, plus he was waiting for Healy, for Molly to report for her shift, and for Suit to get back from the crime scene. Maybe he'd discuss it with Dix if he ever went back to see his shrink. He hadn't thought much about Dix lately. Dix had done him a lot of good. Jesse knew that. Still, the man could be an enormous pain in the ass.

Healy knocked and came into the office without waiting for Jesse's permission. He was dressed in stiff new jeans, an old Boston Patriots T-shirt, and ratty-looking deck shoes speckled with white house paint. Jesse had never seen the man dressed this way, and to Jesse's eye Healy looked even more uncomfortable in this getup than he had in his Tiger Woods outfit. He had a few days of gray stubble on his increasingly jowly face and a sag in his shoulders.

"Heard you had some excitement around here today," Healy said, sitting down across from Jesse's desk as he had a hundred times before.

"Some."

Healy laughed a hollow laugh.

"My old forensics team's going to be in Trench Alley for quite a while, Jesse. I stopped by there on my way over. Looks like the DMZ after a B-52 dropped a load, for crissakes."

"Felt that way, too."

"Don't mind me saying, you look like crap there, Chief. Have you looked in a mirror?"

"Thanks, Healy. How's the wife? Retirement?"

"The docs say the medication is improving her condition, but she's still not feeling great. They say it's going to take time and that she'll be doing pretty well soon enough. Me, not so much. Don't know what to do with myself. I feel about as useful as a lifeguard at a car wash."

That was the moment Molly and Suit walked into the office. The strain had gotten to Molly and it showed on her face. She was a pretty woman who, in spite of having a house full of kids and a stressful job, had always managed to look ten years younger than her birth certificate said she was. But since this thing with Peepers, she'd aged beyond her years. Even Suit, the perpetual kid, had seemed to age and to have taken on an air of seriousness. It had aged them all.

Healy made a face. "Hell, somebody smells terrible."

Suit said, "That's me, Captain. I don't know how firemen get that smell off."

Jesse asked, "Everything under control over there?"

"It's a nightmare, Jesse. The fire spread to the garage and they're trying to contain that, because if the cabs inside start burning and explode, the whole block could go. The gas fire's still burning. There's two engines over there from Salem, too, and they're still foaming it. Robbie's been on the phone with all sorts of people about dealing with the gas in the underground tank. Problem is it's hard to deal with because there's no room to get around back of it. Anyways, it'll be a long time until the ME and the forensics team can get anywhere near the scene. Peter's over there now, but the deputy mayor's pretty POed you're not there."

"Thanks, Suit. I'll head over there in a little while."

"So what are we here for, Jesse?" Molly said.

Jesse reached into a side drawer and pulled out the evidence bag. He held it up for all of them to see what was inside.

"Looks like a target pistol," Healy said.

"Twenty-two Smith & Wesson Model Forty-one. I Googled it the second I got it back here. Very distinctive-looking and very expensive. About sixteen hundred bucks, give or take." Jesse handed it to Healy. "My guess is that it's his."

"Peepers's?" Molly's voice cracked.

Jesse nodded. "It was near the body shop on Trench Alley, right where the Sentra flipped over."

Healy said, "You removed evidence from a crime scene?"

"Good thing I did or, like Suit said, it would be a long time until we'd get a look at it, and that's if it wasn't ruined in the fire." He handed the bag to Healy.

"Hey, hold your damned horses now. I'm retired."

"Funny thing," Jesse said. "Not five minutes ago you mentioned lifeguard duties. Call in some favors. Do what you have to do and maybe we can breathe a little bit easier."

"But if that's his gun and his prints are on

it and the guy in the Sentra —"

"A lot of ifs, Suit," Jesse said. "Too many. Until we get a DNA match, none of us can afford to relax."

As he said it, his old manager's words came back to him again.

FORTY-TWO

There was a knock at the office door. Jesse leaned over, grabbed the evidence bag out of Healy's hand, and stashed it back in his drawer.

"Come in."

Alisha poked her head in. "I'm about to go off shift, Jesse, but I'll stay until Molly's ready, or if you need me to do overtime, I'm good."

"She'll be out in a minute, Alisha," Jesse said.

"Thanks." She began to close the door and then poked her head back in.

Jesse asked, "Is there something else?"

"The envelope in the evidence locker. What do you want me to do about it?"

Healy tilted his head. "Envelope?"

The envelope. Jesse hadn't forgotten about it, not exactly. It was just that the .22 seemed like a more pertinent piece of evidence. But the envelope was the original spark that eventually led to the fire and explosion in Trench Alley.

"Bring it in here," Jesse said, "and then you can take off."

Two minutes later, Alisha handed a larger evidence bag to Jesse. "You sure you don't need me to stay, Jesse? I'm glad to stay."

"No, that's fine. I need you fresh for your next shift. It's going to be a long day tomorrow."

After Alisha closed the door behind her, Molly said, "That looks like the twin to the envelope Jenn's photograph was delivered in."

Jesse retrieved the gun and the original envelope containing Jenn's photo with Peepers's message written on the back. He explained how it was the delivery of the envelope that had initiated the day's chain of events.

Suit said, "So you think he shot out the tire and while that got our attention he came in here and dropped off the envelope?"

"I do. When all is said and done, the bullet in that tire will match the bullets from the earlier incidents and the murders in Salem. The markings on the bullets will match them to this gun." He pointed at the bagged gun. "Otherwise none of what happened today makes sense."

Healy spoke up. "Since we seem to be playing fast and loose with the rules, why don't we have a gander at what's in the new envelope?"

"Suit," Jesse said, "go get us some gloves."

A few minutes later, Jesse and Healy had gloved up. Jesse removed the envelope from the evidence bag. He didn't believe for a second that there were any prints or trace evidence on the envelope or what it might contain, but he couldn't risk acting on that assumption. Nor could he risk the assumption that the man in the Sentra had been Peepers. He carefully squeezed together the two metal prongs that held the flap of the envelope closed, then, using the tip of his gloved finger, lifted the flap. Healy placed another evidence bag around the open flap.

"We good?" Jesse asked.

Healy nodded.

With that, Jesse turned the envelope upside down and pushed in its sides. Two items fell out of the envelope into the second evidence bag. One was a "Howdy from Dallas, Texas" postcard. *Dallas* was written in big, curvy block letters, the outline of each letter encasing an illustration of a famous Dallas landmark. The letters were superimposed on a solid blue background with a lone red star. The other item was a photo of Jenn trying on her wedding dress.

"My God!" Molly gasped in spite of herself.

Suit pointed at the postcard. "Something's written on the back."

When Jesse flipped the bag around, he went cold again. He recognized the neat, plain lettering as Peepers's. But it was what those letters spelled out that concerned him.

SEE YOU AT THE SLAUGHTER HOUSE
DO YOU ASK A PRAYING MANTIS
WHY?

Jesse knew the handwriting would be a match, but to be absolutely certain, he took out that first photo of Jenn and compared the handwriting to the writing on the back of that photo. They all came around Jesse's desk and looked. As they did, they all shook their heads in agreement: It was a match.

And there was that question again, hanging in the air like a shroud. It was on all their faces, in all their eyes. *Was it Peepers in that car?* Suit wanted to give it voice, but he had asked once already. Molly wanted to ask as well, but she knew the answer Jesse would give and she didn't want to hear it. Healy didn't ask, because, as the most experienced man in the room, he knew the answer for himself. Until forensics could investigate the crime scene and gather whatever evidence there was left to gather, there was no way to know for sure. Still, the unspoken reality of the situation didn't stop some of them from praying.

FORTY-THREE

Jesse parked the cruiser by the police barricades and walked along the bent elbow of Trench Alley toward the still-burning fire. All the vehicles that had blocked access to more fire equipment had been driven off the street or, as in the case of his old Explorer, towed to the small police impound lot nearer the station. His Explorer was evidence. The state CSU was already digging bullet fragments and buckshot pellets out of the old Ford. There was no way they could approach the crime scene until Robbie Wilson and the state Department of Environmental Protection declared it safe. That didn't seem like it was going to happen anytime soon.

He'd taken a quick run home to shower and change clothes. He'd called Diana to let her know what was going on.

"Are we still going to Dallas?" she asked.

"Until I have definitive proof that the guy

in the car was Peepers, we're going. Even then, we're committed to going."

"You wouldn't want to disappoint Jenn," Diana said, a bite of snark in her voice. "We wouldn't want that."

"Jealous?"

"A little, I guess."

"When Jenn meets you, you won't be the jealous one."

"So I'm the trophy girlfriend."

"As a ballplayer, I won all sorts of trophies," he said, "but I was never in love with any of them."

"I love you, Jesse Stone."

"Me, too. I've got to go."

He wasn't lying. Robbie Wilson was walking toward him, and the look on the little man's face spelled trouble.

"Where the hell have you been, Chief Stone?" He didn't wait for an answer. "I've been here for hours dealing with this and with the clowns from the state police and the ME's office. I don't have time for this shit. I've got an emergency on my hands here."

Jesse didn't argue with Wilson. "What's the situation, Robbie?"

"Well, we've got things under control. The fire's still burning, but we've almost got it to a point where we can safely gain access to the shutoff valve for the underground tank. Once we're sure we're not dealing with gas and chemicals anymore, we'll spray down any potential hot spots. Then I'll go in with a guy from the state, assess the damage, and make sure the area is safe. Then, and only then, you can let the CSU team do their thing. Though, I gotta tell you, Chief, between the explosion, the exposure to the heat of the fire, and the fire retardant . . . I don't know what sort of integrity any evidence they gather is going to have."

"Uh-huh."

"You sure are an effusive bastard, aren't you, Chief Stone?"

Jesse nodded, but he didn't let Wilson walk away completely empty-handed.

"Chief Wilson," he said, waiting for Robbie to turn back around, "thanks for pulling me out of harm's way before. I won't forget it."

The anger in Wilson's face eased. "Just doing my job."

Jesse waited until the fire chief had walked far enough ahead and then followed, wanting to see the scene for what it was without commentary. It was bad, worse than he had imagined. He could feel the heat from the fire before he even got close to it, but the flames weren't nearly as intense as they had been when he'd left. Robbie Wilson was right, though. The area of the initial crash and explosion was barely recognizable. Jesse looked at where he remembered the overturned Sentra had been. There was nothing there now except foam and char. He tried to imagine the frame of the car beneath the foam, but it was no good. The place was a complete disaster, and he figured he'd be in Dallas by the time the CSU could even access the area. He turned and walked away.

At the edge of Trench Alley, nearing the police barricades, Jesse fished his phone out of his pocket and dialed the number Scott Kahan had given him. He'd rather have called Hunsicker's security man with more definite information, but he didn't have a choice. Before he could dial, the phone vibrated in his hand. When he looked at the screen and saw it was Kahan calling him, Jesse just shook his head.

FORTY-FOUR

"Jesse Stone."

Kahan said, "Heard you've had a little excitement in Paradise today."

"I wouldn't call it excitement. I wouldn't call it little."

"We've had some here today, too."

That got Jesse's attention. "How so?"

"A little over a month ago a young woman named Belinda Yankton was snatched out of her luxury building's garage in the same part of town the Hunsickers live in."

"Vineland Park Village?"

"Exactly."

Jesse wasn't in the mood for twenty questions. "And this has to do with us how?"

"I'm getting there, Stone. Patience."

"I don't have much of that left to spread around today."

Kahan sighed loudly in Jesse's ear. "Okay, but the details are important."

"I'm listening."

"This morning the Yankton woman escaped from her captor. She was found nude and hysterical on a street in West Dallas. Seems she'd been the prisoner of a man this whole time. He kept her naked, tied to a workbench with leather restraints around her wrists and ankles. Kept her pretty drugged up most of the time, but not the whole time. Sound like a familiar MO?"

Jesse could feel heat rising beneath his skin. "Was she sexually assaulted?"

"No. She says her captor claimed he never did that sort of thing."

"Then why the abduction?"

"You'll love this. The guy said it was because she'd been rude to him. She spilled his Shiner Bock on him at a famous barbecue place here in town. He felt she hadn't been properly apologetic and thought she needed to be taught a lesson in manners."

The heat beneath Jesse's skin had nearly reached the surface. "Did he hurt her?"

"Not physically, but he tormented her psychologically."

"Did she get a look at him?"

"I thought you'd never ask," Kahan said.

"I'm asking now."

"I think you already know the answer."

"Peepers."

"It was him, Stone. No doubt. The Dallas

PD have already matched prints he left in the building he was renting to those on file for this particular Mr. Doe. You were right."

"How do you find all this intel out without tipping off the locals about Jenn?"

"Don't worry, Stone. No one knows we're looking for Peepers or why. I have sources inside all the local PDs. They answer my question, not the other way around. You'd be amazed at what tickets to a Cowboys game can get you."

"Not really. So he's definitely down there in Dallas?" Jesse asked, wondering who the man in the Sentra could have been.

"Probably."

That surprised Jesse. "Probably?"

"There was no sign of Peepers when the cops searched the building. It looked as if he'd cleared out a day or two earlier. But he left evidence behind of what he'd been up to."

"Evidence of what?"

"You won't like it."

"I'll add it to the list. Evidence of what, Kahan?"

"Metal shavings, gun powder, drill bits."

"Pipe bombs," Jesse said. "Seems out of character for him."

"Maybe so, but there were also rags with gun oil. He's planning something. I think the Yankton woman was a sideshow. Something to keep him occupied while he prepped."

"But you said he's probably down there, not definitely."

"The woman says he had been drugging her so much lately that she had lost track of time," Kahan said. "She can't be sure of the last time she saw him. It might've been yesterday or three days ago. She wasn't completely coherent. All she could say with any clarity was that he wasn't there when she came to this morning."

Jesse didn't like the sound of it. Something about the woman's escape didn't feel right to him, but he kept his doubts to himself. Instead, he delivered a bombshell of his own. He explained about the shot-out tire, the hand-delivered envelope, and its contents. Then said: "Peepers might be dead."

Kahan didn't overreact. His voice was calm. "Was he the fatality in the police chase and explosion in Paradise?"

"News travels fast."

"Bad news even faster," Kahan said. "Or is this good news?"

"Possibly. General description and MO fit Peepers, but we can't be certain it was him. The car and the deceased were the epicenter of the explosion and the fire's still burning.

I'm not sure there'll be enough of him left to do easy DNA analysis with. It'll take a lot of sifting. And there's no chance CSU will have access to the scene until tomorrow, earliest."

"It'll be a while until you get results even under the best-case scenario. That's unfortunate."

"I did retrieve a weapon at the scene I believe to be the .22 he's been using. It's being tested as we speak."

"You *are* still coming," Kahan said after a long silence.

"Uh-huh."

"You would have been good at my former profession, Stone. Until you have irrefutable evidence to the contrary, always assume your target is operational."

Jesse didn't much like that compliment, but as before, he just added it to the ever-growing list.

FORTY-FIVE

Dawn had come and gone with Jesse Stone behind his desk. His folded garment bag lay across the top of his packed suitcase by the office door. He picked up the ballistics report on the weapon he'd retrieved at the crime scene for the third time in the last hour, reading through it, looking for something that he knew wasn't there: proof the dead man was Mr. Peepers.

He'd been right about the gun. It was Peepers's .22, all right, and, as he suspected, it had been recently fired, but Jesse felt empty of pride or satisfaction. The bullets matched those found in all the shot-out tires — including the one from two days ago — and the slugs retrieved from the victims in Salem. Peepers's prints were on the handle of the Smith & Wesson. They were on the barrel, the trigger, the trigger guard, the clip, and the ammo. He might as well have had the words *praying mantis* engraved on the side of the barrel or bought space on a highway billboard to announce the weapon was his.

Even in the absence of irrefutable evidence, Jesse supposed he would have felt better about being right if the two other reports on his desk aligned in a consistent manner. But they just didn't. None of the slugs the state CSU had dug out of his Explorer were a match for Peepers's .22. The bullets that had been shot through Jesse's windshield and sideview mirror had been .45s. The windshield slug had been recovered from, of all places, his spare tire. The irony wasn't lost on him. Unsurprisingly, the rest of what had been recovered from the Explorer were buckshot pellets. A shotgun, a .45, a pipe bomb . . . it didn't fit.

And then there was the preliminary report on the envelope dropped at the front desk. That made less sense than the two ballistics reports. Except for Alisha's fingerprints, there were no other prints on the outside nor the inside of the envelope. Yet Alisha couldn't recall if the man who delivered it was wearing gloves or not. He must have been. The question was why. Why wear gloves to protect against leaving prints on the outside of the envelope when the postcard and photo in the envelope are covered in prints?

There was a simple answer to all of the questions, to all of the seeming contradictions, to all of the inconsistencies. Peepers was fucking with them. Jesse in particular. Unlike the .45, the shotgun, and the pipe bomb, that fit Peepers's M.O. like a second skin. He'd wanted to confuse Jesse, to torture him psychologically. *Here I am. No, I'm not, I'm here. No, over here. No, over there.*

Jesse wasn't much of a movie fan. He did like Westerns. Loved them, but Westerns were about as popular as musicals these days. Maybe less so. So it was odd that Jesse should remember a movie he watched when he was a little boy, sick and home from school. It was an old black-and-white movie about the French Revolution. What made it okay was that the Scarlet Pimpernel was kind of like the English Zorro: a foppish dandy by day, hero by night. And as he looked at the three reports on his desk, Jesse mumbled to himself: *They seek him here, they seek him there. Those Frenchies seek him everywhere. Is he in Heaven, or is he in hell? That damned elusive Pimpernel.* He laughed at himself for remembering that. If he had been asked to recite any other poem, he wasn't sure he could do better than "Mary Had a Little Lamb."

Then, pulling open his side drawer, he stopped laughing. He reached into the drawer, pulled out the bottle of Tullamore Dew, and placed it on the desk. It really was quite beautiful to look at, and it was calling his name sure as the gate agent would if he didn't get a move on. Still, Jesse couldn't stop staring at the rectangular bottle with its rounded shoulders, the amber liquid within singing its siren song. Jesse folded. He poured himself two fingers and drank. He felt that delicious burn in the back of his throat, the slow warmth rising in his belly. He preferred Black Label. This would do. The disappointment in his weakness would come soon enough. Peepers, alive or dead, had won at least a single victory.

In his surrender, another thought crept into Jesse's mind. It was a thought he had either pushed down or kept at bay during these last weeks. It hit him that Jenn was getting married, that the tangled two-step they had done for years was now finally at an end. It hurt. He couldn't believe that it did, but there was no denying it. And regardless of all the hours he and Dix had spent discussing the dysfunction of their marriage and their even more dysfunctional divorce, he felt he had failed. His wrecked shoulder . . . well, that wasn't on him. Circumstance, misfortune, and the baseball gods were responsible for that. His marriage, though, was something else. He knew Jenn was equally responsible. More responsible. He hadn't been the one to cheat. Still, he saw it as his failure somehow. He poured himself another drink.

Five minutes later, he was in the backseat of a Paradise cab on his way to Logan. He didn't bother chatting with the driver. The disappointment was already setting in. That was the folly of alcoholism, he thought, the pleasures of drinking were so short-lived, and the downside lingered at your door forever.

FORTY-SIX

Diana listened to her Bach, Beethoven, Beatles, Beastie Boys, and Beyoncé playlist to drown out the engine noise, Jesse asleep next to her, his head resting on her shoulder. Even in sleep he seemed utterly composed and uncomplicated. She knew better. When you love someone the way she loved him, you learn to see past the fences they hide behind. You come to know their wounds and their lies, especially the ones they tell themselves. Jesse was a terribly complex man, and for the first time since they'd gotten together, she was scared for him.

She was scared for the both of them, of course. Although her skills were in forensic accounting, she had worked on cases at the Bureau involving men like Peepers: deadly, invisible, sadistic. Men who enjoyed the very act of victimization and the infliction of pain. It used to irk her when her colleagues would refer to them as "animals." Animals killed to survive, to feed their young. They didn't do it for sport. Hunting for the hell of it was a particularly human foible. At the moment, she had a very acute sympathy for prey animals. It hadn't escaped her that she would be nearly as big a prize for Peepers as Jenn would be. That having Jesse watch him destroy her, not Jenn, might actually be what was going on. Nor did it escape her that the woman Peepers had abducted in Dallas resembled both Jenn and herself. But she had accepted that she might be a target from the moment Jesse told her about Peepers's reappearance. Her fears at the moment were separate fears, fears for the man she loved.

He was drinking again in spite of how diligent he'd been about not slipping up. She had smelled the dark grace notes of defeat on his breath when they'd kissed at the gate. Nothing, not the coffee nor the mouthwash, could camouflage it completely. She had also seen the defeat in him, the disappointment in his eyes and the slightest slouch in his posture. He exuded confidence and competence. Not much about Jesse worried her about his personality except this, his reflexive withdrawal. It seemed to be his default setting. He wasn't a man to deflect responsibility or to point fingers. He was stoic in defeat.

It wasn't the drinking that bothered her, per se. She was used to that. In law enforcement, excessive drinking was part of the deal. She also drank too much. Not everyone did it. Not everyone was a drunk, but there were lots of them. High rates of infidelity, divorce, and a whole host of other ugly perks came with the shield and the gun. The thing that frightened her was how the drinking connected to Jesse's need for a sense of control. And if nothing else, Peepers thrived on showing the world who was really in control.

That whole self-contained-man aura was great. Right after she noticed Jesse's rugged good looks and athletic build, it was the thing about Jesse that had captured her attention. When you've been searching for something in a man your whole adult life, you recognize it when you see it. She guessed the great sex didn't exactly hurt, either. But self-containment or self-assurance or self-reliance, whatever you wanted to call it, had its drawbacks.

She saw the seat belt sign pop on, felt the engines cut back, saw the flight attendant marching down the aisle with a plastic garbage bag. Diana pulled out one of her earbuds in time to hear the captain announce that they were making their initial descent into Love Field. When the captain finished his announcement, she put up her tray table, leaned over, and kissed Jesse very gently on the top of his head.

"I love you, Jesse Stone," she said, as much to herself as to him.

"What was that?" the passing flight attendant asked.

Diana smiled, blushing. "Nothing. Sorry."

When she turned back, Jesse, eyes bleary from sleep, was staring back at her.

"You're not bad yourself," he said, and closed his eyes again. "Wake me up when we land."

She laughed at herself for thinking he would ever change. She knew he loved her fiercely, but public displays of affection would never be his thing.

FORTY-SEVEN

At baggage claim, a driver in a black blazer and pants, a white collared shirt, and black shoes stood erect, holding a cardboard sign with Jesse's and Diana's names printed on it. His skin was heavily tanned, his neatly kept black hair wavy and thick. Jesse snorted at the sight of him. Everything about the man, from his posture to the rippling muscles barely contained by his clothing to his reflective orange Oakleys, screamed ex-military. The earpiece and trailing wire were also a dead giveaway that chauffeur had not always been his chosen profession. It was also perfectly obvious, in spite of the sunglasses, that the driver knew exactly who in the crowd he was looking for. Although the need for secrecy was less important now that Peepers had pretty much announced his intentions, Jesse hoped that Kahan's other people were a little more subtle than this guy.

Diana noticed, too.

"What do you think, Jesse, Navy SEAL or Air Force PJ Special Ops?" she asked.

"SEAL."

"Wrong, Stone. He's ex-USAF. You work in D.C. long enough, you can tell."

"What's the bet?" Jesse asked.

"I'm right, you sleep with me when we get back to the hotel."

"And if *I'm* right?"

"You sleep with me when we get back to the hotel."

Jesse laughed. "Deal."

They walked up to the man holding the sign. Jesse introduced them and shook the man's hand. Diana, too.

"Look," Jesse said, "we have a bet going. Are you ex-Navy or Air Force?"

Now it was the driver's turn to laugh and to display his straight white teeth.

"IDF, the *mistaravim.* That's a branch of our Special Forces," he said in a heavy Israeli accent. "I'm Ari and I'll be driving you while you're in town. Now, if you don't mind, we'll collect your luggage and head out."

They followed Ari to the carousel.

"So we both lose," Jesse said.

"I figure we'll both have to pay up."

"Looking forward to it."

255

It was a short walk to where the car was parked. When they stepped out of the terminal they were hit with a blast of devil's breath. To call the heat oppressive was to be kind. The sky was a severe and cloudless blue. It was weather much easier to appreciate from the comfort of an air-conditioned room or car than from the pavement. It reminded Jesse of his youth in Tucson and Diana of her year undercover in Scottsdale. Neither of them said a word about it to the other. As they walked, Ari's head was on a swivel, ready to ditch their luggage and go for his weapon.

The black Escalade with its heavily tinted windows was already running. Ari opened the back door for Diana and Jesse before placing their luggage in the rear. Scott Kahan was sitting in the front seat and turned around, offering his hand to Diana.

"Scott Kahan, Hale Hunsicker's security chief," he said. "You're ex-FBI?"

Diana nodded, shook his hand, and smiled a polite smile, but she saw the same thing in Kahan's eyes as she had seen in men's eyes her whole life: a mix of lust and a lack of respect. She half expected him to turn to Jesse and make some snide comment about how she was even hotter than Jenn. He didn't. Instead he held his hand out to Jesse.

"Stone, how are you?"

Jesse was all business. "Fine. What's the plan?"

"We're heading straight from here to the Vineland Park Village PD, where we'll meet with Jed Pruitt. He's chief and a friend of Hunsicker's. Ari will take Diana to the hotel, get you guys checked in, and issue your weapons. Jesse, what do you prefer to carry?"

Jesse had to think about it. For ages he'd carried a short-barrel .38, but he'd gifted it to Suit and had gotten used to his nine-millimeter.

"A nine-millimeter," he said.

Kahan asked, "Diana, a .40 Glock 22?"

"Well, aren't you just the sweetest thing?" she said in a mocking Southern accent. "A man who asks the question and then answers it for me."

"Sorry," he said. "That won't happen again."

"See that it doesn't. Yes, a Glock 22 is good."

Jesse smirked and kept quiet. Diana Evans brooked no bullshit. He loved that about her. That and about a hundred other things.

Kahan continued. "There's a small reception at the Hunsickers' house this evening. A few friends and family. It's casual. Ari will come get you at a quarter to eight." He turned to Ari, who had settled into the driver's seat. "Go."

And with that, they were moving.

FORTY-EIGHT

Vineland Park's police headquarters was part of the town hall and municipal complex, done in Spanish Mission style with smooth, off-white stucco and red tile roofing. There was an ornate central tower topped with a slight dome and a courtyard with a simple circular fountain. The landscaping was green and lush and fragrant. There wasn't a leaf or petal out of place. The sight of the complex made Jesse smile because it looked like a smaller-scale version of the Beverly Hills town hall. Jesse remarked on that to Kahan.

"Should look like it," he said as they walked from the SUV to the entrance. "Same man designed it. And by the way, Diana is even more beautiful in person than in photos. After what she said to me before, I figured I better not say that in front of her."

"Smart man."

They stopped at the front desk. The sergeant manning it, a fit, bald fellow with a passive *I've seen it all before* expression, smiled at Kahan.

"Hey, Bill," Kahan said, removing a .40 Beretta from his hip holster and placing it on the counter. "This is Chief Jesse Stone of the Paradise, Massachusetts, PD. We're here to see —"

"Chief's waiting. Y'all can go on back. I'll locker this in the meantime," he said, removing Kahan's Beretta from the desk.

As they walked back to Pruitt's office, Kahan explained that Vineland Park cross-trained their police as firemen and EMTs.

"These folks are very good at their jobs and very well paid. Lots of big money around here, so it's not your ordinary small village PD." Then, realizing how Jesse might hear that, he said, "No offense."

"None taken."

"And don't be fooled by Pruitt's down-home cowboy manner. He's retired military intelligence and smart as the day is hot."

They came to a big, high-arched dark wood door. Pruitt's name and title were inscribed in gold on a metal plaque. Kahan knocked.

"Well, come on in, boys."

Pruitt was a tall man, all arms and legs,

with a tanned, weathered face. He had droopy lids over faded blue eyes that had seen a lot of things but that wouldn't give up their secrets without a fight. He had an easy smile and the teeth of a man who had spent some money to bleach out the tobacco stains and had mostly succeeded. He stood a good six-four, and that was with a slight stoop. Still, the man looked sharp in his dark blue uniform.

There was a brief round of handshakes and of sizing one another up. Jesse noticed a hint of disdain in the way Pruitt looked at Kahan. Pruitt noticed Jesse noticed. They didn't need to discuss it. It was understood. No cop, especially a chief, wants to feel like he's got to lick a citizen's boots just because that citizen works for someone rich and powerful. Paradise may not have been Vineland Park in terms of wealth, but Jesse had had to deal with the rich and powerful and their flunkies from the day he accepted the job as chief. But there was something else in Pruitt's eyes beyond disdain that he hoped he'd get a chance to discuss with the chief.

"Have a seat, boys." Pruitt gestured at the rustic, untanned cowhide chairs across from his desk.

When Kahan and Jesse sat, he sat.

Jesse, anxious to get back to the hotel and to call Paradise, spoke first. "Anything more from Belinda Yankton?"

"Nothing that'll help you. That sick bastard played mind games with that poor girl for weeks," Pruitt said. "She may never be right again."

"Well," Kahan said, "she certainly won't be rude again."

No one laughed.

"Why do you think he let her go?" Pruitt asked.

Kahan made a face. "She escaped."

Jesse begged to differ. "No, she didn't. Peepers enjoys killing, pretty women most of all. He had an ulterior motive. He wanted her to deliver a message."

"Which is?" Kahan wanted to know.

"That he's in control," Jesse said. "It's up to him who lives and who dies and when. He also wanted her to feed us information. Chief Pruitt, do you think you could arrange for me to talk to Belinda alone?"

"Ain't a Vineland Park matter, but I'll see what I can do."

Kahan laughed. "That means yes, Stone."

Jesse noticed that disdain in Pruitt's eyes again.

"Like I said, Jesse, I'll see what I can do. But in the meantime, there's been a few other developments we should discuss."

"Developments?" Jesse furrowed his brow.

Kahan's tone turned nasty. "And why don't I know about them?"

Pruitt stood tall out of his chair. "Listen, son." He pointed at the stars on the epaulets of his uniform. "Your boss's money and influence make him someone this department listens to, but he's your boss, not mine. Now, as soon as Chief Stone does me an honor, I'll brief you on the developments."

"What can I do for you, Chief?" Jesse asked.

Pruitt reached into his top drawer. "You can sign this for me."

It was Jesse's Triple A baseball card. And when Jesse saw it, that botched double play in Pueblo came rushing back to him. The glory of those years came rushing back, too. But the knot in his belly came from remembering the swinging bunt in the softball game all those Sundays ago, and the glory of the old days seemed much further away than it ever had before.

FORTY-NINE

Chief Pruitt placed the newly signed base-ball card back in its clear plastic case and put the case back in his drawer. He exchanged the card and case for a file.

"I saw you play back in the day when I was stationed in New Mexico," Pruitt said, still holding the file in his hand. "When Scott here came to me with what was going on and mentioned your name, I Googled you. Couldn't believe you were *that* Jesse Stone. You had a helluva arm there, a helluva arm. Seems to me you could hit a little, too."

"Once," Jesse said. "Once, a lifetime ago."

Before sitting back down, Pruitt handed the file to Kahan. Pruitt was no fool. He had ruffled Kahan's feathers, but he didn't want to push things too far. He knew that he couldn't afford to make an enemy of Hale Hunsicker. So as Kahan scanned the files, Pruitt spoke to Jesse.

"Seems your Mr. Peepers is a smart fella. He didn't get catering jobs with the firms that have been hired by the Hunsickers to work their parties. No, sir. Would have been too easy for him to be tracked down that way. First place we would look. What he did instead was get jobs at other area caterers whose employees work for several companies. That gave him access to people who *would* work the Hunsicker parties and who had worked Hunsicker parties previously. He also worked catering jobs at all the venues at which the wedding week celebrations are to be held, including the main event at the Vineland Park Country Club."

Jesse made a face. "No one said he wasn't smart. What's in the file?"

"Interviews with the catering employees who worked with Peepers, some of whom he befriended. Transcripts of conversations they remembered having with him. Interviews with his supervisors at the three companies Peepers worked for."

"Anything worthwhile?" Jesse asked.

"Not much we got out of it, but the way I figure it, you might see something we don't."

Kahan laughed a quiet laugh as he read.

"I read those reports, Kahan," Pruitt said, "and I don't recall much to laugh about.

Would y'all care to share it with Chief Stone and myself? If you don't mind, I mean."

"Okay, Jed, enough with the *Aw, shucks* routine. You don't like me. You resent Hale throwing his weight around. I get it. What I'm laughing at is the aliases Peepers used at the three jobs he worked: Luther Fish, Jesse Simpson, and Gino Stone. See what I find funny, Stone?"

Jesse smiled a crooked half-smile. Pruitt wasn't smiling. He had his pride and didn't like not being in on the joke.

"Peepers mixed up the three names of the men whom he blames for getting him shot and for interfering with his business. That's what this is all about. Luther Simpson is one of my officers, the one who actually shot Peepers in the shoulder. Simpson got gutshot for that." Jesse held the tips of his right thumb and index fingers close. "He came this close to dying. Gino Fish was a mob boss in Boston who had arranged for me to meet with Peepers."

"Was a mob boss?" Pruitt said.

"Dead. He killed himself."

Pruitt was confused. "Suicide? Why?"

"Peepers had just stabbed Fish's lover and receptionist through the heart and slit his throat. Fish knew the fate that awaited him if Peepers had gotten him out of the office.

266

Fish killed himself to save himself from a slow and horrible death."

"Jeez!"

"Chief," Jesse said, "I know you've taken this seriously, but I think now you can understand why Peepers is so worrisome. He isn't like anyone any of us have ever dealt with. I worked Robbery-Homicide in L.A. for ten years and none of the perps I ever dealt with was a match for Peepers. He's part serial killer, part assassin, part terrorist, and he's invisible."

"But is he even alive?" Pruitt asked. "We're a well-funded department, Jesse, but I can't afford to expend lots of resources chasing a ghost around Dallas. Kahan here filled me in on what happened in Paradise. Says you found his weapon and that the man in the car that exploded matched Peepers's general description."

"I understand, Chief," Jesse said. "I've got a budget, a mayor, and a group of selectmen to deal with. Problem is, we can't be sure if Peepers is dead. My department and the state CSU were only given clearance to go over the crime scene this morning, and the scene is a mess. We can't know if everything Peepers has done is to give us a false sense of security or if he's really dead."

Pruitt looked skeptical. "But he couldn't

have arranged for the car chase and accident in your town. You can't hire someone to die in your place. It had to be him."

"I know it seems that way," Jesse said. "But I think the accident was just that, an accident. If I didn't happen to return to the station house when I did, things would've happened very differently."

"For what it's worth, Jed," Kahan said, "I agree with Stone. We can't assume Peepers isn't a threat."

Pruitt stroked his chin, sitting back in his chair. "Okay. For now, we'll keep the alert on and I'll assign the extra officers as we discussed, Kahan. But as soon as you hear anything from Paradise, I want to hear it second to you, Chief Stone. Break that protocol and I back my people off. Understood?"

"Uh-huh."

There was another round of handshakes, but before Jesse was through the door, Pruitt called to him.

"See you at the party tonight, Chief Stone."

Jesse winked and closed the door behind him.

FIFTY

When Kahan and Jesse left the Vineland Park PD, Ari was outside, waiting in the Escalade to take Jesse to the hotel. Kahan handed Jesse the file and said he'd see him later.

"Aren't you coming?" Jesse asked.

"My car's parked in the lot. Ari will handle it from here. He'll be by later to get you and Diana at a quarter to eight." Kahan turned and left.

Jesse opened the front passenger door to the Escalade, but Ari shook his head no. "It's more secure if you ride in the backseat, Chief Stone. The armor is thicker back there."

"Armor?"

"All of Mr. Hunsicker's vehicles have been . . . what is the word in English? Modified for security purposes. Would take a lot to disable our vehicles."

"He has enemies?" Jesse asked.

"He has money. Money makes for distrust, no? It makes you an attractive target for people with strange notions of how to get money for themselves without working for it."

Jesse shook his head. "Far as I can tell, Ari, all money does is make people paranoid asses."

Ari laughed. "That, too. But Mr. Hunsicker is good to us and generous. I have no complaints."

"I'll ride up front, and call me Jesse."

Ari shrugged. "All right, Jesse."

The ride to the hotel was a short and silent one, but as Jesse got out, Ari once again reminded him about the pickup time. The Escalade remained by the front entrance until Ari was sure Jesse was safely inside.

The out-of-town wedding guests were put up at the Vineland, a boutique hotel in Dallas proper but on the border of Vineland Park. Jesse was never terribly impressed by hotels of any kind. All he required was a clean bed, a bathroom with a shower, and a TV. To him it didn't much matter if there was cucumber and raspberry water in the lobby or coriander-laced soap with microscrubbing particles. He stopped at the desk, showed his driver's license, and picked up a room key.

When he got upstairs, Diana didn't look in any mood to have him pay off his lost bet or to pay off her lost bet. The second after he said hello, she began pacing in front of the big rectangular window that looked out onto the campus of Southern Methodist University. He also noticed the weapons Ari had issued her were on the bed, slides in the locked-open position, two full clips each by their sides. There were holsters and ammo boxes, too. But Jesse didn't think what was troubling Diana had anything to do with the sidearms or even Peepers.

"What is it, Di?"

"What is what?"

Jesse said, "You're pacing a rut in the carpet."

"Tonight."

He was confused. "What about tonight?"

"Men! Christ, sometimes you guys are so thick it's amazing we survived as a species."

"If you tell me what you're talking about, maybe I'll agree with you."

"Jenn! I'm talking about Jenn."

"What about Jenn?" Jesse was still confused. "You knew you were going to meet her at some point this week."

"But I'm not ready. I should have brought different —"

271

"Stop. Stop," Jesse said. "Jenn will always mean something to me, but I never felt about her the way I feel about you. Never, not for five minutes. I thought I was in love with her, but I didn't understand the word until I met you." He kissed her softly on the cheek. "What Jenn and I had was good for a little while, but it was unhealthy. Beyond the physical attraction, we fell in love with the worst parts of us. The neediest parts of us bound us together in ways that were hard to break. That's not me and you. I'm here to help protect Jenn, but it's to protect you, too."

"I know," she said. "But Jenn is — I can't explain it."

"You don't have to. Listen, there's a great spa in this place. Go do the works."

"But Jesse —"

"No, please. I need to call Molly and get an update. Then I could use some sleep."

"You sure?"

He nodded.

"But are you sure it's safe?" Diana asked, pointing to the bed. "I can't very well take my forty-caliber into the mud bath with me."

Jesse laughed. "It's fine. I can guarantee you Kahan has people planted all over this place. Probably has one of his ex–special

272

ops guys hiding at the bottom of the mud bath."

The tension seemed to go out of her muscles.

She shrugged. "Okay. When I come back, I may need you to pay me what you owe me."

He winked. "We'll see."

"What's that file about?" she asked, tilting her head at the top of the dresser.

"Later. Now get out of here before I make you pay up now."

She stroked Jesse's stubbly cheek. "Don't shave until later. I like the way that feels against my skin. And Jesse, have a drink if you'd like. I know. Just please don't hide things from me."

He smiled and watched her until the door closed behind her. She never stopped surprising him. He was glad she was going to escape her worries about Jenn for a little while. Funny she should say that thing about hiding things. What he hadn't told Diana was that, in his way, he was just as nervous about tonight as she was.

FIFTY-ONE

Jesse didn't call Molly immediately. Instead he fell deeply into one of the lies alcoholics tell themselves. He told himself he didn't need a drink. He didn't even want another. That the short ones he'd had earlier at the station were anomalies. That's the thing about addictive behavior. It's not only the substance you're addicted to that's the problem. It's all that comes with it: the patterns, the rituals, the games, the false narrative about loss of control, and the overt lies. He knew all of this, yet felt helpless to stop it once he had taken that first drink.

He remembered an old drunk cop from his time in uniform in L.A. Mikey Barson was a few months away from putting in his papers after thirty-plus years when Jesse was nearing his first full year on the job. In those days, they assigned vets with "problems" to less-than-dangerous duty and allowed them to go gently into the good night. No one was looking to hurt anybody or screw them out of their pensions. Not like when Jesse was shown the door and unceremoniously kicked through it. Anyway, there was one night Jesse and Barson were next to each other at a retirement party or wake. Sort of the same thing, Jesse thought, laughing joylessly.

"Haven't had a drink in three months before tonight," Barson had said, double bourbon in hand, turning to Jesse. "And look at me. Right back to where I was."

"Huh?"

"You'll see, rook. Stop for three days, three months, three years . . . don't matter. You take that first drink and time disappears. You used to drink a half-bottle when you stopped, it'll take a half-bottle when you get back. You never stop being the same drunk."

Jesse didn't suppose anyone had ever told him something that rang so true and for so long. He wasn't a full-fledged drunk back then. At least that was what he told himself. Now what he did instead of calling Molly or taking that inevitable drink was to unload and reload ammo into the clips of their weapons. It was busywork, robotic. It took just enough concentration to distract one's mind and tamp down the thirst. But when the four clips were done, the room got very small. TV worked for a little while, a very little while.

He heard Dix's voice in his head, taunting him. *I told you so. You were only holding your breath again. You were never going to give it up forever. You like it too much. Deep down inside, it's who you are, what you are. Certainly no better than Mikey Barson. Worse. Barson didn't lie to himself the way you do.*

Of course, the script was Jesse's and Jesse's alone. It was Jesse beating himself up. Dix, though tough on Jesse, would never have said "I told you so" or anything of the sort. Jesse felt his eyes searching for the minibar. Unlike in most hotels, its location wasn't obvious. Then, pulling back a door on one of the dressers, he found it.

Relieved, but still resisting, he dialed the Paradise PD's station number. Molly picked up.

"Paradise Police Department, Officer Crane speaking. How may I assist you?"

"I think that's as polite as you've ever been to me," Jesse said.

"Don't be an ass. If I knew it was you, I wouldn't have made the effort. I might've hung up."

"I miss you, too, Crane. Update me."

"First, how's Dallas?"

"You ever stick your head inside a blast furnace? It's like that only prettier and more sprawling. So far I've seen the airport, the inside of the Vineland Park PD, and our hotel room."

"Have you seen Jenn yet?" Molly asked, her voice almost breathless. "Has Diana met her?"

"What is it with you and Diana with Jenn?"

"Don't be thick, Jesse."

"Diana called me thick, too."

"This is big for her. Anyone who knows you for more than five minutes understands that Jenn was the central figure in your life for a long time. Diana wants to see if she measures up. If she could be that meaningful to you. Measuring up is just as important to women as it is to men, only we don't use rulers and parts of our anatomies to do it. And if you don't think Jenn isn't just as anxious about meeting Diana, you're nuts."

"Enough," Jesse said. "So what's going on over there?"

"What you would expect. Crime scene's a mess. Peter Perkins is over there. They've recovered part of the Sentra's chassis and a sawed-off twelve-gauge. Nothing yet on human remains. Peter says the staties think the remains will be skeletal and badly

277

charred but that they should be able to get some usable DNA from the scene. Everything else is calm. Robbie Wilson is POed that you're not here, but screw him."

"No, thanks. Not my type."

"He's nobody's type," Molly said. "Call me tomorrow and let me know how things go tonight."

"Diana will knock her out in the fifth."

"Wiseass."

"That's Chief Wiseass to you."

Molly hung up. Jesse looked at the clock and realized that it would probably be at least an hour until Diana got back to the room. He headed straight to the minibar and removed a little bottle of Black Label. All that was missing was club soda and a poster of Ozzie Smith. He managed without them just the same. He was adaptable that way.

FIFTY-TWO

Suit called in to Molly to let her know he was taking his meal. When she told him that things were quiet and that he should go ahead, he turned the rearview mirror to face him. He removed his hat, finger-combed his hair, held his hand in front of his face to check his breath. He made a face and popped the mint he'd taken from the bowl at the register at Daisy's into his mouth. He checked his breath again. Now satisfied, he collected the flowers he'd picked up at the supermarket and headed for Elena's door.

"Luther," she said, surprise in her voice. "I didn't expect you until later."

"I hope you don't mind, I —"

"Don't be silly. Come in here. I don't want the whole town to see me kiss you."

Inside, with the door closed behind them, they kissed long and hard. It was a minute before they came up for air.

"God, I love the way you make me feel,"

279

she said, touching her own flushed cheek with the back of her hand. "How do you do that?"

"I feel the same way, El." His voice was oddly strained and cracking.

Finally, Elena pointed at the bouquet in Suit's big left hand.

"Luther, are those to freshen up your patrol car?"

He was dumbfounded, then remembered about the flowers and why he was standing there in the first place.

"These are for you." He handed them to her. And, fishing the ring out of his right pants pocket, he said, "This, too." He handed her the ring and got down on one knee. "Elena Wheatley, will you please marry me?"

The longest, most anxious two seconds in the history of the world passed.

"Of course I will, Luther. Of course I will."

She slipped the ring onto her finger, got on her knees opposite Suit, and pressed herself against him. His arms wrapped around her and they stayed that way for several minutes, both of them crying. When they stopped crying, Suit stood, lifting Elena with him.

"Let's do it soon, Luther," she said, wiping the tears out of her eyes. "Please. We've both wasted a lot of time in our lives and I don't want to waste another second apart from you. I don't want to hide us from the world anymore."

He grabbed her shoulders and held her at arm's length. "Soon, but not just yet. We need to keep the secret a little while longer. At least until Jesse gets back from Texas."

"Why? You can ask Jesse to be your best man over the phone."

"It's not that. It's . . ."

"It's what, Luther Simpson?" she said in the same tone she used as a student teacher.

"I don't want to scare you."

"You're already scaring me. Secrets are what killed almost every relationship I've ever had. You can't keep secrets from me if you want me to commit my life to you."

"That's just it, El."

"What is?"

"Your life."

"What about my life, Luther?"

"You know about the explosion on Trench Alley, right?"

"Everyone in Paradise knows about it. But what has that got to do with —"

"The man who shot me . . . He . . . You know, I shot him, too. And . . . well, he's back and he's taking revenge for things."

Elena's expression turned grave. "He's

back where?"

"Here, maybe. He killed two people in Boston. One really, but sort of two. Then he murdered an old woman, a cabdriver, and a dog in Salem."

"A dog! He killed a dog? What kind of monster kills a dog?"

"The real kind. That's why we've got to —"

"But wait a second, Luther. What's this got to do with what happened in Trench Alley?"

"We think the man who was killed in the explosion was him."

"Think? You're not sure?"

Suit shook his head. "Nope. And if we can't get good evidence, we may never know."

Elena winced. It was just slightly, but enough for Suit to notice.

"See, that's why we've got to keep the secret for a little while longer. I want the world to know about us, just not yet."

Elena wriggled out of his grasp, stepped close to him, and wrapped her arms around him. "As long as it's our secret together, I'll keep it as long as you want."

They stayed that way, embracing, each holding on to prop the other up. Five minutes later, Suit was strolling back to his cruiser, his heart racing. He had never been so happy. He had never been so scared, not even when he thought he was dying. Now he knew, really knew, what it was like to be afraid for someone else. He was so caught up in the jumble of emotions that he failed to see the white Chevy Sonic parked across the street from Elena's house, nor did he see the man behind the wheel, the nondescript man with the wire-rimmed glasses.

FIFTY-THREE

He watched as the Crown Vic rode away from the house with the slightly overgrown lawn and empty flower boxes. He had been following Officer Simpson around from the beginning of his shift. The big oaf hadn't done anything except drive in lazy circles through the streets of Paradise. He had stopped once to use the bathroom at a bar and another time to grab a large coffee at a diner. Police work, he thought, snickering to himself, was a great job for a dull-witted moron. It still escaped him how this dolt, of all the people in the world who had been hunting for him, happened to be the one to shoot him.

Thinking about that day at the abandoned housing development made him seethe. Even now, more than a year later, he could barely contain his anger there in the driver's seat of his rental. Sure, things had gone wrong for him before that day, but never so radically wrong. The more he thought about it, the angrier he got. Nothing had seemed to go right for him since. Nothing. First there'd been the debacle at Joe Breen's place in Boston. Outsmarted by a cheap thug. Worse, he'd let a witness get away, a pretty girl at that. He'd barely escaped the cops himself. Then there was the delay in treatment, the botched surgery, the erosion of his skills. Worst of all was the hit his reputation had taken.

It was all he could do not to get out of the car and murder the woman who had let that idiot Simpson into her house, whoever she was. But no, he couldn't give himself away. Not yet, not without a proper audience. For the time being, he had them all confused and chasing their own tails around in the dark. They weren't sure whether he was in Dallas or Paradise or saving a row of seats in hell. Maybe good fortune was finally shining its light back on him, given how things had worked out with the explosion. Talk about a stroke of good luck.

He couldn't help but wonder if the police had recovered his .22 or if the man he'd hired had taken it with him into the next life. That had been the whole point of the little charade: having his proxy shoot out the tire and deliver the envelope, letting the

Keystone Kops find his precious Smith & Wesson. He'd thought long and hard about finding a way to let the crime scene people discover some of his actual DNA in Trench Alley. That would seal the deal. The police would be sure he was dead and he would be able to operate with impunity and actual invisibility. He was positive that most of the fools probably already assumed he was dead. That the body in the Sentra had been his. It was the way cops thought. Cops are as guilty of wishful thinking as anyone, maybe more so. They were a lazy breed, trained to close files, not to solve crimes. But Jesse Stone was different. He knew Stone wouldn't just accept the fact of his death without proof.

Stone. He despised Stone most of all. His bad luck, his missteps, his bullet wound, his loss of status — it all came back to Stone, and it was Stone who would have to pay the biggest price. They would all pay. Some, like that wretched old mobster Gino Fish, had gotten off cheaply. That was good for him, but bad for Stone. The debt would be added to Stone's bill.

But for now he was curious about the woman in the house across the street. If that lumbering clod Simpson hadn't brought her flowers, he didn't suppose he would have given her a second thought. She was little and mousy — at least she looked that way from a distance. What was Simpson doing there with her? He wrote down the address, checked his watch, and then pulled slowly away from the curb. For now, he had to do some reconnaissance at Molly Crane's house, but he would be back later. Yes, he would be back to see about the mousy woman in the house with the empty flower boxes.

FIFTY-FOUR

Hale Hunsicker's house was a posh poke in the eye. It wasn't ugly or even tasteless, and on a five-acre lot it might have even been beautiful. Big as it was, the place wasn't nearly as bold or idiosyncratic as the fussy old Victorians on the Bluffs back in Paradise, the ones built overlooking the ocean by the rich founders of the town. Yet there was something about the Hunsicker place that irked Jesse. Everything about it was just a little too: too big, too showy, too grand, too hungry for attention. In that respect, it was a reflection of the woman who was about to become the lady of the house. There hadn't ever been enough attention in the world to please Jenn, at least not enough of Jesse's.

The manor house — to call it anything else would have been a lie — sat on a low rise beside a teardrop-shaped pond. The gentle slopes leading down to the pond from the house were as manicured and green as the fairways at Augusta. The house, lit up for the world to admire by night, was built of red brick, real red brick, not that sham concrete nonsense. It was vaguely Tudor, but with its tiled roofs and arched doorways and windows, it had Spanish and Moorish elements as well. The things that stuck out to Jesse were the huge windows. Some, like the window over the main entrance, were elegant stained glass. Others were made up of hundreds of individual diamond-shaped panes fit into crisscrossing strips of dark metal. The windows recalled nothing else so much as a medieval cathedral. The house was almost the right size. Jesse was pretty sure there was enough room inside to play a decent game of touch football.

Ari pulled the Escalade up the S-shaped driveway paved with sandy-colored gravel. But the gravel was embedded and meant only to give the sense of real gravel. It was all very English, the sound of tires on gravel. Though it wouldn't do, Jesse supposed, to have actual stones spit out by spinning tires into the fenders of your guests' Lamborghinis or Aston-Martins. Jesse laughed to himself, noticing that there were, in fact, two Lamborghinis parked farther down the driveway. Alongside the Italian supercars

were a Bentley, three Porsches, a few Mer-
cedes, a Vineland Park PD SUV, and a red
Corvette. He pointed the Corvette out to
Diana.

"Probably the cook's," he said, to break
the tension.

The tension wasn't broken. It wasn't even
cracked. She didn't laugh. Why would she?
As Diana and Molly had pointed out to
Jesse, this was a momentous night for her.
For Jenn, too. It didn't help with the tension that a soulless, psycho-killer assassin
might be out there in the falling darkness
just beyond the upturned floodlights, behind
the tan stone wall that ringed the property,
or over the shoulder of one of the security
guards stationed everywhere she looked.
Nor was it comforting to Diana that her
outfit didn't allow her to carry the weapon
Kahan's man had issued her. She'd carried
a weapon on and off for years, though for
her it had never developed into a fifth limb
like it had for many of the other agents
she'd worked with during her time at the
FBI. Suddenly, unexpectedly, she felt naked
without it.

Jesse could read her. That was one of the
differences between Diana and Jenn. He
and Diana had been able to read each other
since the day they met. With Jenn, at least

in the beginning, it was like reading tea leaves or a shaman's tossed animal bones. Jenn would say one thing and mean another. She'd ask for one thing and really want something else. Only after they'd parted and with Dix's help had the veil of Jenn been lifted and her mystery solved. Jesse didn't blame Jenn. There wasn't any anger left, not even any frustration. He knew who Jenn was, that he had wanted her, and that he was complicit in whatever transgressions had occurred.

"You look stunning, Diana Evans," he said. "I didn't even want to come to this damned wedding. Maybe this is what Peepers had in mind as my punishment."

That worked. She laughed, finally, turned, and pecked Jesse on the cheek. She wiped the lipstick off his cheek with her thumb.

"Come on," she said. "Let's get this over with before I explode. I need a drink."

The entrance hall of the house rose up a good thirty feet and the chandelier that hung from the high ceiling was meant to give a rustic, down-home feel. The three black wrought-iron rings, each larger than the one above it by a third, were lit with a hundred low-wattage bulbs meant to suggest candles. The effect was successful. They threw off a soft, welcoming glow. That was about as rustic as things got. The rest of the hall was polished granite, swooping staircases, and stained glass.

One of Kahan's men, an African American version of Ari, dressed in a black blazer, earpiece, et cetera, nodded at them and motioned to the left. When he gestured and his jacket lifted slightly, Jesse noticed the SIG under his arm. Diana noticed, too. They looked at each other and shrugged.

As they moved down the hallway, cocktail party noises pressed to meet them. There was low chatter, shuffling shoes, clinking glasses, a short burst of laughter. There were party aromas, too. The unmistakable smoky fragrance of slow-cooked brisket dominated, with hints of smoked salmon sneaking out of the room as well. Jesse was pretty hungry. Diana not so much. The last thing she was thinking about was food. She stopped just outside the door to the room where the party was going on and did a final check in a hammered silver–framed mirror.

She reached into her cream-colored clutch for her glossy red lipstick, applied a coating, and blew herself a kiss. She winked at Jesse. Her lush blond hair was swept up, revealing the perfect geometry between her tanned neckline, shoulders, and clavicle. She'd had her makeup done to highlight her angular jawline and impossible blue eyes. She'd brought her killer cream cocktail dress with the spaghetti straps. It was at once simple, elegant, and utterly sexy. She ran the back of her hand along her bare thigh, looked at the way her stiletto heels shaped her calves. She smoothed out her dress. Diana may not have had a place for her Glock, but she wasn't going into that room without weapons of her own.

FIFTY-FIVE

When they came into the room, it was as if someone had turned down the volume button. People stopped mid-sentence, mid-laugh, mid-sip, to stare. Nobody wants a train wreck to happen, but no one wants to miss seeing one, either. Jesse swore there was an audible gasp. Apparently, the meeting between Jenn and Diana had been long anticipated by the locals as well. It reminded Jesse of a classic Western where the young upstart comes into town to challenge the fastest gun. The hush and gasp seemed a little over the top, even for Dallas. But when Jenn emerged from the crowd, her hair swept into an updo, wearing a simple cream-colored dress and stilettos, Jesse understood. If the thin straps on Jenn's dress hadn't been covered in what seemed to be real diamonds, you might not have been able to tell it from Diana's.

Jenn walked right up to Diana, squeezed

her hands, and kissed her lightly on the cheek.

"Welcome to Dallas," she said. "You are beautiful, aren't you?" Jenn turned to Jesse, playfully slapping his forearm. "For crissakes, Jesse, did she have to be this good-looking? She does have great taste in clothing."

They all laughed and meant it. Then Jenn kissed Jesse on the cheek and hugged him tight. He hugged her back, noticing Hale Hunsicker staring at them from across the room as they embraced.

When the embrace was at an end, Jesse held his ex at arm's length. "It's good to see you, Jenn. Really good."

Jenn turned back to Diana. "Effusive, isn't he?"

"That's about as talkative as he gets."

Jenn nodded.

"Hey, you two, I'm standing right here."

Hale Hunsicker had been as patient as he was going to be, stepping over, taking Jenn by her still-svelte waist, and pulling her close.

"You mind if I join the party?"

"Hale, nice to meet you in person," Jesse said, shaking his hand. Neither man let on that they'd done anything more than talk briefly on the phone. "This is Diana Evans."

Hale took Diana's hand gently in his. "Pleasure."

She said, "Thank you so much for having us. You've got a lovely house, Hale."

He opened his mouth to say something, but Jenn spoke first.

"It's enormous, but so cool. C'mon," Jenn said, looping her arm through Diana's. "Let me show it to you."

And with that they were gone.

"That went better than expected," Hale said, shaking his head. "The crowd seems disappointed."

"The night is young."

"And Jenn said you barely had a sense of humor."

"I have my moments. Jenn looks wonderful, Hale. She's happy. I can tell. She's never really been happy before. I couldn't make her happy. You seem to agree with her."

Hunsicker smiled in spite of himself. "Thank you, Jesse. This may sound silly, but it means a lot coming from you. I'm proud of my girl. She's taken to her life down here. Couldn't have been easy for her tonight, with all eyes on her and Diana being so ungodly beautiful and all."

"She's always had it in her, but I was damned if I could bring it out in her. She was great just now. She wasn't going to give people the show they wanted."

"No, she wasn't, was she? No, sir, she was not."

"Old Jenn would have done it just for the buzz and for the audience's attention. I'm glad for her and for you."

"First there's that little ole something about keeping her alive," Hunsicker said, his voice turning chillier. "Heard about that trouble you had up Paradise way."

"Uh-huh."

"So . . ."

"Nothing solid yet. CSU people were first allowed onto the scene of the explosion earlier today. I'm sure Kahan told you it was a mess. Where is your man, anyway?"

Hunsicker made a careless wave of his hand. "Around somewhere, I expect. He's got a lot on his plate this week. Would have whether Peepers reared his head or not."

Jesse didn't like the sound of that, but was in no position or mood to cause trouble.

"Come on, Jesse," Hunsicker said, casting a mammoth arm over Jesse's shoulder. "Let me introduce you around. You may not be as pretty as Diana, but we'll make do."

As they strolled over to a group of people, one of whom was Chief Pruitt, Jesse complimented Hunsicker on his performance.

"You didn't give us away when you came

over," Jesse said.

"I'm not so sure. Jenn's pretty sly that way."

An unpleasant reality was dawning on Jesse: He didn't really know Jenn anymore. They had been apart longer than they had been married. And it had been years since they lived in close proximity. He couldn't quite understand why that realization was accompanied with sadness, but it was. He couldn't deny it, and denial, at least about things disconnected from drinking, wasn't his style. He wondered what would have become of their relationship had Peepers not resurfaced. *Would they have drifted even further apart? Would the phone calls have become less frequent? Would they have stopped?*

"Chief Jesse Stone of Paradise, Mass," Hunsicker said. "This is Chief Pruitt of the Vineland Park PD and his lovely bride, Emma."

Pruitt caught on and made like this was their first meeting. After the introductions to the small group of people, Jesse excused himself and got a drink at the bar. There was another round or two of introductions. These included Hunsicker's parents, siblings, business partners, and neighbors; the owners of the Dallas Cowboys and Mavericks; and the mayors of Vineland Park and Dallas.

That done, Jesse found a quiet corner and another Black Label. Chief Pruitt found Jesse.

"Okay, Chief Stone," Pruitt said. "It's arranged. You can talk to Belinda Yankton tomorrow. She's back home now, but under a doctor's care. They thought it would be good for her to be in a familiar environment."

"What time?"

"I'll come collect you at eleven in the a.m., all right?"

Jesse nodded.

"Good. Then I'll take you for some real Texas barbecue for lunch."

"Sounds good."

They shook hands again as Diana and Jenn reappeared, both smiling.

FIFTY-SIX

Sitting down the quiet street from the neat ranch house, watching the comings and goings of the Crane children, he supposed Molly would have been the ideal target all by herself. She would be perfect in a hundred ways. She was still quite pretty for a woman her age, though she buried her looks beneath her uniform. Her looks were more genuine somehow, so different from the rude blonde's. The blonde's looks were so brittle and superficial. By their second day together, after the makeup had smeared and the sweat had soaked her hair, there wasn't much beautiful about her. She cracked so easily and he hadn't even hurt her, not really, not the way he would have liked to. He'd only ever touched her to reset her shoulder, to stroke her hair, or to clean her up.

Molly would be different. She was stubborn. She would put up a fight. She would die hard even if, in the end, she would break. In the end they were all alike. They all begged for him to kill them. He had gotten to know Molly over these last few months as he had gotten to know them all: by watching, by listening, by hiding in plain sight in their midst. He had been careful to stay out of Jesse Stone's line of sight. He was the dangerous one. Not the rest of them. That buffoon Simpson had once held the door open for him at the Gull. No wonder they called him Suitcase. He seemed to be about as intelligent as one. He had sat across from Healy in a doctor's office. But that was easy. Healy was so distracted by the state of his wife's health.

He sat there in the driver's seat, windows down, enjoying the hints of fall in the air. Dallas was still like an oven, though not as horrible as it had been during July and August as he cemented his plans and crossed paths with Belinda June Yankton. He kind of missed her. He had never experienced that kind of close proximity with a woman for that long without the cycles of pain. He laughed at himself, not something he did frequently, thinking that he had liked knowing she would be there waiting for him when he got back from his stupid catering jobs. There were times he had found his mind wandering, planning their time together when he got back to West Dallas. He missed the feel of her hair against his fingertips and the palm of his hand. He even wondered how she was doing, because that wasn't the type of information the police released to the media. Maybe he would drop in on her someday. Just the look on her face would be worth the risk.

And as he sat there, he thought again of the perfection of Molly Crane in terms of Jesse Stone and the debt to pay. It seemed to him that of all the people in Stone's life, Molly knew him best. She was closer to him in ways no one else was or would ever be. At a bar one night after he had shot out the rear tires of two Hondas, he had overheard two of Stone's cops discussing Jesse and Molly. They were speculating that they had probably slept together once and that it had gone badly.

"That's got to be why they're always sniping at each other," the one cop said.

"No, you idiot, that's exactly wrong," said the other. "It's 'cause they haven't and they want to that they're always busting on each other."

The trouble with Stone was that he collected women the way some men collected memorabilia or coins. And the insane part of it was how devoted they were to him, how devoted they remained years after they had parted ways. Even his first girlfriend from when he had played baseball still had feelings for him. And it was to save her life that Stone had started this. He had considered going back to pay her a visit as well, to finish the job he had started. *Maybe someday* was his new mantra. He repeated it over and over and over again because he liked the sound of it and the fantasies attached to it. But he had to focus on the now and the near future.

He grew bored with his surveillance of the Crane house. Molly, for all of her camouflaged good looks, was not very exciting to watch. She was just another tired small-town housewife with too many kids and a husband she had probably tired of long ago. The smallness of most people's lives was shocking. He used to like the thought that his coming into a person's life was finally a bit of excitement. Exciting for him, at least. He was fairly certain his targets would have some different words for it. He started up the Sonic and made a U-turn. There was nothing more to gain by his staying here.

He had planned another bit of mischief before leaving Paradise. It was intended to throw Jesse Stone, who he knew was probably already in Dallas, even further off his guard. But as he drove toward Salter Road, where the rear tire of yet another old Honda Civic was waiting, he felt the pull of something else, curiosity, or perhaps opportunity. He slowed down. Stopped. The Honda could wait. He thought about Luther Simpson and that bouquet of flowers. He made another turn and backtracked, heading to the mousy woman's house, the one with the empty window boxes.

FIFTY-SEVEN

Jesse couldn't sleep. It was mostly silent in the hotel room except for the low thrumming of the air conditioner. Normally, he could have slept through carpet bombing, but not tonight, not even after too many Black Labels and the most intense sex he and Diana had ever had. And that was really saying something. There had been nothing normal about tonight.

Normal had been getting squeezed out of Jesse's life from the second he'd picked up his mail that day two months ago and noticed a Vineland Park, Texas, address on a fancy envelope. After Gino Fish's suicide, normal had seemed to be less and less of a possibility. What was normal about chasing a vengeful ghost, a killer who might or might not be dead? What was normal about Jenn and Diana, arm in arm, dressed alike, giggling and pointing? What was normal about Jenn belonging to someone else, living in another man's house, marrying him? Jesse didn't use words like *surreal* very often, but there was no other way for him to describe the scene or the way he felt about it.

And then there was Jenn, pulling him aside and practically begging for them to have some time together, alone. What was he supposed to do with that? Jenn and her drama, it had all come rushing back at him. He'd told Diana about Jenn's request. He wasn't going to hide things from her. He wasn't going to lie to Diana. She wasn't like Jenn in that way. There were times when they were together, even after they were together, that Jenn had wanted him to lie to her. Jenn had always wanted Jesse to fix things, to make the world right, and in the next moment she would work to screw it all up again.

Jesse hated that he was still vulnerable to Jenn's gravity. At least Jenn's pull on him no longer carried the weight of the sun. It was more like the moon, a tug at him, not an irresistible force. It ate at him, though, that she would even ask. Besides, where and how could they meet and spend time alone together? There wasn't any doubt that Kahan's men were watching every step Jenn, Diana, and Jesse took while they were in town. Then there was Peepers. Even if they could escape all the watchful eyes, it would be foolish to do so. It would be presenting Peepers his dream scenario on a silver platter. *Come and get us.*

"Go," Diana said earlier. "I'm sure she has some things to say to you that she's meant to say for a long time, and I'm sure that's true for you also."

"What do I have to say to her?"

"Gee, I don't know. How about wishing her luck and that you're happy for her? Unless you're not."

"Please."

"Well, then," Diana said, "give her a chance to say what she has to say. Maybe she needs this to be sure she's doing the right thing."

"Be sure? Why did she agree to marry Hale if she wasn't sure?"

"Is anybody ever sure about marriage?"

"You've got a point."

"Of course I do," she said.

"What did you two talk about when you disappeared?"

"She showed me the house. What a place."

"That's not much of an answer."

"What do you expect me to say, Jesse, that we compared notes on you?"

"I don't know what I expect."

"Your nose is growing, Chief Stone."

"Come on, Di, give me a break."

"We made the best of what was a really uncomfortable situation," Diana said. "We talked about how all the other guests seemed to be waiting for us to scratch each other's eyes out or spill drinks over our heads and how we were glad neither of us had given the crowd what they were spoiling for. We made small talk about the house and the wedding parties and her wedding gown. And . . ."

"And?"

"And she asked if we were getting married."

"*We?* As in you and me?" That'd gotten Jesse's attention. He had sat up in bed. "What did you say?"

"Yes."

"What? Wait. Do I get a say in this?"

"I'm sorry, Jesse." She turned away from his stare. "It just came out of my mouth. I didn't mean for it to happen, but there was Jenn showing me this grand house, and her amazing ring, and telling me how happy and in love she was and —"

"But I thought you could never be happy in a place like Paradise. If I get married again, I don't want to get divorced again. I won't do that. For better or worse, Paradise is my home now, Di. I'm not pulling up roots again."

"I know. I know." She sat up, too. "I didn't mean to say it. It was an impulsive, defensive thing I blurted out."

"When were you planning to let me in on the happy news?"

"Please, Jesse, I already feel like a complete idiot. I'm sorry. You have to believe me that I didn't mean to say it."

He reached out his right arm and tucked some loose strands of her hair behind her ear. "What's done is done. I believe you didn't mean to say it, but did you mean it?"

She grabbed his hand. "I'm not certain what you're asking me."

"I'm asking you if you want me to ask you to get married."

"Yes!" she said.

He tilted his head at her and gave her a grave look. "No one's here besides us. There's no need to compete with Jenn. There's nothing written in —"

"Jeez, Jesse Stone, shut up and ask me before I change my mind just to piss you off."

"Will you marry me?"

"I already said yes."

She leaned over and kissed him. That began something that didn't stop until they had once again fallen breathless and sweating in each other's arms.

Now Diana was sound asleep, snoring softly, curled up in a top sheet on her side of the bed. Jesse, staring up through the darkness at the green light on the smoke alarm, was rehashing how his proposal of marriage had come about and contemplating the word and the state of normalcy. He got out of bed and pulled the last little bottle of Black Label out of the minibar.

FIFTY-EIGHT

Chief Pruitt was right on time. His Vineland Park PD Suburban pulled up to the hotel entrance at exactly eleven. A few minutes prior to the sheriff's arrival, Jesse, drinking his third cup of coffee, strolled over to a guy who was clearly one of Kahan's minions. He stood beside him but didn't look at him.

"I'll be with Chief Pruitt all day until the party tonight," Jesse said, flipping through a stack of *Wall Street Journal*s. "Don't waste your time on me. Keep eyes on Miss Evans. If you follow me, I'll know it. And I'll make an ugly scene. You copy?"

"Copy that," Kahan's man said, his voice barely a whisper.

Pruitt was in good spirits. He gave Jesse a firm handshake and a pat on the shoulder. Told him how beautiful he thought Diana was.

"You're looking a little rough around the

edges, there, Jesse," Pruitt said when he noticed Jesse hadn't said much. "A few too many?"

"That obvious, huh?"

"Like a flashing neon sign, son."

Jesse laughed. Pruitt, too.

"It's not only the scotch," Jesse said.

"Pressure getting to you?"

Pressure comes in all shapes and sizes, Jesse thought, considering he'd just committed himself to Diana for the rest of his life. But he understood what Pruitt was referring to.

"Not me I'm worried about, Chief Pruitt. It's everyone else."

"Call me Jed. And worrying about everyone else, that about describes a chief's job, doesn't it?"

Jesse nodded, staring out the window of the big SUV.

"Problem this time is that everyone involved is someone I care about. It's one thing to worry about your town. You can have some distance from it most of the time, enough to be rational. It's something else when it's the people closest to you that you're worrying over. No distance. Hard to make clear choices."

"I hear you, Jesse. I surely do."

That was when Pruitt wisely changed the

subject to baseball. That pleased Jesse. He didn't get to talk much baseball with anyone except Healy, and until Peepers reared his head again, Jesse hadn't seen much of his old state police friend. And these days, given Healy's retirement and the health of his wife, baseball took a backseat when they got together. Suit was more of a football fan. The rest of his cops were such dyed-in-the-wool Sox fans that it was impossible to have a baseball discussion that didn't include the Sox and the hated Yankees. For them, the other twenty-eight teams were inconveniences, games to fill in the spaces between Sox–Yankees games.

Pruitt recalled games Jesse had played in. They discussed the guys Jesse had played with in the minors, the ones who had made it to the show and those who hadn't. Vic Prado's name came up, of course.

"So was he really mixed up with the Boston mob like the media reports said?" Pruitt asked.

"Uh-huh, but he paid a big price."

"Yes, sir, he'll be spending a lot of time behind bars."

"That, too, but I meant something else," Jesse said. "Peepers was the guy who nearly tortured Vic to death. That's what started this whole mess. Long story."

"We got a few minutes."

"Maybe some other time, Jed. Okay?"

"Sure thing."

There was a moment of awkward silence, the kind that happens between people who are getting along but don't really know each other. Pruitt broke it up by going back to an earlier part of the conversation.

"I hear your Diana can really handle herself. Ex-FBI, right?"

"Uh-huh. A few weeks ago, she chased a mugger down in Boston. Didn't hesitate. Saw it happen and was out of the car before I could move."

"She sounds like a woman full of surprises."

"You've got no idea."

They didn't speak much for the rest of the ride, but the awkwardness was gone. Pruitt had a satisfied smile on his face that he kept there right up until the moment he pulled the Suburban into the semicircular front drive of an apartment and hotel complex that smelled of money. But by the time the VPPD chief put the SUV in park, the smile was gone. From his serious expression, one might've believed he had never smiled in his life.

FIFTY-NINE

The two-building complex was done in that same smooth, tan stucco finish as the Vineland Park town hall had been done in. The accents were all Spanish, including the rounded red tile roof over the front portico, under which Pruitt had parked. The buildings were located in a lovely area of low hills, running trails, wooden footbridges, and a network of streams. There was some cloud cover that morning, so the searing power of the Texas sun wasn't at its fullest. Still, the heat was pretty intense as they stepped out of the SUV.

"These buildings here are called the Park Mansion. That tower over there," said Pruitt, pointing to his right, "is the hotel. Whenever big musical acts or celebrities come to town, that's usually where you'll find 'em. And the Park Place Bar in the hotel is the finest cocktail bar in all of North Texas. Pretty fair collection of fine scotches and women, too. I'm sure you, Hale, and the boys will be stopping by there tonight."

"You're not coming?"

"I'm too old for this party-every-night shit, and tonight's going to be all about drinking, let me tell you. Between the cigar bar at Javier's and Park Place . . . no, sir. My liver won't take it. C'mon with me."

The doorman stood from behind a security desk as the front doors parted and the two police chiefs entered. They were hit with a blast of arctic air. The doorman was a short, smiling fellow with dark brown eyes, brown skin, slicked-back black hair going gray, and a once handsome face with a lot of rough mileage on it.

"Mornin', Champ."

"Good morning, Chief Pruitt," the man said, a heavy dose of Mexico in his English. "This must be Chief Stone. Good morning to you, Chief. Please sign in, gentlemen." He handed them a tablet and stylus. "Just follow the prompts."

As he waited to sign in, Jesse noticed the not-too-subtle bulge beneath the doorman's gray tunic. As Jesse signed, Pruitt explained that he and Jesse would first go down to the garage and then head up to Miss Yankton's condo. The doorman didn't object. Instead, he issued an electronic passkey to Pruitt.

"That will get you where you have to go, gentlemen."

As they rode the elevator down to the garage, Pruitt said, "Recognize the doorman?"

"Should I have? He had a flattened nose, a lot of scar tissue around the eyes, and you called him Champ, so he was a boxer."

"Rodrigo 'Rodeo' Robles. Was the flyweight title holder for about five minutes in the late nineties. Good man. Tough as nails."

"Carries, too."

"Didn't use to until this abduction happened. Already too many damn guns carried by too many damn fools, but Rodrigo took our course. He won't be stupid with it."

The elevator stopped and the doors spread open. The exhaust fans whirred as they had whirred the evening Belinda June Yankton had been snatched by Peepers. Pruitt walked Jesse over to where Yankton's red Audi convertible was parked. As they walked, the faint background odors of car exhaust, gasoline, and motor oil brought back the car chase and explosion in Paradise. He wondered how the evidence collection was going and how soon it would be before he could relax. Jesse had tried not to dwell on it, but he knew that if Peepers wasn't dead and he slipped through his grasp this time, he might never be able to relax again.

"Clever bastard, Peepers. Stole a parking pass and waited down here in the spot next to the woman's. She was headed out for a night with some girlfriends over at the Jungle Bar at Vineland Park Village. Never made it."

"Drugged her. She was unconscious before she knew it."

"How'd you —"

"It's what he did to a woman in Boston."

"Next thing she knew, she was naked and strapped to a workbench with leather cuffs and restraints."

Jesse nodded.

"Same as he did to the woman back in Massachusetts?" Pruitt asked.

"Uh-huh."

"C'mon. Nothing much else to see down here."

As they rode up in the elevator, Pruitt explained more about Belinda Yankton's delicate mental state.

"I don't want to hit this too hard, Jesse, but you've got to be careful with her. I figure, based on what Kahan told me about your experience with the LAPD, that you'll be just fine with her. Still, I had to warn you."

"I understand," Jesse said. "I get the sense you don't much like Kahan."

"He's all right as far as it goes. Good at his job. Thorough."

"But you don't trust him?"

"Not as far as I could toss a fat steer. Man has his own agenda. He operated on his own way too much for my taste, if you know what I mean. Covert-ops types have a different kinda mind-set in the way they go about their business."

"We're on the same page, then, where he's concerned."

The smooth-as-silk elevator came to an almost undetectable stop and a woman's voice announced that they had reached the twelfth floor. No annoying bells or blips at the Park Mansion. Only the best.

SIXTY

The uniqueness of the building didn't stop with the elevator's female voice. A voice that would have set the adolescent Jesse Stone's mind areel. The hallway floors were done in a mosaic of vibrant azure, white, and corn-yellow Mexican tiles. The entrance to each condo was framed with an ornate terra-cotta surround the color of sunbaked red clay with granite accents and topped by a fanciful arched cornice. The doors them-selves were massive: double-sided, paneled, and sun-bleached as if reclaimed from an old desert mission. The hardware was heavy hand-hammered iron. Jesse had seen many such entrances to houses back in Tucson, but never inside an apartment building.

Pruitt rapped his knuckles on the wood. When the doors pulled back, they were surprised to see a black face staring back at them, a man's black face. And the man at-tached to that face did a pretty good job of filling up the doorway. He had a tree-trunk neck with thighs to match, and his arm muscles rippled with even the slightest movement. He wore a pink golf shirt, khakis, and deck shoes, which did little to soften his intimidating look.

"IDs, gentlemen," the big man asked politely enough.

Both men did as they were asked. This was no time for a testosterone fest, not with Belinda Yankton likely within earshot. When he returned their badges and credentials, Pruitt inquired as to his identity.

He didn't give a name, just "Private security provided by Miss Yankton's ex. She's expecting you. Kitchen."

They stepped inside, past security. The spacious living room was beautifully appointed with an eclectic mix of Asian, Mexican, and African objets d'art. The furniture was oversized, featuring lots of wood, leather, and woven fabrics. Pruitt described it as Texas-ranch rustic. The tiled floors were covered in colorful American Indian rugs. There were two sets of windows twice the size of the front doors, yet the room was dark. The windows were shuttered, slats facing so that almost no outside light could leak in. The place smelled of cigarette smoke, must, and fear.

Belinda Yankton sat at the kitchen island, smoking a cigarette burned down to the filter, an overfull ashtray and a big mug of coffee in front of her. She was still thin and had put some effort into prettying herself up for her guests, but Jesse guessed her heart wasn't in it. You could see she was a very attractive woman who had aged years in a very short time. Her cigarette hand shook. Jesse had seen this before with people who had survived traumatic events: rape victims, hostages, people who'd been in a bomb's blast zone. He had seen it in Suit. The physical wounds heal, but the trauma is never far away. Pruitt and Jesse waited for Belinda to make the first move, because the woman's state of mind couldn't have been more evident if the word *fragile* had been tattooed across her forehead.

"Hey, guys, please sit," she said, her voice surprisingly calm and steadier than her hand.

Jesse and Pruitt sat across from her.

"Can I get you some coffee?"

"That'd be great," Jesse said.

Pruitt shook his head. "No, thank you, ma'am. I'm just fine."

She tamped out her cigarette and poured a mug for Jesse. Watching Jesse fix the coffee to his liking, Belinda Yankton lit another cigarette.

"So," she asked, "how are we going to do this?"

Jesse turned to Pruitt. "Chief, you think you can give Miss Yankton —"

"Belinda, please. I'd like it if you called me Belinda. For weeks he called me the rude blonde. Even after he knew my name, he'd call me that. The rude blonde. The rude blonde," she said, repeating it over and over.

"Sure, Belinda. Call me Jesse. Chief, could you give Belinda and me a few minutes?"

"That okay with you, Belinda?" Pruitt asked.

"Yes, Chief Pruitt. I'd like that."

They waited until Pruitt had left. When he was gone, Belinda offered Jesse a cigarette. He said no, that the coffee would suit him for now. He had thought a lot about how he would approach this conversation if he got the opportunity to have it. And seeing how brittle Belinda was, he decided to go ahead with his first impulse.

"Listen, Belinda, I'm sure you're sick to death of rehashing what happened to you and that you can't be looking forward to telling another cop about how you were afraid for weeks at a time and the rest of the things you went through."

She nodded, unable to look Jesse in the eye, a stray tear rolling down her cheek.

"So I'm going to tell you about my encounter with the man who held you and if anything comes to mind to say, no matter how silly or trivial it may seem, please say it. Interrupt me whenever you'd like, okay?"

She nodded again, her hands shaking more violently now than they had only a minute before.

"You know what my therapist always says when he sees something going on with my hands?" Jesse asked, pointing at her cigarette hand.

"You have a therapist?" She sounded surprised, her voice less steady than before.

"I do."

"What does he say to you, Jesse?"

"He'll nod at my hands and say, 'Put that into words.' So, Belinda, put your shaking hands into words."

"I'm ashamed to say it."

He smiled his most comforting smile at her. "No need for shame around me. I don't think you could embarrass yourself any worse than I have embarrassed myself. So come on and say it. We're going to have to trust each other."

"Okay, Jesse. Will you hold my hand,

please? I really need to hold on to someone. Everyone's so afraid to touch me. They're afraid I'll crack or something. Please, Jesse."

He didn't answer with words. Instead he reached over the island countertop and tamped out her cigarette. When that was done, he took both of her hands in his and he told her about how he had met Mr. Peepers.

Sixty-One

They were back down in the Suburban before they discussed what had gone on upstairs in the condo between Jesse and Belinda Yankton. First, Jesse explained about how he'd done most of the talking. Pruitt smiled at that.

"You would've been a natural in intel, Jesse. That was sharp of you to take on the burden and do the talking, putting her at ease."

"She asked to hold my hand. Held it the whole time."

"Yeah, she probably feels so disconnected from her old life. Needed someone to hold on to, if only just for a little bit. We all need an anchor at one time or another."

"That's right. Also helped me gauge if anything I was saying hit a nerve. I watched her, too."

"And?"

"I found out some things that didn't come

out in the original reports."

Pruitt was curious, but was more interested in the scowl on Jesse's face. "You don't mind me asking, what's that nasty expression about?"

"Some things Belinda said about Peepers . . . I don't like them."

"Not much to like about the murderous son of a bitch to begin with."

"You're right, but it's not that," Jesse said.

"You mind sharing?"

"Belinda said that she got the impression that Peepers was kind of fond of Jenn."

" 'Fond'?"

"Her word, not mine. She told me that Peepers would sometimes talk to himself when he thought she was out of it. Usually when he was working on something or cleaning his weapons out of her line of sight. She said, 'The more drugs he gave me . . . they didn't always work the way he thought they would. There would be times I would be out of it, but I'd snap to and be aware of everything, but I wouldn't be able to move at all. I couldn't even will myself to blink. It was kind of like those stories you hear about folks being on an operating table and being awake. I was conscious, but I must've looked totally out of it to him. If he even noticed me.' "

"And he talked to himself about Jenn?" Pruitt asked.

"Jenn and other subjects, usually less pleasant ones. He also talked to himself about things he would have liked to do with Belinda. No wonder she's freaked out. I'm pretty sure you don't need me to repeat that stuff."

"No, sir, I do not. Don't take much of an imagination to figure that out. But why not do them to her? Between you and me, Jesse, there wasn't anything she could have done to stop him, and he had all the time in the world to do whatever he desired."

Jesse nodded. "That's one of the things I don't like about what Belinda said to me. It was as if Peepers grabbed her for one reason and then decided to use her for something else."

"Like what?"

"Good question, Jed. To deliver a message. To throw us off his scent. To mislead us. I don't know."

"What about Jenn?"

"One time, when Peepers took Belinda's gag off to get some fluids in her, she got up the courage to ask about Jenn. At first Peepers's face twisted up with anger. Again, Belinda's words, not mine. She begged him not to hurt her and he calmed down. She said it was weird because he became almost kind. Mellow, even. His voice was less angry and threatening. He told her about the month or so he'd spent in L.A. tailing Jenn before she met Hunsicker and moved to Dallas. He said he'd felt kind of sad for her. That she had seemed very lonely."

Pruitt was incredulous. "Peepers feels things? This guy killed an old lady and a dog because they were inconveniences."

Jesse shrugged. "I used to hunt killers for a living. You can only know them up to a point, even when you have them in custody. They all have weak spots, but what those weaknesses are is hard to figure."

"Did the Yankton woman say more about Peepers's feelings toward Jenn?"

Jesse said, "She did, and this is the other thing I don't like. Belinda said she got a strong sense that Peepers would never hurt Jenn, not really. In fact, she said, talking about Jenn seemed to arouse Peepers. Soon after they talked about Jenn, Peepers drugged her, but not enough. She had one of those lucid moments of waking up and not being able to move. When she came to, Peepers was fondling her breasts in a very clumsy manner. 'I was glad I couldn't move,' she said. 'I think if he knew I knew he was touching me like that, he would have killed me for sure. From what happened between him and me in the restaurant, I just knew he hated being embarrassed probably more than anything.' "

"What do you make of it?"

"Nothing good, Jed. Nothing good. Especially since he promised he would never sexually assault her and swore he had never touched any of his other victims."

"Inconsistent behavior is trouble."

"Uh-huh. Do Peepers's feelings about Jenn make him less of a threat to her or more of a threat? Does he harbor fantasies of snatching her and being with her? Or is he so freaked over his feelings about her that he feels a need to kill her?"

"Well, come on and let's get some lunch," Pruitt said. "There's never been a puzzle some good Texas barbecue couldn't help solve."

Jesse didn't know about the truth of that, but it certainly couldn't hurt. And maybe it would help him stop itching for a Black Label.

Sixty-Two

It was an hour before the beginning of their shift and Molly showed up at the Gull ten minutes early. It was in her nature to be early. Today her earliness wasn't about her nature. Molly was early because she was burning with curiosity. What could Suit want to discuss with her that they couldn't talk about at work or over the phone?

They had shared a strange relationship over the years. Paradise lifers and colleagues, they weren't exactly friends. They weren't enemies, either, but they were occasionally rivals. Jesse Stone, his opinions and affections, were most often at the center of this rivalry, though not always. They were just very different people.

Molly was long married with a houseful of kids, some soon heading to college. She took her job seriously. It seemed to Suit she took everything seriously, too seriously. Yet she had more leeway with Jesse. She could bust on him, humble him, in a style Suit could never pull off. And it wasn't because she was so good-looking. In his most self-honest moments, Suit knew it was because Jesse thought so highly of Molly. Jesse respected Molly in a way Suit was sure Jesse didn't respect him. Jesse loved him. He never doubted that. But it was painful and painfully obvious to everyone that Jesse thought Molly could have been a big-city cop and that he thought Suit was right where he belonged. He was a small-town kid and a small-town cop.

Poor, dumb Suit. Jesse never said it. Maybe he never even thought about Suit that way, not in so many words, but sometimes Suit read them in Jesse's eyes. It was never worse than after Peepers shot him in the belly and he'd been forced to work light duty for a few months. Working the desk while Molly took his place on patrol was as serious a wound to his ego as the bullets to his gut.

Molly ordered a coffee, checking her cell phone for the time. *What has Suit gotten himself into now?* He'd never crossed the line, but he was occasionally indiscreet. His affairs with older married women weren't ever front-page news. In fact, she was sure that Suit and Jesse thought they had done a good job of keeping her out of the loop. She wasn't judging Suit. Who was she to judge Suit? She had crossed a line that she swore she would never cross, though only once. She liked Suit. It was hard not to like Suit. For one thing, he tried hard. He was funny and, because of his size and boyishness, there was something teddy bear–ish about him. He could be charming, too. He wanted people to like him. Needed to be liked. Molly, not so much.

"Let's go to a table," Suit said, stepping up to the bar and flagging down the waitress.

As they were sitting down, Suit ordered two glasses of champagne. When Molly objected, Suit repeated the order and shooed the waitress away.

"Champagne? What's going on, Suit?"

"I need your help."

"I knew it," Molly said, exasperated. "What is it this time? You know, champagne isn't going to soften me up, especially before a shift."

But instead of becoming glum and defensive, Suit laughed.

"I knew you'd think that, Molly. That I screwed up somehow."

"It's usually why people need help. It's always why you do."

"Jeez, thanks for the vote of confidence. At least Jesse pretends I'm good at my job."

Molly felt a twinge of guilt. She was being too hard on Suit. He had done plenty of good as a cop. He'd saved people's lives, and when he'd messed up in the past, nobody had suffered very much for his mistakes. Even his getting in the middle of Jesse and Peepers and the mess now following in its wake was done with the best intentions.

"Sorry, Suit. I'm cranky. It's all this stuff going on with Peepers, and I'm worried about my family. And with Jesse out of town . . ."

"That's okay. I guess you'd be right most of the time, but not this time. I didn't screw anything up," he said, smiling with pride. "I need your help because I did the right thing, Molly. The rightest thing I've ever done."

Before Molly could ask what that was, the two glasses of champagne arrived and were set out in front of them. Suit thanked the waitress and asked her to bring him the bill. They clinked glasses and sipped. Suit made a face.

"Is it any good?" he asked Molly.

"It's good enough."

"I hate champagne."

Molly shook her head. "Then why'd you

order it, genius?"

"Because it's what you're supposed to drink when you get engaged."

It was all Molly could do not to spit out her second sip. "Engaged! To who?"

"You don't know her, I don't think. Elena Wheatley. She used to teach at Paradise High. We've been seeing each other a few months and . . . you know. It just felt right. I asked and she said yes."

"Why is this the first I'm hearing about it?"

"It's the first anyone's hearing about it. Not even Jesse knows. And please, don't tell anyone. Okay? I want to be the one to tell people when this thing with Peepers blows over."

"Sure, Suit," Molly said. "But why tell me, and why do you need my help? Seems to me you're doing just fine."

"Because I trust you to make sure I do stuff right, to tell me how I'm supposed to go about things. I know you know all that stuff. I really love her, Molly, and I don't want to hurt her feelings or screw this up for her."

"Stand up," she said.

"Why?"

She repeated. "Stand up."

This time he stood. Molly came around

the table, kissed him on the cheek, and hugged him.

"Congratulations, Luther. Best of luck to you and Elena."

"We're going to need it."

"Don't worry," she said. "I'll make sure you keep in line."

"Thanks, Molly."

"Shut up and get out of here. You've got to be on patrol in forty-five minutes."

"But what about the check?"

"It's my treat. Now get!"

As she watched Suit leave, Molly noticed she was smiling. She hadn't done much of that lately.

SIXTY-THREE

Done up in the same Spanish Mission style as the town hall and the Park Mansion complex, Vineland Park Village was a kind of Rodeo Drive turned into a square strip mall. The bulk of the businesses were designer clothing and accessory shops, with a movie theater, restaurants, and a few bars thrown in. It was the sort of place created to burn your cash and melt your credit cards faster than a casino. The cars in the lot were like the cars parked in the driveway at Hale Hunsicker's house: expensive, luxurious, and fast. The place was impeccably landscaped with flower beds carpeted in burnt-orange-, yellow-, and periwinkle-colored Texas wildflowers. Cactus, too. The sidewalks were shaded by rows of acacia trees.

"Right across the street there," Pruitt said, "that's the Vineland Park Country Club, where the wedding reception will be."

"You think I can get a look at the place before the wedding?"

"I'm sure Kahan will take care of that for you. Kind of exclusive. Only reason they let me in is 'cause the members think it's smart to keep the chief of police happy."

"Speaking of Kahan, I haven't seen him lately."

"Like I said, Jesse, you got to watch out for fellas like him. No telling what he's getting up to. But come on, let's get you an after-barbecue drink."

"Is that a Texas tradition, too?"

"No, sir, not a Lone Star tradition, but it sure is one of mine."

"Just one," Jesse said. "After listening to Belinda Yankton's tale, I could use one."

Alcoholics were full of such lines. There wasn't a situation where a drinker couldn't come up with a snappy rationalization. Jesse Stone was no exception.

"You'll be upstairs tonight," Pruitt said, sipping his bourbon and water. They were at Ace's Bar, a notorious local watering hole, at least according to Pruitt. "Vineland natives call the upstairs lounge the Jungle Bar because . . . well, that's where the big cats and kittens prowl. You'll see."

Jesse was already through most of his Black Label and soda. He was about to ask for more info on the Jungle Bar when his cell phone buzzed in his pocket.

"Excuse me," he said, waving the phone at Pruitt and retreating to a quiet spot near the restrooms.

"Jesse Stone."

"Jenn Soon-to-be Hunsicker here. Where are you?"

"Ace's Bar with Chief Pruitt."

"Are you drunk, Jesse?"

"Jenn, we've talked about this. You lost the right to ask me those kinds of questions a long time ago. But no, I'm not. The chief and I have had a long day and we had stuff to talk about."

"Jed's a good man," she said, trying to recover. "Do you think you could ask him to leave you there? I want to talk to you, Jesse. Alone."

"Look, Jenn, I'm not up for any drama. Okay?"

"Does Diana know you're out drinking in the afternoon?"

"What did I just say, Jenn?"

"I'm sorry, Jesse. I'm sorry. Of course what Diana knows or doesn't know isn't any of my business. Please, just ask Jed to leave you there and I'll be over in ten minutes. Please, Jesse. Consider it a wedding gift."

"A wedding gift is for both the bride and

groom. Do you think Hale will see our visit that way?"

"You're impossible, Jesse Stone. I'm coming over. If you want this conversation to happen in front of Jed, that's up to you."

She hung up.

Jesse went back to his drink and asked Jed Pruitt if he wouldn't mind giving him some time alone.

"I'll be okay. Peepers won't make his move here."

"You sure about that? Remember what Belinda Yankton said to you today."

"I'm sure. I'll call Ari to come get me when I'm done. Are you sure you won't come tonight?" Jesse asked. "I feel like I could use an ally."

"You look like a fella that will hold his own around Hale's crowd. Mention your baseball career and all them master-of-the-universe types will shrivel up. Money may be good for a man's ego, but it don't measure up to really doing something. Remember, most little boys grow up dreaming of being a cop or a professional athlete. I'd say you got that covered."

"Thanks for the barbecue and the company."

"Truly my pleasure. I'll catch up with you at tomorrow's festivities."

When Jed Pruitt's back vanished into the shadows of the bar, Jesse hurried to order a second Black Label. He thought of Jenn and thought of how he could use that second drink. He laughed at himself, because even he realized he would have had a second drink regardless.

SIXTY-FOUR

Jenn came and sat right next to him at the bar.

"Is this seat taken, handsome?" she said.

"It is now."

Jenn was dressed in a red spaghetti-strap tee and a gauzy white shoulder wrap splashed with vaguely floral shapes of sky blue and pale yellow. Her slacks were white and tight. Her high, wedged shoes were a few hundred bucks' worth of casual. One thing Jesse had noticed in his brief time in the Lone Star State was that Dallas women had a different sense of casual than women did almost anywhere else he'd been. It included perfect makeup and expensive, if not necessarily fancy, clothing.

"Can I get you something to drink?" Jesse asked, shaking his glass so that the ice cubes rattled about.

"For goodness' sakes, Jesse, you have to go out with Hale in a few hours."

Jesse stared at Jenn in the bar mirror as he had stared at Vinnie Morris in a bar mirror the month before. He couldn't believe how his life had been hijacked. Between the wedding and Peepers, he had thought of little else. He realized that even Diana hadn't gotten his full attention and that maybe he had missed some cues and signs. The whole marriage thing had caught him totally off guard, not that he wasn't excited at the prospect. A little worried, too.

Mirrors sometimes reveal things to you that eye contact just can't. That's what Jesse thought as he took in the sight of his ex-wife's face. She had aged well, growing gracefully into her good looks. The myth is that only men grow into their looks with age. Jenn put the lie to that. The small lines around her still-sparkling blue eyes and around her full mouth added to her beauty. She looked like she had lived a little and learned a lot. It was easy to see what Hale saw in her. But he sensed that she still hadn't fully shed her hungry insecurity, the thing that had been at the center of their inevitable divorce and, paradoxically, the thing that had tied them together for so many years afterward.

Jesse knew he was as much at fault as she was. It was a dance and they both knew

343

their steps, who led and who followed. Jenn had a problem. She came to Jesse to fix it. He fixed it. He liked fixing it. It made him feel good to fix it. But once things were fixed, she went AWOL. Well, until the next time. And then the music played and the dance began again. Dix was the man who helped Jesse lift the needle off the record and stop the music. Maybe Hale found Jenn's needs charming. Maybe he liked coming to her rescue. Maybe with him she didn't disappear after things were fixed.

"This is my last one, Jenn. I'll be fine later."

"Jesse Stone is always fine. That's what the rest of the world thinks, but we know better, don't we?"

"Did you come here to give me a hard time and make me regret coming to your wedding, Jenn? Because if you did, you're doing a good job of it."

"That's just it, Jesse. Why did you come?"

He didn't like where this was going.

"In the end," he said, "I thought it was the right thing to do. You know about me and doing the right thing. I want you to be happy and I wanted to see for myself that you were."

She laughed without joy and ordered a glass of Australian chardonnay. "Not as oaky as American chardonnay," she said to Jesse.

"I'll have to remember that."

"Like you remembered that answer you just gave me about why you're here. You recited it like it was written on a cue card and you practiced it on the plane down here." She lifted her glass. "Cheers."

"Cheers. Okay, Jenn, I wasn't lying, but the truth is I wanted some closure for myself. It's one thing for me to say I'm completely over you. It's another to test it. And maybe I wanted you to have a close look at Diana."

"That's better," she said, dabbing a drop of wine off her lip with a bar napkin. "Especially that last part about Diana. She is ungodly beautiful and she's definitely a match for you. She can talk shop with you and seems like she can handle herself like Sunny could. No need to come to her rescue, huh, Jesse? Probably the other way around. Still . . . I'm not buying it. We're not what we once were to each other, but I know you, Jesse Stone. Once you've made up your mind, no one's going to change it. So what changed your mind about coming?"

He swirled his drink and polished off the rest. "Asked and answered."

345

Jenn turned to Jesse, grabbing his forearm. "Stop it. Just stop it. I know something's going on. I saw the looks between you and Hale and then between you and Jed. Remember, I was an investigative reporter for a while."

That was sort of accurate. Jenn had worked on a short-lived show that wasn't exactly fluff, but wasn't exactly *Frontline* or *60 Minutes,* either.

"It's nerves, Jenn. It's pre-wedding jitters. You're imagining things."

"And you're lying. You want to tell me I'm imagining looks between you and Hale and Jed. Okay. Maybe. But why do we suddenly have twice the number of security people around than we had a month ago. Why did I have to wait upstairs last night before the party until Hale gave me the all-clear?"

"Why ask me? Ask Hale."

"Don't you think I have?" Jenn said, her voice strained with emotion. "He just says it's nothing. I know he's lying. He's not as good at it as you. He's a tough guy in his way. Big and strong and ruthless in business, but he's not as to himself as you are. He doesn't have the walls around himself you have, and the ones he has aren't as tall or sturdy. It's one of the reasons I love him so much. I can reach him in a way I could never reach you, Jesse. Please, I'm begging you to tell me the truth. I can't have the both of you lying to me, not during my wedding celebrations."

Jesse swallowed hard, took her hand in his, and lied some more.

SIXTY-FIVE

The invisible man got off the plane at Will Rogers World Airport in Oklahoma City. He might just as well have actually been invisible for how much notice anyone took of him. On his flights from Boston to Baltimore and then on to Oklahoma City, his seatmates paid him no mind. He could hear the passengers around him — in the row behind, to the side, and before him — greeting one another, asking what they did for a living or where they were ultimately headed. Saw people shake hands. No one spoke to him. No one shook his hand. Occasionally a bored businessman or old lady would give him a half-smile or a nod. The longest conversation he'd had on both flights consisted of "Water, please. No peanuts for me."

It was of little consequence to him. What could anyone in the seats around him possibly say that would interest him? Though he was sure there was plenty he could say that might interest them, at least until they ran screaming. He snickered to himself as he made his way to the rental counter, imagining that scene and conversation at thirty-five thousand feet. Nowhere to run. Nowhere to hide. But he had no need of inane chitchat or brief, meaningless encounters with people he would never see again. He had plenty to occupy his mind now that he had decided finally on how the payment of his debt to Jesse Stone and Suitcase Simpson would play out.

He checked his watch. With no traffic, he'd be back at the storage unit in Dallas within four hours. Just under three, if he pushed it, but that wasn't his style. Drive ordinary cars. Stay in the speed slot where the cops won't stop you. Walk on the shadowed side of the street in daytime. Keep in people's blind spots until its suits you not to. For now, he was enjoying and would be exploiting the fact that most of the world believed he was probably dead. They might fool themselves that they were being as diligent as they had been before the fortuitous car chase and explosion in Paradise, but it wasn't so. It was only human nature to relax, to let their guard down, if only a little. And he knew human nature in a way that most people never would. He knew humans like a rat-lab scientist knew rodents. He had seen humans under the most intense stresses imaginable. The only human he worried about was Stone.

Stone wasn't the type to relax or assume. He was willing to bet that Stone was even more suspicious now than he was before the explosion and fire. Stone had always been the wild card in all of this. The one he had to plan for and hedge against. The one he had to distract and keep off balance. And that's what this trip back to Dallas was all about, peeking out of the shadows and grabbing Jesse's attention at precisely the right moment.

At the rental counter, he stood waiting for a long time until the woman behind the counter called for the next person on line.

"Oh," she said, "I'm sorry. I didn't notice you standing there."

Of course she hadn't.

"That's all right . . . Victoria," he said in his nasal, high-pitched voice, reading her name tag. "It happens all the time."

Walking away, he smiled his special smile, repeating the name "Victoria" over and over again. At least she had apologized for her transgression and seemed to mean it. He thought of the rude blonde and wondered if

his lessons had stayed with her. He just
might have to find out.

Sixty-Six

When Jesse got back to their room, Diana threw her arms around his neck and kissed him on the mouth. She pushed back and said, "Jesse Stone, I love you something awful. Do you know that?"

"That or you're certifiable."

"Both. Me, too, apparently. After all, I agreed to marry you."

But instead of smiling, Jesse's face got serious.

"What's wrong, Jesse?"

"First things first."

He nodded for her to follow him over to a cowhide sofa next to the window in their room. He sat her down and then sat next to her.

"Listen to me, Di, we both got really caught up in things last night. And I meant everything I said to you last night."

"But . . ."

"But I screwed up one marriage. I won't
—"

"I'd say Jenn played a pretty big role in
what happened between the two of you."

"Yeah, but like I said, we got caught up in
things last night. I want to make sure you're
sure. We can walk back from this if you're
having second thoughts."

Diana scowled at Jesse. "Sounds to me
like you're the one having second thoughts."

"Nope. No second thoughts. Just concerns
about you being happy in Paradise."

She laughed. "Hard not to be happy in
Paradise."

"Not according to Genesis."

"Now I've heard it all. Jesse Stone referring to scripture."

"I guess that is pretty strange, but you
know what I mean. Paradise will bore you
to tears, and I can't ask you to do that to be
with me. I respect you and love you way too
much to ask that of you."

She didn't laugh at him, but smiled her
white neon smile at him. She leaned over
and kissed him softly on the lips.

"I said I would marry you, Stone. I didn't
say how that marriage would work. You're
right, if I stayed home and had kids and
cooked for you, I'd lose my mind. But we're
not having kids, at least not yet, and I'm

not staying home and cooking for you. I've got my consulting business and it's doing really well. I already make more money than you do, and I could expand anytime. I've got agents from the Bureau who are about to retire looking to me for jobs. No, Jesse, we'll be good. I won't be home a lot of the time, and when we see each other, it'll be amazing. We'll have the best parts of a long-distance relationship and a close marriage."

"And you thought of all this between last night and . . . five-thirty-seven p.m. central time today?" he said, looking at the clock radio beside the bed.

"Jackass. Of course not. I think I knew I wanted to be with you forever the morning after we woke up back in New York. I was so comfortable with you even then, when I was pretending to be someone else. If you didn't ask me, I would have asked you."

"When?"

"Eventually."

He smiled. "What makes you think I would have said yes?"

She punched him in the arm again and said, "And don't ask me if I'm sure ever again. Come on, let's go shower. We've both got big nights ahead of us."

But when they came out of the shower, Diana spotted something she didn't like in

Jesse's expression as he shaved.

"What's wrong?" she asked. "It's not about us, is it?"

He shook his head, stopped shaving, and turned to face her. "When I saw Jenn at the bar before, she asked me what was going on."

"Shit!"

"She's many things. Stupid isn't one of them. She's noticed all the extra security and that I changed my mind about coming to the wedding. She believed the part about me coming to show you off to her and that I needed some peace of mind that her marriage to me was truly all in the past. She didn't buy anything else I told her, until . . ."

"Until what?"

"Until I told her that a disgruntled ex-employee of Hale's had made vague threats against him and his properties."

"Talk about opening a can of worms, Stone."

"It was either that or a can of spiders. I chose worms."

SIXTY-SEVEN

Ari picked Diana and Jesse up at eight. It was a casual-dress night, so that allowed Diana to carry her piece under a loose-fitting blue blazer. She got dropped off at the Hunsicker place. Ari took Jesse over to Javier's Gourmet Mexicano Restaurant. Jesse didn't know about that gourmet thing, but he was pretty anxious to have some authentic Mexican food again. You can get great ethnic food in the Northeast, even in the towns close to Paradise. Of course, there was always Boston. But Mexican food up north was always a disappointment to Jesse. Having grown up in Tucson, playing ball in Albuquerque, and living in Los Angeles for more than a decade, he was a tough audience.

Ari half turned to Jesse and said, "The boss is pissed off. I thought I should warn you."

"Kahan?"

"Mr. Hunsicker. I don't know at who for certain, but my nose says it's you."

"Such a handsome nose."

Ari smiled a big white smile. "And a very accurate one," he said, his Israeli accent showing through. "Just be ready. Do you know why the boss would be so mad?"

Jesse laughed. "I've got a pretty good clue."

"We're here, Chief. The food is quite good."

"Thanks, Ari. And thanks for the heads-up."

"*Yasher koach.*"

"What's it mean?"

"In Hebrew it means *Order the guacamole.*"

They both laughed at that and were still laughing when Ari came around to open the door for Jesse.

"It really means *May you have strength.*"

Hale Hunsicker wasn't laughing and he wasn't smiling. He was fuming like a cartoon character. All that was missing was the smoke coming out of his ears and flames out of his nostrils.

"What the fuck are you laughing at," Hale yelled at Ari, who immediately stopped and couldn't get back behind the wheel of the

Escalade fast enough.

The valet's eyes got wide with fear and he stood clear of Hale Hunsicker. Hunsicker was a big, imposing man, and to the valet he probably looked like a man ready to throw down. Jesse was more concerned about someone overhearing, but luckily, no one except the valet was within earshot. Jesse didn't want the whole town knowing about Peepers. For added insurance he gave the valet a twenty and asked for a few minutes of privacy. The kid nodded, smiled, and walked around the other side of the building. Jesse braced himself for the onslaught. He knew that preemption wasn't an option with a man like Hunsicker.

"Two things, Stone." Hunsicker was in full voice and in Jesse's face. "What are you doing meeting with Jenn at a bar with no one around? And —"

"The bartender was there," Jesse said, to take some of the steam out of Hunsicker's rant.

"What?"

"We weren't alone. The bartender was there."

"That's not the point," Hunsicker said, his voice already calmer. "She was unprotected."

"She was with me and I was carrying

this." Jesse pulled back his sport jacket to expose the nine-millimeter on his hip.

"But what about her getting there and getting home?"

"Look, Hale, she asked to meet me. I figured she'd have one of your guys drive her there and back. Ari came and got me. And like I said, Peepers, if he's still alive, won't do anything yet," Jesse said with a lot more confidence than he actually had. "I thought she wanted to talk about us, about our marriage and divorce, or about old times. But what she wanted to talk about was —"

"Yeah, I know. She's noticed . . . things."

"So what did you want me to tell her, Hale? That she was crazy? That all the muscle and guys with earpieces were figments of her imagination? I had to tell her something she would believe."

"I guess."

"And I made it sound as if there's no specific or imminent threat to you personally and that all the extra security is just you erring on the side of caution."

"I just wish you'd given me a friendly warning, so I could have prepared."

Jesse shook his head. "No, your reaction had to be authentic or else she would still be suspicious."

"I still don't like it."

"I don't like any of it, either."

"Come on in, then," he said, throwing his arm over Jesse's shoulders. "Meet the boys."

None of "the boys" had been at the party the night before. There were black and brown faces among them and not in the security detail. They were all about Hunsicker's age, some as big or bigger. Some were dressed in that millionaire casual look: the thousand-dollar tan suede blazer, the faded jeans, the hand-tooled and silver-buckled belt, and customized cowboy boots of some exotic creature or other. One or two wore Stetsons. But others wore Costco casual: Kirkland jeans, Carhartt shirts, Dickies belts, and Payless shoes. Still, it felt very familiar to Jesse. These were Hunsicker's old teammates. Being around guys like this always left Jesse with mixed feelings. There was nothing quite like the shared experience of a team. At the same time, there was a kind of sadness to it that your best was behind you. And for these guys, that meant their best was already behind them at twenty-one.

SIXTY-EIGHT

Jesse had the *pollo mole poblano.* It was, as was all the food, authentic and delicious. It turned out that although Jesse might not have recognized the faces of any of the men with him that night, he had seen a few of them play ball. Four had gone on to have long NFL careers and one, Da'Reese Murray, was a new Hall of Famer. All of the guys referred to him as Canton, after Canton, Ohio, the location of the Pro Football Hall of Fame. As dinner went on and the drinks flowed, everyone relaxed, some a little too much. Many a tale was told out of school. Many that, if the wrong sets of ears had overheard, would have resulted in expensive divorces.

Even though none of the experiences or stories were his, it was oddly comfortable for Jesse, having long ago been a part of many teams. The LAPD was the closest he'd come to that feeling since he'd had his shoulder ruined in Pueblo, but he'd screwed up his detective career so badly that just thinking of his time in L.A. knotted his belly. How strange that it had come full circle and that the end points of the circle should meet in Dallas at Jenn's wedding. It was Jenn's cheating on him that had started his slide so deep into the bottle that he'd lost his way and his shield. In Paradise, Jesse was more like the coach than he was like one of the players. He guessed he would always miss the camaraderie of a team.

The number of guys had whittled down. Many of the less-well-to-do men, the Costco casual crowd, had work in the morning or had long drives. The rest of them moved from the restaurant into the cigar-bar area of Javier's. The atmosphere in the cigar bar was completely different. Back here, the smells of warm tortilla chips and fried onions were overwhelmed by the aromas of burning tobacco and money.

Jesse, who'd had a few beers with dinner, was working slowly on a second Johnnie Walker Blue Label and ignoring the Cuaba Tradicionales in the ashtray on the table in front of him. Hale, with a skinful of Pappy Van Winkle's Family Reserve and feeling generous, prodded Jesse into both the scotch — he would have been happier with

Black Label — and the cigar — he would have been happier without one. But it was Hale's celebration and Jesse didn't want to create any more tension between them than already existed.

"You know that's a hand-rolled Cuban cigar from my own personal stash you're letting go to waste there."

Jesse ignored that, raised his glass, and tapped Hale's glass. "Thanks for inviting me along. I know my being here under these circumstances isn't what you would have wanted."

"It's what Jenn wanted and that's what matters to me."

"You love her that much?"

"More than you know. She saved me from myself. From making the biggest mistake of my life. Even if things didn't lead to us getting hitched, I would have been grateful to her till the day they threw dirt on my sorry ole ass."

"How's that?"

"I expect you'll see a little later this evenin'," Hale said and thumped Jesse on the shoulder.

"Where's Kahan, Hale?"

"On assignment. If things work out, we should be seeing him tomorrow or the day after. Now, don't you go worryin' 'bout him." The bourbon was starting to get to Hunsicker, who was slurring his words and dropping letters.

Then Jesse noticed something in Hale's eyes. He wasn't sure what it was, but whatever it was wasn't good. Jesse followed Hale's eyes as they moved away from his face and stared over his shoulder. As Jesse turned around to look, a booming voice rang out, cutting through the smoke and the background chatter.

"Well, how do, Hale Sapsucker? Mixed company prevents me from calling you what I should."

The man behind Jesse was a baby-faced toad and built in inverse proportion to his voice. He was round and squat and had probably dreamed of being five-eight for forty-plus years. From his oversized Stetson cowboy hat to the embroidered lapels of his garish red sport jacket to his silver-toed boots, he was dressed like a Texan out of a fifties Hollywood movie.

"Jesse," Hale said, "meet Elroy Cates. Elroy, meet —"

"I know who he is, Hale. Nothing goes on in this town I don't know about. Pleasure to meet you, Chief Jesse Stone." He extended his little hand to Jesse and Jesse shook it. Cates's grip was more like his voice than his stature. His handshake was steel. "Question is, does Jesse know who you are, Hale?"

Jesse didn't know what was going on, but it was pretty clear there was blood between Hunsicker and Cates and it was all bad. He could also see Hale struggling with himself not to take the bait, and maybe, if there hadn't been quite as much bourbon in him, Hunsicker could have restrained himself.

"What's that supposed to mean, you little —"

Cates cut him off. "Means that your host here has a taste for things that don't belong to him. At least he had the good sense to —"

Things went quickly south. Before Cates could finish his sentence, Hunsicker threw a haymaker that would have felled a tree, but trees stand still. Cates did not. He leaned back, and the only casualty was Cates's cigar. Instead of throwing a punch of his own, Cates goaded him.

"Hey, Hale boy, maybe time's come to stop picking fruit from other people's trees."

That did it. Hale jumped at Cates, but before he could get at him, Jesse and Da'Reese Murray grabbed his arms and held him back. Cates just laughed, collected his still-lit cigar off the floor, and walked away. Hunsicker shrugged out of Jesse's and Murray's grasp.

"C'mon," Hale said, "let's go. Something stinks in here and it ain't the cigars."

SIXTY-NINE

Now there were two: Hale Hunsicker and Jesse. Ari drove them over to Ace's and dropped them by the front door. The noise from the upstairs lounge was a low roar.

"Just a nightcap," Hale said, as they got out of the Escalade. "Besides, you haven't been to Vineland Park until you've been to the Jungle Bar."

"Where the big cats and kittens prowl."

Hunsicker laughed, shaking his head as he did so.

Vineland Park Village was more impressive at night than it had been during the daytime. Every branch of every tree was strewn with strings of lightbulbs, so many that you lost sight of the individual bulbs and the trees themselves seemed to glow. The effect was enhanced by the hot breeze gently swaying the trees in the clear Texas night. Or, Jesse thought, maybe that was more a product of the beer, scotch, and descending fatigue. The dome at the top of the movie theater was lit up like a beacon. In Paradise the only light that bright was the one on the old Quilty Lighthouse up the coast, a few miles offshore on Indian Rock.

Jesse recognized the bar downstairs at Ace's from his earlier meeting with Jenn. It was pretty crowded, but sedate in comparison to the scene upstairs. In some ways the Jungle Bar was the same as any other bar of its type in Boston, L.A., or New York. It was a moneyed meat/meet market. Jesse was impressed because of the absurdity of it. There seemed to be a dress code, though not one as simple as jacket, collared shirt, no sneakers. It appeared far more specific than that. The men's sport jackets were limited to three colors: black, gray, or camel. Cowboy boots were a must, though showy was frowned upon. White, pale blue, or gray shirts were all collared, top button open. Too much jewelry was a no-no. Wedding bands were optional, yet watches the size of Fiats were everywhere. There was an awful lot of carefully managed facial scruff as well as salt-and-pepper hair worn swept back, not slicked back. Bald heads and neatly trimmed beards were also acceptable.

But it was the women who fascinated

Jesse. It was like the Dallas Cowboys Cheer-leaders meet the Stepford Wives, only they weren't wives, at least not most of them, not anymore. Jesse hadn't seen this many blond heads in one place, not even in L.A., a place where sun-streaked blond hair was everywhere. And their dress code seemed more restrictive than the men's. Tight pants, tight dresses, or tight skirts, frequently white. The operative word being *tight.* Heels were high. Tops were silver or black, often shiny, always showing cleavage. There was more jewelry on the women and it ranged from diamond necklaces to silver-and-turquoise bracelets. The makeup was all perfect, if generally too heavy to suit Jesse. There was no smoking in here, but between the spicy aftershaves, grassy colognes, and exotic perfumes, there was almost as much alcohol in the air as was in the bottles at the bar.

"Amazing, isn't it?" Hale asked.

"Uh-huh."

"It's like this from Wednesday to Sunday. What are you drinking?"

"Black Label, rocks."

With Hale waving at the barman and Jesse facing the same way, neither noticed the woman walking up behind them.

"Hey, Hale Hunsicker. Don't you dare

ignore me." She had Lauren Bacall's voice with an exaggerated Texas twang.

Jesse turned his head around to see a stunning black-haired woman with fire in her copper eyes. She was folding her long, sinewy arms around Hale's shoulders and chest. Her legs were long, too, and she took the definition of tight and white to new extremes. Her shiny silver blouse was open down the front in such a way as to expose a large, tapering V of tan, lightly freckled skin stretching from her clavicle to a point beyond her cleavage. She kissed Hale's neck in a way that couldn't be mistaken for a friendly peck. He turned around, handing Jesse his drink. But as stunning as this woman was, and she was all of that, Hale seemed as pleased to have her holding him as he had been at the sight of Elroy Cates.

"Aren't you going to introduce me to your handsome friend, Hale, or are you goin' to get all jealous on me?" she asked, leaning into Hunsicker as if performing a vertical lap dance.

"Jesse Stone," Hale said, turning to face the bar to get his own drink and to put some space between him and the woman. "Meet Cassie Cates."

"Cates as in Elroy Cates?" Jesse asked, shaking her hand. "A pleasure."

"Pleasure's all mine, honey. I can assure you." She squeezed Jesse's hand a little too tightly. "So you've met that human fireplug masqueradin' as my ex-husband?"

Jesse nodded.

"Wait just one second," Cassie said, screwing up her face. "Jesse Stone. So it's your ex that's set to marry this fool? Shoulda been me, ya know, taking the vows, but this big coward over —"

Hale cut her off. "C'mon, Cassie. We've been over this territory till there's ruts in the ground. There's no need to involve Jesse and Jenn in our drama."

"Drama! Hale Hunsicker, you weren't calling it drama when you couldn't get enough of me, now, were ya, honey?" She showed Jesse the back of her left hand, wriggling her naked ring finger. "When I was still married."

Jesse saw that look in Hale's eyes again. This time he understood its implication and turned to see Elroy Cates, head down, charging at Hale. Jesse stepped in front of Cassie and nudged her out of the way. Hale slammed his drink-holding hand down on the top of Elroy Cates's hat, splashing bourbon all over Elroy's hat and clothes. Cates caromed into the base of the bar and went down to the floor. Jesse stepped between Cates and Hunsicker, extending his hand to help Cates up. It might've ended there or at least not escalated if Cates's friend hadn't decided to appear out of the crowd.

He was bigger than Hunsicker and a few years his junior. He rammed his shoulder into Hale's midsection. He caught Hale in just the wrong spot and the air went out of him with an audible *ooph.* Hale doubled over and the big man landed a short, chopping right to Hunsicker's jaw. Hale went down. Jesse threw the point of his elbow into the big man's ribs to get his attention, then kicked the back of his right knee and sent him sprawling. By this time, Elroy Cates had scrambled to his feet and caught Jesse in the belly with a straight right. It was quite a punch for a toad. Reflexively, Jesse's right arm shot out and the back of his hand caught Cates in the mouth. Jesse felt Cates's lips split open and felt the scrape of his teeth rip the skin of his hand.

Now Hunsicker was up and grabbing his attacker by the back of his hair. He slammed Cates's friend face-first into the bar rail. Everything paused for a second after the sickening dull cracking sound the big man's nose made against the rail. There was blood everywhere as Hunsicker let go of the big man's hair. He slumped to the floor, choking on his blood and mucus. That's when Jesse became conscious of the sirens. He was about to pull out his shield when Hunsicker turned his attention to Cates. Hale had Elroy by the throat, hoisting him off the ground. That was trouble, the kind that led to crushed windpipes and manslaughter charges.

Jesse had to do something and fast. No one in the crowd seemed willing to join the fray, and asking Hale to kindly put Cates down or demanding it didn't seem like viable options. He tried, anyway, to no avail. He grabbed Hale's arms. Same lack of results. Jesse threw a punch at Hale's solar plexus, but because of the angle, he missed and it glanced harmlessly off his ribs. Hunsicker swung Cates around so that Cates was now between him and Jesse. Jesse slid the nine-millimeter out of its holster and racked the slide. That sound alone was usually enough to stop people from doing what they were doing. It doesn't do any good if no one can hear it. So Jesse stepped around Cates and stuck the barrel of the gun to the side of Hale's neck.

"Let him go, Hale. Now!"

As Cates hit the floor, half the Vineland

Park PD came charging up the stairs and into the Jungle Bar.

SEVENTY

He was exhausted from his day of travel and the drive down from Oklahoma City. It had taken longer than he anticipated. There they were again, he thought, those unanticipated circumstances. This time they took the form of a semi and a church bus, not some dumbass deputy cop swimming at the wrong end of the pool. The semi had rammed the church bus on I-35 just north of Ardmore, causing a ten-mile backup and a ninety-minute delay.

Things at the storage unit had gone more smoothly. He had considered bunking at the unit for the night. He always kept a sleeping bag and MREs, bottled water, and a first-aid kit in his storage rental units, wherever he was operating. He also kept ten thousand dollars, a SIG nine-millimeter, a Taser, an assault knife, a roll of duct tape, and a change of clothes in a bag just in case. But he knew that his movements would be on closed-circuit TV — every self-storage facility he ever used was monitored — and he didn't want to draw unwanted attention by entering a unit at night and failing to leave. Instead he ate an MRE, which tasted worse than the packaging it came in, washed it down with a bottle of water, loaded up his car with what he had come for, and left.

He drove a few miles below the speed limit in Vineland Park because he'd scouted the area and discovered the VPPD was renowned for speed traps. Not even the residents of Vineland Park speeded, not ever. Their money and clout might get them good tickets at Cowboy games, but not out of speeding tickets. He was particularly careful because this was one of the few places in the country where his taste in automobiles worked against him. Subcompacts were the exception in Vineland Park and were as conspicuous as a tarantula in a basket of downy yellow chicks.

He didn't care if the cops ran his plates. A car rented to Milton James of Pewaukee, Wisconsin, wouldn't raise any red flags. Even if he was pulled over, he looked like a Milton James. That's why he had chosen the identity. Just another plain face from a faceless place in a cold northern state. The trouble wouldn't be getting pulled over. Nor would it come from a cop typing his name into his computer. No, trouble would come only if the cops asked him to pop his trunk.

He didn't think he'd have any trouble explaining the old Lee-Enfield rifle in the trunk. This was Texas, after all. Texans respected gun rights, they hunted here, and a classic rifle with a scope wouldn't necessarily raise any eyebrows. The three bombs, on the other hand, would be an issue. There would be no explaining those away. If a cop took one step toward the trunk or asked to inspect the car, he would have to be put down. But there was no reason for him to be pulled over and no reason for him to borrow trouble at this point.

And just as he felt himself relax, pulling up to a stop sign, he spotted a VPPD cruiser hidden behind a row of hedges to his right. He made sure his stop was a full one. He counted to three before moving on. He didn't turn to look at the cop as he passed him. He kept his eyes straight ahead and his speed at a steady twenty. A block away from the cop, he exhaled. He'd already surveyed the vantage point from which he would spring his surprise, and would be out of Vineland Park soon enough. He heard his motel bed calling him.

He was another two blocks ahead when

he heard something else: a siren. He shrugged his rounded little shoulders. *So what?* If you listened carefully, you could hear sirens of one sort or another every few minutes. And since the uniformed services in Vineland Park were all cross-trained, a siren around these parts was just as likely to mean a brush fire was burning or an old millionaire had fallen down and broken his hip as a crime being committed. But then he saw the flashing lights in his rearview mirror. He immediately pulled over, watching the cruiser come flying his way.

He reached under the seat, feeling for the butt of the SIG he had taped there at the self-storage warehouse. It hadn't moved and would be easy enough for him to reach if and when the time came. He heard another siren and another. When he looked back up out the front windshield, there was another cruiser headed toward him and a third coming up the street to his left. This wasn't good. One cop, two, he could handle, but it was unlikely he could put down all three before fire was returned. And the cops in Vineland Park weren't slouches, as far as he could tell. Certainly not by reputation. These weren't the Keystone Kops of Paradise, Massachusetts. His shoulder ached, remembering the bullet Luther Simpson had fired into it.

He took deep breaths, trying to clear his mind so that when he made his move he could do so without hesitation. *One bullet each. Tap. Tap. Tap. Wound them in the gut. Then finish them one at a time. Quickly. Head shot. Head shot. Head shot.* He cleared his mind of any idea of failure or of being wounded. As the cruiser rushed up behind him, he forced himself to take another deeper breath. *Wait. Wait. Wait. React, don't act.* But the Impala screamed by him, its tires screeching as it swung a hard right. The cruiser that had been racing toward him turned hard left, following the first cruiser. The third cop followed the first two and their sirens faded quickly into the night, not nearly as loud as they had been when they were coming at him.

He pulled away from the curb and continued on his way to his motel. He felt his shirt glued to his back by sweat. About five minutes later, he passed Vineland Park Village and saw where all those cops had been headed. He didn't waste time wondering what the trouble was all about. He had one more errand to run in West Dallas, and before surrendering to the song his motel bed was singing to him.

SEVENTY-ONE

They were at the Vineland Park station. Funny, no matter how pretty the exterior, no matter how comfortable the station décor, jails were jails, though Jesse had to admit that these holding cells were better than some of the accommodations he'd been forced to put up with as a minor-leaguer. Hale and Jesse were in one of the fenced-in cages; Elroy and his buddy were in the other. Cates was handcuffed to a steel bar in his cell as one of the cops attended to his pal's newly realigned nose. A cop at the scene had already attended to Jesse's hand and Cates's mouth.

"So," Jesse said, leaning over to Hale, "I take it that Cassie is who Jenn saved you from."

"You know it."

"I can see the attraction. She is something."

"She's all of that. But she's like a whirlwind that won't never die out," Hale said, lapsing into his good-ole-boy persona, a wistful look in his eyes. "The thing about it is that we would have burned each other out in a few years. It's hard to keep a woman like Cassie's attention. She's the type of gal just as soon fight you as fuck you. You know what I mean?"

Jesse nodded. He had known a few women like Cassie. His relationship with Jenn had had some of the same components, but he was thinking more of Maxie Connolly. An older woman he'd met very briefly the year before. Maxie was in her sixties, but she had once been the talk of Paradise, a true force of nature.

"You two do realize I can hear y'all," Cates said. "That's my wife you're discussin'."

"Not to put too fine a point on it, but she's your ex-wife, Elroy. That aside, is there anything I've said about Cassie that ain't the truth?" Hale asked.

"Can't argue with the veracity of a single damned word of it, Hunsicker. Cassie is a woman worth fightin' for."

"Well, Elroy, it's a little late to be closing that barn door."

"I suppose, but there's no gettin' around the fact that you were sleepin' with another man's woman, Hale Hunsicker. That's nothin' to be proud of or to be braggin' on."

"No arguing that," Hale said, "but she was worth it."

"And then you just dumped her. Broke her heart, you know? She don't show it, but she ain't healed yet. Then you got to go to the bar and rub your getting married in her face. I hate your guts, Hunsicker, but I would've expected more of you than to do that."

Hunsicker had no answer for that. Instead, he rubbed his jaw where Cates's friend had landed the punch. It wasn't broken, but it was red and swollen. There'd be a hell of a bruise there by morning. Jenn wasn't going to be pleased. It seemed both of them realized that at once.

"Jenn's going to have my balls on a platter for this," he said to Jesse. "She wanted everything to be perfect for the wedding and now I'm going to look like I got an eggplant growing out of my jaw."

"They'll get you ice and some anti-inflammatories. With a little makeup, you'll be fine for the wedding."

"Jenn may look past the bump on my jaw, but not the reason I got it. Cassie Cates is a sore subject with Jenn."

Jesse was about to ask a question when

Jed Pruitt walked down the hallway toward the cells. He didn't look pleased. Angry. Simmering, but not boiling over. He had two of his cops behind him.

"Okay, boys, you had to have your fun, I suppose, but I'm not laughing," Pruitt said, his demeanor making it clear he wasn't yet finished. "I've assured Ace that reparations will be made and that there will be some charity event or other that somehow compensates this department for the time and manpower it wasted breaking up an overgrown, drunken bunch of babies playing at being men."

"Sure thing, Jed," Hale said. "Sorry about the trouble."

Cates seconded the motion. "Absolutely, Chief Pruitt. 'Sorry' don't quite say it."

"Officer Ambler, you done tending to King Kong over there?" Pruitt asked the cop working on the big man's broken nose.

"I've done all I can do with him, Chief." Then he turned to Elroy Cates. "Mr. Cates, you should take your friend over to Vineland Memorial and have the nose reset."

"All right, then, let 'em go," Pruitt said, motioning to the cops behind him.

The cops stepped around Pruitt. One opened Cates's cell door and stood aside.

"Hale, let's let Mr. Cates and his pal here

exit the station first." Pruitt's tone made it evident that it wasn't a friendly request.

The cop who was working on the big man's nose uncuffed Cates and busied himself with cleaning up and packing away his equipment. Cates and company left the cell, the cop who had opened their cell door in tow. When the hall door slammed shut, Pruitt nodded to his cop to open the other cell door. Hale left, still rubbing his jaw, but when Jesse tried to follow, Pruitt stopped him.

"Sorry, Jesse, I truly am, but you're staying. This may be Texas, but it's Vineland Park's little parcel of it. And here, no citizen pulls a weapon in a public place and gets a walk. We'll put you in a decent cell for the night as soon as Hale leaves. I'm sure the judge will see it your way and you'll be out by noon tomorrow."

Jesse nodded, knowing that this was a possibility when he pulled his nine. He turned and sat back down.

"But —"

"No buts, Hale. From what everyone tells me, Jesse's sitting in there because you didn't give him much of a choice. Anything happens to Jenn because he's in there, that's on you, son. Now get."

SEVENTY-TWO

It had to be one of the best-attended arraignments in Vineland Park history. Chief Pruitt, Hale Hunsicker, Jenn, Diana, Hunsicker's parents, a few of Kahan's men, and even Cassie and Elroy Cates, looking a bit sheepish and the worse for wear, were there. An older gentleman with long gray hair, holding a black Stetson under his left arm, had introduced himself as C. C. Peacock to Jesse when Jesse was marched into the courtroom.

"I'll be representing you, son. I hear you're a police chief, so you don't much like lawyers. I also hear you're a sharp fella, so you know to just stand there and let me do the talking. We'll get you right out of here."

Diana wore a bemused expression on her exquisite face. *Bemused* was not a word to describe the look on Jenn's face. She kept alternating her gaze from Hale to Jesse, and it had murder written all over it. Hale Hunsicker wore a kind of distressed expression, but Jesse didn't think it was about the ugly bruise on his jaw or about Jenn's anger. He didn't like it. When they'd brought him into the courtroom, he'd raised his cuffed and chained hands and waved at Diana. She just shook her head at him and smiled in spite of herself. She also mouthed "I love you" and winked at him. Jesse winked back.

There was something amusing about the entire situation, but somehow it was lost on the judge, a desiccated older woman who reminded Jesse of an angry substitute teacher with little patience for student hijinks.

The judge read the charges out in a nasty monotone.

"How do you plead, Mr. Stone?"

Peacock said, "My client pleads —"

She banged her gavel. "I asked your client, Mr. Peacock. Now, Mr. Stone, how do you plead?"

"Not guilty, Your Honor."

She raised a single skeptical eyebrow at him.

"Good thing I won't be on your jury, Mr. Stone," she said, and then repeated his plea to the court clerk.

"Can we now discuss the matter of bail,

Your Honor?" Peacock asked.

She nodded at the ADA. "Mr. Spiegelman, what do the People say?"

Spiegelman looked back at Cates and Hunsicker and said, "While the People acknowledge the seriousness of the charges, Your Honor, we have faith that Mr. Stone, a decorated former LAPD detective and current chief of police of Paradise, Massachusetts, should be released on his own recognizance."

The judge looked about ready to explode. "I'm confused here, Mr. Spiegelman."

"How so, Your Honor?"

"Are you the prosecuting attorney here or Mr. — excuse me, Chief Stone's — public relations man?" She turned to Jesse's lawyer. "I'm not sure your services are required here, Mr. Peacock. It seems Mr. Spiegelman is already doing your work for you. Maybe you have a place for him in your firm."

Spiegelman flushed and Peacock laughed, but not too long or loudly. He also knew better than to speak again before spoken to. Spiegelman did not. Flustered, he tried to explain, digging the hole for himself even deeper. The judge let him finish.

"Well, I've heard about enough," said the judge. "Chief Stone."

"Yes, Your Honor."

"What should I do with you? My guess is you're as guilty as guilty could be of what you're charged with. This may be Texas, young man, but at least in Vineland Park, we take a dim view of loaded weapons being drawn in public. A very dim view."

"May I say something, Your Honor?" Jesse said.

Peacock looked displeased and grabbed Jesse by the forearm.

She nodded. "Please."

"Given my training and expertise, I did what I did as a last resort and not carelessly or without respect for the law, Your Honor."

"That's the first sensible thing I've heard this morning." She addressed the court officers. "Release Chief Stone. Mr. Peacock will be informed of the trial date within the next several weeks, though given Mr. Spiegelman's questionable prosecutorial zeal and the lineup of people in the gallery, I doubt there will be a trial. Next."

Jesse rubbed his wrists and walked back toward the gallery. Diana still had that bemused look on her face. Pruitt was smiling, too. Even Elroy Cates seemed relieved. Jenn, on the other hand, looked about as happy as the judge had been. Angry heat was coming off Jenn in waves, and Jesse was thankful to be in a crowded public place. But it was Hale's expression that really concerned Jesse. Something was up. He'd see about that soon enough. For now, he was just happy to be with Diana.

Jesse asked Hunsicker if he and Diana could get a ride back to the hotel after he collected his personal effects. Hunsicker balked.

"Why don't you guys come to the house? We'll fix you up with some food and clothes, Jesse. Let you get a shower or a dip in the whirlpool."

Jesse could tell it wasn't a request, and he was curious about what was going on, anyway. Diana also read Hale's body language and heard the strain in his voice.

"Sure, Hale," she said. "Let's do that, Jesse. Okay? With the wedding in two days, I'm sure Jenn could use some help."

It seemed the only one unhappy about the plan was Jenn, but she said nothing.

SEVENTY-THREE

Back at the house, Jesse actually did shower and shave. He didn't know how Hunsicker managed it, but there were new clothes in the right sizes waiting for him when he was ready to get dressed. The jeans were fine, as were the running shoes, as was the burnt-orange-and-white Longhorns T-shirt. The four of them even managed a civil if somewhat awkward breakfast together, Jenn glaring at Jesse through most of it. As he ate his omelet and drank his coffee, Jesse couldn't quite figure out exactly what he was supposed to have done to prevent what had gone on the night before. It wasn't as if Hale had given him a choice of venue for dinner or drinks, and there was no accounting for Elroy Cates's movements.

As the meal drew to an end, though, it dawned on him. The reasons for Jenn's anger were suddenly obvious. Jenn had a problem, one that Jesse didn't fix. Worse, he couldn't fix. Oh, he'd prevented Hale from killing Elroy Cates. He'd fixed that, all right, managing to get himself arrested in the process. The deeper problem lay not with Jesse, but with Hale Hunsicker. For his part, Jesse had nearly forgotten who'd been the root cause of all the trouble. Although Elroy Cates was the instigator, it wasn't him. The root cause was Cassie Cates. Cassie got under Jenn's skin way more than Diana ever could. And it seemed to Jesse that Hale had wanted Jesse to meet Cassie or, at least, knew running into her at the Jungle Bar would be a distinct possibility. Jesse didn't want to think about it, and Hunsicker saved him from having to.

"Ladies, if you'll excuse us," Hale said, standing and putting a hand on Jesse's shoulder. "We have some things to discuss."

Diana said, "Sure."

Jenn pouted but kept quiet.

The two men moved into a room in the house Jesse hadn't been in or seen before. Well, there were about twenty of those, but this one was on the ground floor and not far from the room where the party had been held that first night he and Diana arrived in Dallas. It was what Hale politely referred to as a library, but it was more accurately a home office. The twenty-five-by-thirty room with twelve-foot ceilings was full of glass, steel, hardwood, and leather furniture. At least it looked used and worked in and not strictly for show. There were plenty of built-in bookshelves lined with books, most of which seemed never to have been touched by human hands. Jesse didn't judge him too harshly for that. Hale Hunsicker wouldn't be the first rich person to try to look like he'd read a lot more literature than he, in fact, had. What he did judge Hunsicker harshly for was walking him into his drama with the Cateses while they were in the midst of this thing with Peepers.

It took a few seconds for Jesse to notice that Scott Kahan had reappeared and was standing behind Hunsicker's desk, staring out the big leaded windows of diamond-shaped panes at the small lake beside the house. He didn't acknowledge Jesse's or his boss's presence, which suited Jesse just fine. Jesse had something to say to Hunsicker before they moved on.

"What the fuck was that about last night, Hale?"

Hunsicker tried to look shocked, but failed badly. "What about last night?"

"That whole thing with Cassie Cates. That wasn't an accident, and please don't insult my intelligence by claiming otherwise."

"Can't this hold for a little while longer? Scott's got some —"

"No, Hale, I don't think so." Jesse pointed at Hale. "Your heart's torn about your old girlfriend, okay, I understand that. But you better not walk down that aisle with Jenn if you're going to screw around on her with Cassie. Jenn's not my business anymore, but that doesn't mean I don't care. I wouldn't be here if I didn't care. Jenn isn't stupid. She knows something's up with you."

"I know she's not stupid, and yeah, I guess that I was the stupid one last night, dragging you to the Jungle Bar. And I won't claim it was the bourbon, though it helped. I just wanted to see Cassie one more time before the wedding is all. I knew she'd be all over me, and I guess I wanted to test myself."

"Pass or fail?"

"Don't worry about Jenn and me, Jesse. I won't blow up the best thing that's ever happened to me. Promise."

Jesse didn't bother carrying it any further. What was he going to do, threaten the man? To what end? Hale and Jenn were adults, and Jesse hoped they both knew what they were getting into. One thing Jesse wasn't going to get into was some bullheaded at-

393

tempt to save Jenn from herself. He'd said his piece and that was that.

"Besides," Hunsicker said, "Scott here really does have some important information."

"I'm listening."

Kahan turned around to face Jesse. He nodded hello. Jesse nodded back. Kahan picked a file up off the top of his boss's desk and walked it over to Jesse. He didn't hand it to him. Instead, he looked Jesse in the eye and said, "Peepers is alive and he's here."

SEVENTY-FOUR

Jesse had sensed as much about Peepers. Even in the immediate wake of the explosion and fire, even after the results on the .22 he'd recovered at the scene, he had never felt confident that the man who died in that car was Peepers. He simply had been willing to let himself hope just a little. Still, he needed more than Kahan's word.

"Proof?"

Kahan handed Jesse a time-stamped photo.

"That was taken from surveillance footage at Will Rogers Airport in Oklahoma City. As you can see by the stamp, he got in from Baltimore yesterday afternoon."

Jesse didn't say anything as he studied the image. It wasn't exactly high-resolution, though the man pictured certainly resembled Peepers.

"Looks like it could be him," Jesse said at last.

"I figured that would be your attitude. And I can understand your hesitancy, but it's definitely him. Check this out."

Kahan went back to Hunsicker's desk, scooped up a tablet, tapped the screen, and offered it to Jesse. "Watch."

It was surveillance video of the man in the still photo, showing him as he moved through the terminal. There he was, on line at the rental counter. Jesse felt sudden discomfort as he watched the man who Kahan claimed was Peepers standing impatiently, being ignored by the woman behind the counter. He remembered what Belinda Yankton had told him about Peepers's distaste for rudeness. Then Jesse exhaled when the woman at the rental counter waved the man over and smiled at him. There was nothing extraordinary about the remainder of their exchange.

"The silver Honda Fit with Arizona tags was rented to a Mr. Milton James of 2231 Moony Road, Pewaukee, Wisconsin," Kahan said. "Only problem is there is no such person and no such street address, though the credit card he used was valid. This guy, whoever he really is, is good. Probably has twenty different identities, credit cards, passports, phony addresses."

Jesse listened but continued watching.

Then he saw it, that smile. Until he saw that smug, self-satisfied smile, the one Belinda Yankton had so eloquently described, he was willing to be unconvinced that the man he was watching was Peepers. But it was frightening how accurate Yankton's depiction of the smile was.

"It's like he's the king of the world and ruler of the universe," she'd said to Jesse as he held her hand at the kitchen table the previous morning. "Lord Jesus, that smile would chill me, Jesse. It was as if he had some secret knowledge or he found something amusing the rest of us couldn't possibly get."

Jesse put the tablet down at his side. "You wouldn't want to tell me how you got access to this footage, would you?"

Kahan laughed. "I asked for it. You just have to know who to ask."

"Okay, even if I'm ninety percent sure this is —"

"It's him. It's good not to just accept things at face value, Jesse. It's one of the first things you learn in intel. Don't act immediately on information unless there's no choice. Question. Question. Question. And when you're sure, question it again. Then test it. But that's him."

"What about the guy in Paradise?" Jesse

asked. "I checked with my people there last night before I went with Hale to Javier's and they said the CSU people still weren't finished with the scene."

Kahan handed Jesse the folder he'd been holding since just after Jesse and Hale had walked into the library.

"See for yourself. The man killed in the car you were chasing in Paradise was Michael Scott Atkinson, a former Army Ranger with a history of violence both in and out of the service. Came home from his tours in Iraq and Afghanistan and went into business for himself, putting his skills to more profitable and less patriotic uses. Peepers might work alone, but he's in the business. It's a different business than most, but it's a business just the same. You hear about people, know their reps. Peepers probably hired Atkinson to screw around with you and then things worked out better than Peppers could have dreamed. And look at Atkinson's photo. He's bigger than Peepers, a little more imposing, but you wouldn't necessarily remember his face."

Jesse studied the photo. He didn't look much like Peepers, yet Kahan had a point: This guy had an unremarkable and forgettable face. Jesse could see how Alisha, already busy on the phone, might have been suggestible to Jesse's questions. She saw who Jesse had prompted her to see and Jesse leapt to conclusions because the delivery of the plain envelope fit a familiar scenario.

"We've also got photos of the car headed toward Dallas," Kahan said, his voice nearly as smug as Peepers's smile. "He's alive and he's here."

But when Jesse flipped the photo over and saw a DNA report that proved the body in the car was Atkinson's, he was confused.

"How did you —"

"I called in a few favors," Kahan said. "There are people in several governments, including ours, who owe me a few. It's amazing what kind of results you can get when people are properly motivated."

For some reason Jesse found he was furious with Kahan. He should have been glad that they knew things for sure now. They knew Peepers was alive and in the Dallas area. Yet it was all Jesse could do to contain his anger. Maybe it was Jesse's innate uneasiness about unequal justice. How the rich and powerful could get what they wanted just because they could, not because they earned it. They could get access to things the rest of us couldn't dream of. Maybe it was that he resented Kahan's treatment of the law and procedures as mere inconveniences. Less than inconveniences. But you couldn't shove the genie back into the bottle and un-know things. So Jesse kept quiet. Keeping Jenn safe and putting an end to Peepers was what was important.

Hunsicker spoke up for the first time in several minutes. "So what do we do? Do we finally alert the media and bring down the weight of all the law enforcement agencies? I mean, look, fellas, we know where he is and he doesn't know we know."

"Don't be so sure," Jesse said. "He took the precaution of landing in Oklahoma, but he did everything but wave at the camera. When he killed Gino Fish's assistant, he disguised himself from the cameras. You can't try and outthink him, you have to think along with him."

Kahan nodded in agreement. "He's right, Hale. We may know he's here, but we don't know where here. He's already most likely ditched the rental and either stolen another car or rented one under a different alias."

As if on cue, Kahan's phone buzzed. He excused himself and answered it. Mostly he nodded and made noises that let the person on the other end know he was listening. He put the phone back in his pocket.

"A contact in the Dallas PD," Kahan said. "They just found Milton James's rental over in West Dallas, not too far from where he kept Belinda Yankton. And before you ask, no, there are no new reports of a stolen car from that area yet."

"What do we do?" Hunsicker asked, looking more than a little worried. "The rehearsal and rehearsal dinner are tonight."

Kahan looked at Jesse, and Jesse back at him. There was no need for words between them. They tilted their heads at Hunsicker as if to say "Who's going to tell him?" Jesse pointed at himself. Kahan nodded.

"We do exactly what we were supposed to do. We go ahead with the rehearsal and the dinner. I doubt Peepers will make his move in front of a small audience. He wants the big stage."

SEVENTY-FIVE

Jesse made three calls after his meeting with Kahan. The first was to Healy.

"It's not him."

Healy was confused. "Who's not him?"

"The body in the car on Trench Alley. It's not Peepers."

"And you know this how?"

"I've got photos of him at the Oklahoma City airport yesterday afternoon and positive DNA test results for a Michael Scott Atkinson. He's in the state database."

"Bullshit on that. Our people have barely gotten done —"

"It wasn't your people who got the samples or did the test."

"Cut it out, Jesse. Next thing you're going to tell me is that there are black helicopters circling Paradise and snipers in the trees."

"I wouldn't be surprised. Hunsicker's chief of security is ex-CIA or -NSA or some other alphabet soup, and he's got a long reach."

"You want me to let Molly know?"

"I'll do that," Jesse said.

They had a brief talk about Dallas, Healy's wife, and Healy's limbo of semi-retirement.

"This thing better come to a conclusion and soon," Healy said. "I'm officially retired, but I've been in the office more in the last week than I was when I was on the job. People are getting suspicious and I'm running out of favors to ask and people to ask them of."

His second call was to Molly and it went pretty much the same as his conversation with Healy had. There was a lot of disbelief and disappointment. The small-talk part of the conversation was more about how the meeting had gone between Jenn and Diana. There was something bugging Jesse about Molly's tone during the call that he'd been willing to attribute to the news about Peepers being alive, but by the end of the call he was convinced it wasn't that.

"Is there something you're not telling me, Molly? Are you holding back?"

Suit's engaged. Can you believe it? That big, goofy bastard is serious. He actually asked me to help him with the wedding prep-

arations. "No, Jesse, nothing" is what she said.

His last call was to Vinnie Morris.

SEVENTY-SIX

Jed Pruitt pulled his VPPD SUV up the steep, winding driveway of the Vineland Park Country Club. As he drove, Pruitt pointed out features of the golf course. *They keep the fairways flat and the greens furry so the members will be happy with their scores. Apparently keeps the membership levels high. And when you charge the dues and fees this place does . . .* The clubhouse loomed before them as they came up to the crest of the hill. Both Diana and Jesse were shocked. Jed Pruitt laughed at their stunned expressions.

"Hideous, ain't it? They spent about twenty mill to redo it about two years ago. Turned a perfectly classy old Tudor-style building into this monstrosity."

Diana said, "It looks like a cross between something out of *Macbeth* and one of those all-the-beer-you-can-drink steakhouses, only uglier."

Pruitt laughed again. "Exactly. Some of our unkinder residents refer to it as the Beef and Brew."

"At least it's big," Jesse said.

Pruitt agreed. "It's all of that. *Cavernous* is the way I'd put it."

Almost before Chief Pruitt could put the vehicle in park, a silver-vested valet who looked like an escapee from the cover of *GQ* was at his door. He had arranged for Jesse and Diana to do a walkthrough of the place, the venue for the wedding and reception. Scott Kahan had assured Jesse that there was no possibility of Peepers successfully pulling anything off at the country club on the day of the wedding.

"We've scouted every inch of the place. Analyzed where a sniper might hide. We're going to have a portable X-ray scanner for the gifts and scanners to see who might be carrying. We're going to have temporary barriers set up outside so that a truck can't be rammed into the place. I'll have men everywhere and a response team will be on-site. We've got dummy limos set up for the drive from the house to the venue and from the venue to the airport."

But Jesse, not Kahan, was the cop. He had worked security details in uniform and in plain clothes. As he knew only too well, and as Kahan himself had said during their first meeting, there was no such thing as a totally secure location. Diana was a valuable second set of eyes. She had a knack for seeing things that even fellow agents hadn't been able to see. Better still, she was willing to speak up and act if the situation called for it. Like her looks, that knack and her willingness to act were as much a curse as a blessing. It's what had caused her to get jammed up at the Bureau and eventually led to their parting ways. More important, Jesse trusted her. He didn't trust Kahan as far as he could throw him, nor did he have much faith in Hale Hunsicker after the events at the bar. Oddly, other than Diana, the one player in all this he trusted to do his part was Peepers. That's why they were all here, because he could count on Peepers to keep his promises.

Diana and Jesse sat at the rear of the main ballroom at the country club, watching the preacher, the wedding planner, and the catering manager block out the wedding party's movements. *Okay, best man, you stand right here . . .* They hadn't originally been invited to the rehearsal, because neither was a part of the wedding party, but they asked if they could tag along. And with

Hale pleading their case, Jenn relented, though it did raise her already high level of suspicion.

"Why do you want to come?" Jenn had asked them, even after she'd given her permission. "The rehearsal dinner is at the restaurant in the lobby of your hotel. You could spend the time together and then just ride the elevator down from your room."

Characteristically, Jesse shrugged. But it was Diana who saved the day.

"Look, Jenn, I know this is awkward having us there at the rehearsal, but we just got engaged and we want to soak in the atmosphere. We'll be doing this soon enough ourselves. And we'd want you and Hale there with us."

With that, Jenn's suspicions had seemed to evaporate, and she kissed Diana on the cheek. She whispered in Diana's ear, "You'll make him happier than I ever could. He loved me. I think he still does, in his way, but he looks at you like he never looked at me. Good thing I'm only a little jealous."

They had laughed about it. For her part, Diana was only half lying. Even in the midst of all the danger and drama, she was excited at the prospect of being the second Mrs. Jesse Stone, and she intended to be the last one.

What Diana and Jesse were actually doing there was assessing how things might go if Peepers did try something during the ceremony. It was one thing to do a walk-through of an empty building as they had done with Jed Pruitt earlier in the day. It was something different to see how events might unfold with people in the room. One was static. One was dynamic. And it was seeing how the people would move, where and when, that helped Diana and Jesse figure out how Peepers might come at Jenn. All of Kahan's planning and precautions were good and valuable, but as former boxing champ Mike Tyson is famous for saying, "Everybody has a plan till they get punched in the face." And what might happen after that punch was what Diana and Jesse were worried about.

"I don't see it," Diana said. "I just don't see how he could pull it off here. Not by himself."

"Uh-huh."

"You don't agree?"

"Just the opposite. The problem is I do agree," Jesse said. "It's those pipe bombs that he built that concern me. If I could see how he could use them, I'd feel better about it."

"As a diversion."

"But not here. Peepers isn't stupid. He's done his research. He knows that Hunsicker has a security man and who he is. He's figured out by now that we must be waiting for him and that a simple diversion won't work. He'll know we won't fall for it. That we'll be prepared."

SEVENTY-SEVEN

The valet at the Park Mansion Hotel and Spa accepted the ten-spot tip from the little man as he handed him the keys to his rented Maserati. The valet handed him a receipt stub.

"When you want your car, just hand that to the valet on duty. And thank you for your generosity."

"My pleasure," he said to the valet, though it was a lie. His pleasure lay ahead of him.

The bellman collected the luggage out of the trunk and rear seat of the little man's car, placing the items on a wheeled cart.

"I'll take that," the little man said, pointing at the attaché case, and handed out another ten-dollar bill. "You can have the rest brought up to my room."

"Thank you, sir. Very good, sir," the bellman said, handing the man the cordovan leather case. "Heavy for an attaché case."

It was all the little man could do not to

glare at the bellman and declare that the weight of his attaché case was none of the moron's business. Instead he simply winked at the bellman, who, in turn, winked back to indicate that he understood the case contained valuables. He understood nothing, of course.

"Going to do some fishing while you're here?" the bellman asked, retrieving the long, round hardened case from the Maserati's backseat.

"Fishing, yes. Smart man. Now, please, just get that stuff up to my room."

"Right away, sir."

At the front desk, an exotic-looking woman with high cheekbones, almost translucent skin, raven-black hair cut in a neat line halfway down her neck, and ice-blue eyes greeted the little man.

"Good evening, sir. My name is Dijana," she said with a slight Slavic accent. "Do you have a reserv—"

The little man handed her a Massachusetts driver's license and a ruby-colored credit card. "Dijana," he said. "That's a beautiful name."

She smiled a glowing white smile. "Thank you . . . Mr. Stone." She read his name off the credit card. "It's Serbian for Diana."

The little man laughed in a disquieting way.

"I am sorry," she said. "Did I say something —"

"No, no. I'm sorry. Just an inside joke. Please, forgive me, Dijana."

"Of course." She tapped her keyboard. "Yes, sir. We have your reservation right here. Mr. Jesse Stone. One night, a king-sized bed. All of our rooms are nonsmoking. And you specifically requested a west-facing room with a balcony above the tenth floor. Is that correct, Mr. Stone?"

"It is."

She screwed up her lovely face. "May I ask you, Mr. Stone, why you made that request?"

He fought himself really hard not to explode at her.

"Personal quirk," he said. "I don't enjoy the sunrise. Why do you ask?"

"Oh, I suppose I was a little curious, but also because your credit-card status allows us to upgrade you to a spa-level room on the eighth floor. Those rooms include room-service breakfast free of charge, three newspapers, a huge discount on our spa facil—"

He interrupted her for a third time. "That's very kind of you, but no, I'll keep my original reservation."

"I assure you, Mr. Stone, it's no bother at all, and the amenities are fantastic."

"Again, Dijana, I appreciate the offer, but no."

She considered trying one last time as per her training, but there was just something about Mr. Stone that told her not to go there. He had been perfectly polite, yet he made her uneasy. She handed him two key cards in a small cardboard folder.

"That's room ten twenty-one. The elevators are to the left of the lounge to your right," she said, gesturing with her arm. "Please let us know if the room meets your specifications, and thank you very much for staying with us."

"You're welcome, Dijana."

"Is there anything else the staff at the Park Mansion Hotel and Spa can do for you this evening, Mr. Stone?"

"As a matter of fact, there is." He placed his attaché on the counter. "I'd like to check my attaché into the baggage room until I check out. Would that be okay?"

"Absolutely, sir. Cliff, our concierge, will be only too happy to do that for you. He'll give you a check stub when he takes your case. If there's anything of value in your case, we do have a more secure area."

"No," the little man said. "The baggage

room will be just fine."

And with that, he turned away from Dijana and moved to the concierge's desk. As he did, he smiled that smug smile of his and laughed to himself about the Serbian Diana to his Jesse Stone. He wondered if the real Jesse and Diana would appreciate the irony. Somehow he doubted it.

SEVENTY-EIGHT

The restaurant was called Edge and, as everyone who worked at the hotel had pointed out, it served the best steak in all of Texas. And that, as they had all added, was really saying something. As if to make the point, the first thing a patron saw when entering Edge, even before reaching the hostess's desk, was the glass-faced meat locker in which the steaks were aged.

"Those are our pride and joy," the hostess said, seeing Jesse and Diana stop to peer into the glass case. "Those rib-eye steak racks are dry-aged one hundred and fifty days. You will never have a more flavorful, richer piece of steak in your lives. Are you folks here for the Hunsicker party?"

"Uh-huh."

"Right this way."

The décor of the place was eclectic: Asia meets Texas somewhere in Europe. There was an open kitchen with roaring flames and broilers, and the place smelled like a beef lover's paradise. The sweet, smoky, and alluring aroma of charring beef fat and flesh filled the air. Most of the rehearsal participants were already seated when Diana and Jesse — who'd stopped in their room to freshen up — were shown to the two long ebony tables. Both of them breathed a sigh of relief at being seated at the other table, far away from Jenn and Hale. They were keenly aware that the confrontation with Peepers was at hand, that their obsession for the last five weeks would come to some sort of resolution within the next thirty-six hours . . . or not. They just wanted to spend one meal together and enjoy their food without Peepers or Jenn or Hunsicker or anyone else imposing themselves.

They were between two other couples, neither of whom seemed to be interested in talking too much about anything but the food and wine. That was fine with Diana and Jesse, who found themselves actually discussing wedding plans. The discussion didn't last long because, after the steaks were ordered and the celebratory champagne poured, the inevitable and excruciating toasts to the happy couple began.

When Jesse's eyes were about to glaze over, his cell phone buzzed in his pocket.

He excused himself. As he walked out of Edge and into the lobby, he noticed that Kahan nodded to Ari to follow. Jesse looked at the screen. He didn't recognize the number and decided not to pick up. The phone stilled in his hand. As he turned to head back to the table, the phone buzzed again. Same number. He thought about not taking it, but realized he wasn't very anxious to listen to any more toasts.

"Jesse Stone."

"Hello, Chief Stone. It's rude not to answer your phone."

"Who is this?"

There was a high-pitched snicker in Jesse's ear. "Do you ask a praying mantis who?" It was Peepers. "Hello, Chief Stone," he said a second time.

Jesse's heart turned cold and his guts burned with anger, but he knew that he dared not show his cards to Peepers and had to play things steady.

"Hello, Milton James," Jesse said, aware that calling him Peepers would send the man on the other end of the line completely off the rails. During their one meeting, Peepers had threatened to shoot out both of Jesse's kneecaps if he referred to him as Mr. Peepers. "Are you still Milton James?"

There was that snicker again. "Not tonight, Jesse. I've turned over a new leaf. You know, I've always called you Chief Stone, but I know you prefer to be called Jesse. Is it all right if I call you Jesse?"

"If you'd like."

"I *would* like. Do you know why I'm here, Jesse?"

"Uh-huh."

"Poor Jenn," Peepers said. "I am quite fond of her, really I am. It is her misfortune to have gotten mixed up with you. I owe you, Jesse. I've a blood debt to repay to you and that moron Simpson. It's a shame that Jenn is the one to have to receive the payment of debt. Alas, blood for blood and all of that. Do you understand, Jesse?"

"I speak the language."

"Stick to police work, Jesse. You're more suited to it than to standup comedy. Suited! Ha, I made a pun, but I, too, am better at other things. Do you know why I'm calling?"

"You're lonely."

The phone almost turned icy against Jesse's ear. "No, Jesse, not because I'm lonely. The world is full of victims to keep me company."

Jesse ignored that last part. "Why, then?"

"To give you fair warning the festivities are about to begin."

"Festivities?"

Peepers said in a snide, sarcastic tone, "Festivities: the celebration of things in a joyous and cheerful way."

"Like I said, I speak the language."

"Not the language I'm speaking, Jesse. Until tomorrow."

"What about tomorrow?"

But it was no good. Jesse was shouting at a soulless man on a dead phone. And when he stepped back inside Edge, the toasts were still going on. He couldn't help but wonder if Jenn would live long enough for any of her guests' wishes for health and happiness to come true.

SEVENTY-NINE

After the toasts and before the meal, Jesse nodded to Kahan to meet him by the restrooms. Kahan waited a minute before following Jesse.

"The phone call? Ari told me you didn't look happy and that you were raising your voice at the end of the conversation."

"It was him," Jesse said. "Peepers."

"He called you? Why?"

"Why do you think? To taunt me. To remind me that he was going to return a debt to me and Suit by hurting Jenn."

"He does like telegraphing his moves to you. He's consistent in that way." Kahan held out his hand. "I'll let Pruitt know. For now, give me your phone, Jesse."

Jesse did as he was asked. Kahan called the number back. No answer. When it went to voice mail, all he got was a recording that the message box had yet to be configured. He shrugged.

"I'll have the number checked out, but it will be a prepaid phone. My guys will probably be able to trace it back to the cell tower, but I doubt we'll get a specific enough location to act on it."

"He's close," Jesse said. "I can feel it."

"We know he's here."

"No, Scott, I mean close. Maybe not in this hotel, but close."

"Besides taunting you and threatening Jenn, what did he say?"

Jesse recounted the call pretty much verbatim, adding his observations about Peepers's inflection, tone, the length of his pauses, et cetera. Kahan listened impassively, taking in all the details.

"What do you think he meant by saying 'until tomorrow'?"

"He's got something planned for tomorrow," Jesse said.

"How do you know he didn't mean he was going to call you tomorrow? Isn't that how you would normally understand someone saying 'until tomorrow'?"

"The way he said it. I'm telling you, he's going to do something tomorrow."

"But there are no events planned tomorrow. It's the day before the wedding. Jenn and Hale built in a kind of day off for themselves and the guests so everyone could be well rested and looking good for the wedding. They're even eating all their meals in. It doesn't figure. Look, Jesse, I know you think this guy is some kind of ghost. He's good. I'll give him that, but there's no way he'll be able to get anywhere near the house."

"What about the pipe bombs?"

"At its closest point, the wall around the house is nearly an eighth of a mile away. Tough to hurl a pipe bomb, even a small one, that far. And it's not as if I won't have my people everywhere."

"How about a sniper rifle or an RPG?"

"A rocket-propelled grenade! This isn't Tikrit, Stone. And you're forgetting your own theory. He isn't going to hurt Jenn if you're not there to see it. Up close and personal, isn't that the way he likes to operate? If you're not going to be anywhere near Jenn tomorrow, and we'll make sure you won't be, then she's safe. No, I'm betting on the wedding day. He's going to call you tomorrow and taunt you again. That's what he meant."

"It didn't feel that way, but maybe you're right. And tomorrow, put an extra guy or two on the hotel. Maybe close to Diana. He might be pointing us at Jenn, when it's Diana he's after."

Kahan smiled a not-altogether-smug smile. "I've had people close to her since the day after we met in New York. Nothing's going to happen to either Diana or Jenn on my watch . . . or you, for that matter. What's wrong, Stone? Upset you didn't spot my people?"

"Something like that."

"You're not the only person on earth good at his job. Now go back inside and enjoy your steak. It is amazingly good. We'll have plenty of time until Peepers comes after Jenn. And when he does, it will finally be over."

Jesse walked away from Kahan feeling reassured, but not completely. Something he couldn't quite put his finger on was gnawing at him, but nothing concrete. Every time he thought he had a grasp on what it was, it slipped away. So he headed back to the table, still trying to figure out what was eating at him.

EIGHTY

He awoke to the soft, synthesized sounds of wind chimes dancing in a light breeze. He reached his short left arm across to the nightstand, tapping the sleep button. The second time the gently ringing chimes sounded, they got his full attention, his eyes snapping open. He shut the alarm, slipped on his glasses, checked the time, and swung his pale white legs off the bed. He surrendered to nature, his little body and face distorting as he stretched the sleep out of his muscles and joints. His shoulder ached, as it always did in the morning. He sometimes wondered if the real Jesse Stone's shoulder ached this way in the morning. At the moment his focus was elsewhere, though he was sure Jesse Stone's focus and attention were squarely on him. If they weren't, he was about to make sure Jesse's focus was squarely on him. Hopping out of bed, he smiled at the thought and in anticipation of the kill.

Thirty minutes later, cup of coffee in hand, he went out to the valet on duty, gave the Mexican kid his parking stub and a ten-spot. He said, "Please have my car at the east hotel exit. Leave the keys in the ignition, please." He looked at his watch. "Have it there in precisely twenty minutes. That's at nine-fifteen. If the car is there as I ask, there'll be another ten in it for you."

"Yes, sir. Nine-fifteen," the kid said, throwing his thumb at the east side of the building. "It'll be right there where you ask."

He went back up to his room, blind to the activity in the lobby, blind to the men and women in their athletic gear, heading out to the running trails across the way, blind to the mother struggling with her two-year-old son, whose stomping feet and angry tears were just the first steps toward a full-blown tantrum.

Upstairs, he hung the *Do Not Disturb* sign from the outside door handle, closed the door, clicked the security lock closed, and swung the triangular door latch over the little arm and knob attached to the jamb. He removed the lamp and clock radio from the nightstand, placed them on the bed, and wriggled the nightstand to a spot a few feet behind the French doors that opened onto the room's small balcony. He repeated the steps with the nightstand from the other side of the bed, hefting the second nightstand on its side atop the first one. He swung open the French doors and stepped out onto the balcony. He looked across to the adjoining building, the residential tower of the Park Mansion complex, counted nine floors up and two windows to his left. He looked up to the sky. It was a clear day and there might be some glare off the windows, but not enough to trouble him.

He retrieved his rifle from the black "fishing equipment" case, the magazine and scope from his duffel bag. He affixed the scope to the rifle, threaded his arm through the strap, placed his elbow on the second nightstand, and lined up the shot. He made minor adjustments to the scope. When he was satisfied, he unthreaded his arm from the rifle strap, clicked the magazine into the weapon, and laid it down on the bed. He checked his watch and retrieved yet another one of his many prepaid cell phones. He dialed Jesse Stone's number. It took only two rings for Jesse to pick up.

"Jesse Stone."

"Good morning, Jesse," he said. "Tick, tock. Tick, tock. Wedding bells are almost ready to chime. Consider today a free preview of things coming your way. And when you're contemplating the damage done, remember that it all comes back —"

"Damage? What —"

"It's rude to interrupt. I don't like rudeness. Remember that. And remember that if you had only let things be, neither of us would be here in Vineland Park today. How many people are dead already because you just couldn't let things alone? Tick, tock, Jesse. Tick, tock."

He clicked off, undid the guts of the phone, stomped on it, and dropped it in the toilet. He checked his watch once more, picked up the rifle, and rethreaded his arm through the strap. He lined up the shot again. This wasn't about precision. If he hit her, all the better. If not, it would serve to reinforce his message about minding her manners and to remind her that she would never be free of him. That she would always be his prisoner, tied to that workbench in the old building in West Dallas. In any case, the shot, and the rest of what was about to unfold, was for Jesse Stone's benefit and, in its way, for Jenn. A sort of wedding gift to her. He smiled that smile of his, remembering just how beautiful Jenn had looked as she tried on her wedding gown.

He waited. He knew that he probably wouldn't feel the attaché case explode on the tenth floor. It was meant to be more lightning than thunder anyway, a means to distract and misdirect, not to inflict much damage or do harm. What he knew was that the fire alarm would ring immediately in the wake of the explosion, and that would be his cue. And . . . there it was, the shrill electronic shrieking, the grating chirping, and the announcement from speakers mounted in the hallway to evacuate the building in an orderly fashion using the stairwells only and not the elevators.

He put in his earplugs. He worked the bolt, placing a cartridge into the rifle's chamber, took aim, and just as he moved his trigger finger off the trigger guard and onto the trigger, a silhouette appeared against the curtain in the window across the way. He couldn't believe his good fortune and did not hesitate. The glass shattered across the way and the silhouette was no longer visible. The shot was loud, he knew, and under any other set of circumstances would have attracted unwanted attention. But with the alarm sounding, the announcement repeating, people running for their lives, no one was going to stop to investigate.

By the time anyone did, he would be long gone.

When he climbed down the east exit stairs, the car was where it was supposed to be, but the Mexican kid was nowhere in sight. He snickered because he hadn't meant to give the kid the extra ten bucks, in any case.

EIGHTY-ONE

Although they responded to both immediately, it had taken a while for the Vineland Park PD to connect the explosion in the luggage room at the hotel to the killing at the residential tower across the way. By that time, the little man registered at the Park Mansion Hotel and Spa was gone with the wind. It was Jed Pruitt himself who showed up at Jesse Stone's hotel to fetch him and Diana and bring them to the crime scenes.

"You know the situation?" Pruitt asked, pulling away from the hotel and heading toward the Park Mansion complex.

Jesse said, "We heard the sirens, then Kahan called. Filled us in on what he knew. Told us that Hale's house was pretty much in lockdown mode and that they were prepared to put Jenn in the panic room or to evacuate. But he didn't have all the details on what had happened at the Park Mansion."

"He didn't have all the details because neither did we. Here's how it stands: That guy we met who was guarding Belinda Yankton is dead. A clean headshot through glass and drapes from the tenth floor of the adjoining building. The room the shot came from was registered to — and you're not going to like this part even a little bit — Jesse Stone of Paradise, Massachusetts. I can't say that I much appreciate his sense of humor."

Diana asked, "How's Belinda Yankton?"

"She's safe for the moment. We've moved her to an undisclosed location."

"That's not what I meant, Chief."

Pruitt apologized. "Sorry, Diana, I was thinking like a cop there and not like a human being. She's a wreck, as you might imagine. It took her a few minutes to gather herself to go into the next room after she heard the glass break and the thud. Then a few more minutes to finally call nine-one-one. When we showed up at her address, she refused to let us in. We had to break into the condo and, as Jesse can attest, those front doors of hers were not easy to breach. My people found her barricaded in her bedroom closet, smeared with blood and clutching a Bible. Had to sedate her."

"You've gone wide with this," Jesse said.

Pruitt nodded, but not enthusiastically. "Had to, Jesse. We could play it close, keep it between us, as long as we thought Jenn was the only target and nothing else happened. But this is homicide, a bombing, and you know Homeland Security is going to be up my ass about it being a terrorist attack. The god-danged media's already reporting it as such, though that don't make a lick of sense."

"Was anyone hurt in the bombing?" Diana asked.

"No, ma'am, no one. Apparently, it wasn't much of a bomb, as near as we can tell. A lot of sound and not much fury. At least we can all be thankful for that."

"He didn't want anyone to get hurt or a lot of people would have gotten hurt," Jesse said. "This was all for my benefit." Jesse explained about the phone call he'd gotten from Peepers earlier. "I was set to call you when we heard all the sirens coming from Vineland Park."

"Kahan called last night and told me Peepers had called you at the restaurant, but what could we have done? We had no way of knowing where he'd strike or if he even meant his threats. We couldn't have stopped him. Still likely I'm going to catch hell over this. Probably lose my job."

"The great frustration of law enforcement," Jesse said. "Criminals act. We react."

They pulled up to the curb outside the Park Mansion complex.

Pruitt said, "We can look at the homicide scene later, if you'd like. Really not much to see over there now but the broken glass, the drapes, and bloodstain. I think we should check out the hotel room first. There's stuff in there I think you need to see."

When they entered the hotel they saw a team of cops photographing and sifting through debris from the explosion. Shards of wood from the door that had once kept the luggage room secure as well as scraps of clothing, shreds of leather and plastic suitcases, and bits of metal had been blown out into the lobby.

The tenth floor of the Park Mansion Hotel and Spa was teeming with police, and not all of them from Vineland Park.

"We asked for an assist from the Dallas PD," Pruitt said. "As good as I'd like to think we are, we don't have much expertise with these sorts of crimes. Come on down here." They walked halfway down the hall. "Peepers's room has already been gone through and dusted, but I had them leave a few things for you to see."

The cop at the door nodded to Pruitt and

stepped aside to let the three of them enter.

"You can see he used the nightstands as a shooting platform. If you stand behind it and look slightly to the left, you'll see the window he shot into."

"But you didn't bring us up here to show us this," Diana said.

Pruitt shook his head. "I did not."

"Then what?" Jesse asked.

"We found these in the closet." Pruitt handed over three evidence bags to Jesse. "They're schematics for the electrical, plumbing, heating, and cooling systems of the Vineland Park Country Club. "He's a thorough son of a bitch. Gotta give him that."

Jesse didn't like it. Thorough people aren't usually sloppy, and leaving those schematics behind was sloppy.

"What's wrong, Jesse?" Diana asked.

"I'm not sure."

Pruitt yanked the cell phone off his belt and excused himself. He didn't look pleased when he came back into the room.

"They just found his rental ditched about three miles north of here," Pruitt said.

Jesse made a face. "What was it, a Honda Civic?"

"No, as a matter of fact, it was a blue Maserati. Guess he wanted to seem like he belonged here."

Jesse stared at Diana and they seemed to have the same thought at the same time.

Diana said, "Something's not right."

"Very not right," Jesse agreed.

Pruitt was dumbfounded. "I'd say. The man just set a pipe bomb off in a hotel lobby and murdered a man he never met through a window."

That wasn't what they meant, but neither Jesse nor Diana wanted to argue or explain.

Jesse said, "Can you have someone take us over to Hunsicker's place?"

Pruitt made a face. "Sure, but don't you want to see —"

Jesse shook his head. "We need to get over there, Jed."

Diana reached her arm out and placed it on Pruitt's shoulder. "As soon as possible, Chief."

"Look, you two. I'm not having anybody do anything until you explain what the rush is all about."

Jesse and Diana looked at each other again, but it was Jesse who spoke. "He played us. I don't think Jenn's his target, at least not anymore."

Pruitt understood without any further explanation.

"Officer Moore," the chief said to the cop

guarding the door, "take these folks over to the Hunsicker house, and do it now." He turned back to Jesse and Diana, shook their hands. "I'll call ahead for you. Be safe."

They left without another word.

EIGHTY-TWO

The pilot got on the intercom and told them to buckle up. That they were beginning their descent and would be on the ground at Logan in less than twenty minutes. If the situation wasn't what it was, Jesse thought, he could get used to private jet travel. Hale Hunsicker's Gulfstream G280, complete with flight attendant, had been waiting for them when Ari dropped them off at Love Field. Suzanne, the flight attendant, came out of the galley of the aircraft and asked them if there was anything else she could get for them before they landed. Jesse waved her off and smiled. Diana, too. She nodded at them and went back to securing things in the galley.

Jesse, who'd been pacing, sat back down in his seat. He had his stoic game face on, but Diana knew there was a lot going on inside him. He wasn't a man to show his weaknesses or worries. He didn't make elaborate gestures or make public displays of affection, and he was a man of his word, but he was more complicated than the parts of him he showed to the world. He showed them to her and that was enough.

"Listen, Jesse," she said, "we both got caught up in things back in Dallas. No one here knows you asked me to marry you and the way it all happened with me blurting it out just because I was with Jenn and . . ." Her voice drifted off. "I mean that if —"

"You don't have to explain. Same is true for you. You gave a great speech back in Dallas about how we'll make it work, but I know a life in Paradise isn't what you want. If you want to change your mind, that's okay. That won't change what I feel about you."

She looked gut-punched. "I don't want to change my mind. You?"

Jesse shook his head.

Diana smiled at him. Jesse smiled back at her. The smile didn't remain on Jesse's face for more than a few more seconds, because he and Diana had made some hard choices over the last several hours, choices that might determine their own fates and the fates of the most important people in Jesse's life. Both of them had taken big risks before, with their careers, their lives, and others people's futures, but never the lives of others to whom they were so closely attached. The easiest choice was to leave Dallas and skip the wedding. Although much of their time there had been less strained than they had anticipated, had even been fun on occasion, neither of them had really wanted to be there in the first place.

"I've never been much of a believer in fate, but now I'm not so sure," Diana said after a minute of quiet between them.

Although leaving Dallas to get back to Paradise was the obvious choice for them to make, it hadn't gone down well with Hunsicker.

"You can't be serious. Jenn'll skin me alive if you're not there tomorrow. She's really counting on you both being there. Frankly, I can't believe I'm saying this, but I think she wants Diana there as much as you. There's some weird bond they have that has to do with you."

"At least you know she'll be safe, Hale," Jesse said. "And you can't tell her. Everyone has to think we'll be there at the country club. If this goes the way we hope, Mr. Peepers will never trouble anyone again. We all want that. You've seen the damage he's done and what he's capable of."

Kahan had been the easiest to convince.

He immediately understood the intentions behind what Peepers had been up to and had even offered to send some of his people with Jesse and Diana back to Paradise.

"Look, at least take Ari with you. He's got experience at this sort of thing. He's the best man I've got."

"I appreciate the offer, Scott," Jesse said, shaking Kahan's hand, "but we can't afford to send out the wrong signals, especially if Peepers has a plant at the wedding. And we can't have people showing up in Paradise who don't belong or fit in. The risk is too big. Peepers has to believe we still think he's coming after Jenn. And I can't chance you weakening things here if I'm wrong about this and he really is coming for Jenn."

"Okay, but I'll have a car waiting for you at Logan and it'll drop you off wherever you want in Paradise."

The hardest decision they had to make was keeping things quiet and not letting Molly, Suit, and Healy in on what they thought was going on. His reasoning was much the same as it was for rejecting Kahan's offer of help.

"It's okay if Peepers is aware the cops and everyone else is looking for him in Dallas. He expects that. He wants that. The more focus on Dallas, the better. But we can't give him an inkling that we know where he's really headed."

Diana played devil's advocate. "If we let word get to the media and warn everyone in Paradise, we might be able to buy some time and prepare for when he resurfaces. I can probably get an old pal at the Bureau to set up a task force focused exclusively on him. After the bombing and the sniper stuff he pulled today, I can probably get him a terrorist designation, and you know how the government is about terror suspects."

"You know that won't work. If he slips away from us now, we'll never see him coming the next time. He won't be sending me photos or making goading phone calls to me next time. He'll come at us the way he came at Gino Fish. And even if we all built fortresses around us, he'd win eventually. No, Di, now is our chance and we better take it. We won't get another."

But all of those decisions were easy for Jesse compared to his decision to tell Diana the truth about what he thought was going on. His first impulse had been to lie to her, that he should do anything to protect her, to keep her in Dallas, far away from where he thought the confrontation with Peepers would go down. He was old-fashioned that way. He had always watched out for Jenn and he had always been more comfortable with Molly in the cop house with him than on the streets. But first with Sunny Randall and up to now with Diana, he had treated them as super-competent equals. The thing is, the minute he asked Diana to marry him, that all changed. Maybe it shouldn't have. Maybe it wasn't right. Maybe that made him a relic, but he couldn't deny his feelings. Still, when the time came for them to discuss their reactions to what Peepers had done at the Park Mansion, Jesse found the truth coming out of his mouth.

The pilot got back on the intercom one last time to tell the flight attendant to buckle up and prepare for landing. Diana reached for Jesse's hand and squeezed it. He turned and smiled at her, then looked out the cabin window at the night sky and the welcoming lights of Boston. He couldn't help but wonder what they were being welcomed home to.

Eighty-Three

It was cool out for September, the wind whipping in off the Atlantic right into the heart of Paradise. Quite a change from the Dallas heat. Though it was too dark to see the color of the leaves, Jesse knew they had already turned more yellow and red than they had been only in the hundred hours since he and Diana had gotten in the car to Logan. The limbs of the trees seemed to have sagged some, turned down like lips kissed by a lover for the last time. There were signs of surrender in them, an acknowledgment that there was yet another fall and winter to come that they were helpless to stop.

Jesse turned up the collar of his jacket against the wind, collecting himself as he prepared to climb the fence at the edge of the small woods that bordered the Cranes' property. He was convinced now more than ever he needed to move back into town.

That it had taken a dangerous amount of time, too much time, to collect what he needed at his house and to sneak back into town. He had looked at the *For Sale* sign in front of his house and wondered if there had been any more bites. If not, he'd lower the price. Like always, he'd do what he had to do.

Suddenly, a whole list of "have-to-dos" rushed into his head. He had to replace his old trusty, now bullet-ridden, Explorer. *With what?* he wondered. But it was the house sale that came back to him. Diana would want to be at the center of things. Paradise wasn't exactly Boston. Not even close, but he knew she needed some sense of action to keep happy, and whatever action there was in Paradise wasn't out where his house was now. He had been alone long enough. In a bizarre way, he guessed he owed a debt of his own to Peepers for the circumstances that had pushed him over the edge to commit to marriage. But he couldn't smile about it. Too much blood had been spilled and too many lives lost in the name of a stupid vendetta.

Then he remembered his last at bat in that softball game back in August that had seemed to start all of this. Remembered the news about Gino Fish. Remembered hearing about the murders in Salem, the dog's in particular. And that reminded him of who he was dealing with and why it had to come to an end, sooner rather than later. And that snapped him out of his own head and right into the moment. He knew exactly why he was there at the edge of Molly's property in the dark. He stopped thinking of what had been and what might be. He boosted himself up and over the fence.

During the flight, he and Diana had agreed to split up so that they could cover Peepers's most likely targets. Jesse made sure to put Diana on Peepers's least likely target: Healy. Healy hadn't been directly involved with the original incident, the one in which Suit was nearly killed and had wounded Peepers in the exchange of gunfire. But if Peepers was paying attention — Jesse and Diana had no doubt that he had been — then he would know how close Jesse and Healy were and now just how vulnerable Healy was because of retirement and his wife's bad heart. Diana wasn't oblivious to Jesse's impulse to protect her. She didn't like it, but it was hard for her to argue with Jesse's rationale for his looking after Molly and Suit.

"I know Paradise," he said. "I know how to approach their houses unseen from places not even Peepers would be aware of. You don't know Paradise at all, not really. Besides, Suit and Molly are my cops, my responsibility. If you're with Healy, then you'll both have each other's backs and we won't be presenting Peepers with even more incentive. You and Molly or you and Suit together would provide too good a target for Peepers. Remember, in some ways it's about making me suffer. And with you and Healy together, I won't be distracted worrying about the both of you."

Over the fence, Jesse lay flat on his belly, watching, listening for anything out of the ordinary. If Peepers was already inside, there would be obvious signs. He would gather everyone in the house into one room or the basement. That was if he hadn't already hurt Molly's girls and her husband. Jesse's guts churned at the thought of that, of Peepers torturing Molly's girls in front of their parents. But Jesse pushed those thoughts down, way down. He'd never be able to do what he'd have to do if he let his head go there. He would be lost if he let his imagination control him or if he now started questioning all the decisions he'd made over the last twenty-four hours or over the last six weeks. No, he had to focus on the present, on what was happening in real time.

He'd already been to Suit's house and done a quick check. Nothing was happening there. Suit's family had all relocated and Suit was on patrol until eight in the morning. The way Jesse figured it, Suit was probably safe, at least until the end of his shift. By then, he would have Suit covered, and when the time came, he'd go back over to his house. He might also call Suit, maybe give him a heads-up, or have him come by Molly's house. He'd worry about that when the time came.

Molly was moving around the kitchen. Two lights were on in upstairs bedrooms. Shadows moving, TVs on. That was all to the good. No way this much activity would be going on in the house if Peepers were present. Still, Jesse had to be careful not to assume Peepers wasn't close by, doing exactly what Jesse was doing. Watching. Waiting. Looking for a weakness, an opening. He meant to stay here, to watch the house all night if need be, but he was determined that there had already been enough blood. It had to stop here. Now.

EIGHTY-FOUR

His body ached something fierce, but it had been worth it. He had kept his position in the Cranes' backyard until all the lights had gone off in the house and then given it another hour. At that point, when he was sure Molly and her family were all asleep, he checked the perimeter of the house by going back over the fence and making wide circles of the area on foot. Each circle a little bit closer in to the Crane house than the previous one. If Peepers was here, he was even better than everyone assumed he was. He would have to have been a ghost.

As Jesse had walked his tightening circles, he had been careful not to make assumptions that would get people killed. Peepers obviously had skills other than torture and invisibility. The way he'd murdered Gino Fish's receptionist said he was good with a knife. The way he'd killed the old woman, the cabbie, and the dog in Salem said he was great and accurate with a handgun at close range. That he had made a successful head shot through draperies at a few hundred yards said he was good with a rifle. He could also manage to build a working explosive device. So as he walked those circles, Jesse checked up trees and under cars, searched for cases and packages, anything that didn't seem to belong. He took no comfort when he came up empty.

After he watched Molly's husband leave for work, waiting for her to put her girls on the school bus, Jesse returned to her backyard. It was a day off for her. He hadn't risked approaching her when her family was home and he could not approach through the front door. There was always the chance that Peepers was watching. Even when he was certain the house was empty, Jesse didn't approach her back door directly, either. Instead, he threw pebbles at her kitchen window and back door windows from the cover of the side of the shed. Molly, an annoyed scowl on her face, flung the door open and stepped out onto the small back deck.

"Okay, wiseass, who's —"

"I'm the wiseass," Jesse said in a voice not much above a whisper, "and I'm over by the shed. Come over here and pretend to fuss with the bushes."

The scowl left her face as she seemed to immediately understand the situation. She stepped off the small deck, opened the shed door, got out some pruning shears, and snipped away at a few leaves.

"Is he here?" she asked, fear in her usually steady voice.

"In Paradise, yes. But I don't think he's near here, at least not yet. I've been watching your house since last night."

"Where, then? He can't hurt my kids, Jesse. What if —"

"Stop it, Molly. Don't go there."

"But how and why are you even here?"

He did a brief rundown of what had transpired over the last twenty-four hours. As he spoke, Molly's hands began to shake and her pruning became angry and erratic. It was clear to Jesse that Molly could think of nothing else but the danger to her kids. And once again, he felt that sense of relief at never having had kids.

"Who's on the desk this morning?" Jesse asked.

"Alisha."

"When we're done here, call her and tell her to put Gabe on patrol at your girls' school. Don't have him sit on the school. Have him circle."

"Thanks, Jesse."

"I don't think he'll go after your family, but I can't have you worry too much."

"So what's the plan?"

As Jesse opened his mouth, the phone rang in the house. Molly didn't move to answer it.

"Go get that, Molly. Don't do anything out of the ordinary. Just put the shears down and answer. Maybe it has something to do with Peepers."

Molly came back out onto the deck a few minutes later, her face white. Her expression screamed to Jesse. He shot out from behind the shed and ran to her.

"What is it?"

She didn't answer him, but kept staring off into the distance. Jesse took her by the biceps and shook her. As he did, he repeated the question. Then, "Is it your kids? Your hus—"

"Suit," she said.

"What about Suit?"

"He hasn't come back in off patrol and he won't answer his radio."

"Fuck!"

"Alisha has the guys out looking for his car."

"Did they check his house?" Jesse asked, even as he pulled his cell from his pocket.

"He's not there." Molly's voice was near cracking. Suddenly, something like a smile came across her lips.

"What is it?"

"I think I know where he might be." The smile disappeared. "Oh, no. Oh, shi—"

"What?"

"While you were gone, Suit got engaged."

"Engaged?"

"To Elena Wheatley. She used to teach at the high school before you came to town. She moved back to Paradise a few months ago when her mom passed. Suit reconnected with her and they've been quietly seeing each other since. He wanted to tell you about it himself when you got back because he wants you to be best man."

"Get dressed and go to the station. Alisha is good, but she's not ready to handle what you can handle."

"Should I call the staties and get everyone over there?"

"No! I don't want a cruiser or another cop within a half-mile of that house. I'll handle this. What's Elena's address?"

"But —"

"No, Molly. That's an order. This is on me. You just be ready if I need you."

"Should I drive you over there?"

Jesse shook his head. "It'll be almost as

fast if I cut through the woods. Besides, I don't want you anywhere near Peepers or that house."

He turned and walked to the back fence.

"Jesse," Molly said, calling after him, "be safe. I can't lose you."

He smiled at her but didn't say a word.

EIGHTY-FIVE

Jesse came upon Elena Wheatley's house much as he had Molly's, from behind. But unlike Molly's house, there were no woods to cover his approach nor much of a real fence. Only a three-foot-high stone wall separated the rear of Elena's lot from the rear of her backyard neighbor's lot. He surveyed the house as he crept slowly along the side wall of the neighbor's house. Nothing about the back of the house gave anything away. Like many houses in Paradise, Elena Wheatley's had a small one-car garage tucked behind the house, and it was only when Jesse climbed over the low stone wall and took a look through the dingy garage window that his worst fears were realized. His guts twisted up at the sight of Suit's cruiser.

Leaning against the side of the garage, Jesse sent a text message. Then he put his phone away and collected his thoughts. If he had been a praying man, this would have been the time to get to it. But Jesse knew that this was it, and one way or the other, Peepers was never going to have another chance to spread his brand of terror and fear. Somehow Jesse had known that when the final confrontation came, it would be on Peepers's terms and that it would be between the two of them. That all of Kahan's and Healy's machinations wouldn't be enough. He took one last deep breath, racked the slide of his nine-millimeter, and walked up onto the square patch of concrete at the back door to Elena Wheatley's house.

He found the three of them tucked cozily in the little den just beyond the front vestibule. Suit, naked from the waist up, was lying on his left side on the floor. His arms were behind him, wrists cuffed with his own cuffs, his feet bound together with duct tape, nylon rope binding his taped ankles to the handcuffs. He was semiconscious, his face a swollen, bruised mess, and there was a small bullet wound to his right shoulder. It was bleeding, though not profusely. But it was Elena Wheatley's situation that startled Jesse.

She was dressed only in a beige sports bra and white cotton panties. There were tear stains on her face, but no tears. She had cried herself out. Although she was shaking with fear, her face was impassive, as she had apparently retreated into herself. She was on her knees in front of a fussy old couch, an assault knife in front of her, a ring of duct tape around her neck, which was attached to the barrel of Suit's pump-action shotgun. And there seated on the couch, holding the butt end of the shotgun, was Peepers, his pale white little fingers close to the trigger.

"Hello, Jesse Stone, it's been a while," he said, a smile in his nasally, high-pitched voice. "I knew you'd figure it out in the end. I would never hurt Jenn."

"That's what Belinda Yankton told me. She said she thought you were fond of Jenn."

"Very fond. How is my rude blonde these days?"

"How do you think?"

"Well behaved and properly mannered, I expect."

Jesse held his nine-millimeter up and began to kneel in order to place it on the floor.

"Oh, no, Chief, don't do that," Peepers said, a smug smile now on his face and in his voice. "You'll be needing your weapon very shortly."

"Why's that?"

Peepers's smile broadened. "You know better than to ask a praying mantis why. It's quite simple, really. You're going to kill that imbecile officer of yours by rolling him onto his back and shooting him in the liver. I missed his liver last time, but you won't miss it, Jesse, not from this range," he said, kicking Suit's wounded shoulder. Suit groaned in pain. "Then you're going to slit your own throat with that knife there in front of our mousy little hostess."

"No, I'm not."

"Then I hope you have a dry cleaner who is good at removing blood, skull, brain, and hair from clothing, because you'll be wearing a lot of this woman's head in a few seconds."

Jesse lied. "The house is surrounded. You won't get twenty feet."

Peepers removed his glasses with his free hand and patted his eyes dry against the sleeve of his blue polyester sport jacket. He replaced the glasses, and when he did, the smiles had vanished from both his face and voice.

"You will be beyond worrying about my exit, and please don't treat me like a fool, Jesse. It's beneath the both of us. You know there's a debt to pay. I'm here to both pay mine and collect yours. Get on with it."

"Let her go."

"I will, but only after we've settled accounts. I imagine you know exactly where the liver is, Jesse. And please, no more talking. I give you my word that I will release the woman after you do what you must. One more thing, don't even attempt to swing that sidearm my way," he said, pulling a .22 out of his jacket pocket and aiming it at Jesse. "She'll be dead before you can fire and so will you."

"Let them go and I'll do what you ask."

Peepers was laughing a twisted laugh. "Bargaining. They always bargain. I usually enjoy this part of things, when they try to trade things as if they had any control of things anymore, as if they had anything at all to trade. But not today, Jesse, no bargaining today. I love the begging as well. I really love the begging. Again, not today. The bill is the bill and it must be paid in full. Now do it." Peepers yanked on the shotgun. Elena gasped. Peepers raised the .22. "Now!"

"Sorry, Suit," Jesse said, rolling his friend onto his back, "I'm really sorry."

Suit nodded. "Do it," he slurred. "Just save her." Then he squeezed his eyes tightly shut.

As Jesse was about to fire, he heard footsteps behind him. He fired into the floor next to Suit. That got Peepers's attention just long enough. Jesse turned to see if the wild card he had played was enough to win the hand. But when he saw who it was and caught the look on Peepers's face, he knew it had all gone wrong.

Eighty-Six

Peepers did not hesitate. With amazing speed, he wacked Elena in the back of the head with his .22 and shoved the shotgun forward. As Elena fell unconscious, face-first into the carpet, Peepers swung the .22 up toward Jesse's right side and fired. And in that briefest of seconds between the muzzle flash and explosion, Jesse dived to his right to try to catch the bullet with his body. As he dived he prayed. He bargained, too. He prayed for the bullet to hit him, to hit him anywhere, as long as it didn't make it past him. Dying was the least of his fears. As he fell, there was a second shot, and a third, louder shot. Then the front door flung open and Vinnie Morris, Jesse's ace card, came into the den. It was already too late.

Jesse thumped to the floor, unwounded, waiting. And there it was, the thing he had prayed so mightily against, the thing he had bargained silently to prevent: a second thud.

He rolled over, sick with fear and regret at what he knew he would find. There was Diana Evans, a red dot above the bridge of her nose and blood on her blouse above her heart, dead on the floor behind him. Healy stood behind her, in his hand an old Smith & Wesson .38, smoke drifting up out of its barrel.

Peepers was screaming. Jesse turned to look at him, and when he did, Peepers smiled at him through the pain. The little man's lower abdomen was covered in blood.

"Let me have him, Jesse," Vinnie Morris said. "For Gino and for you, let me have him."

Jesse looked up at Healy and over to Suit, who was wriggling his body to get close to Elena. Both men nodded yes as the wail of sirens imposed themselves into the conversation.

"Out the back," Jesse said.

And with that, Vinnie Morris slammed his fist into Peepers's face. He gathered the man's lapels in one hand and dragged him up to his feet. They were out the back door a full twenty seconds before Molly, Peter Perkins, and Gabe Weathers came barreling into the house. When they got there, Healy was cutting the tape off Elena Wheatley's neck and checking to make sure the cut on the back of her head wasn't severe. Suit had managed to get close enough to her to lay his head on her thigh. And Jesse was cradling Diana in his arms.

EIGHTY-SEVEN

They had each told roughly the same story to the state investigators. Peepers had an accomplice who came bursting into the house just after the shots had been fired. He grabbed Peepers, knocked Healy over, and exited through the back door. They didn't get a good look at the accomplice and had no idea where he'd taken Peepers. Elena, who suffered a severe concussion, had no light to shed on any of the events of that morning or the day before. There was a small blessing in that.

None of it seemed to matter much to Jesse, who had been AWOL since receiving Diana's autopsy results. He'd buried himself in his house, blaming himself and drinking himself into a stupor. Whenever he would come out of it, he would beat himself up again for neglecting to order Molly not to share information with Healy or Diana. So when Healy, impatient for news, called

Molly that morning, she told him about Suit's engagement and their assumption that Peepers had gone to Elena Wheatley's house. It didn't help Jesse's state of mind that Diana's father had made it clear he didn't want Jesse anywhere near Diana's funeral. What did it matter? She was dead because of him and there was no getting over that.

Tamara Elkin had come to the station to try to comfort Jesse and to enlist Molly's help.

They were discussing how to approach Jesse when he came out of his office. He smiled at seeing Tamara. It was a sad smile, the saddest smile she thought she had ever seen or was likely to see. Then again, most people don't smile at the medical examiner. The ME seldom has the kind of news anyone is apt to smile about. She had handed Jesse the autopsy file, but without the photographs. She knew that not even Jesse Stone, the toughest man she had ever met, would be able to forget those photos. Still, she knew Jesse would want to see the report for himself. Molly and Tamara sat by helplessly as Jesse read the results.

"Did she feel it, do you think?" he asked, putting the folder down.

Tamara shook her head. "No, Jesse, death

would have been pretty much instantaneous."

"But she knew. There had to be a split second when she knew."

Tamara stood up and came to stand by him. She placed her hand on his shoulder.

"I don't know that, Jesse. No one knows the answer to that."

"I don't like thinking that she knew or that she felt pain."

"Jesse, please don't —"

There were no tears in his eyes, but he looked as shaken as Molly had ever seen him. "Do you think she felt pain?"

Tamara pointed to a line in the report. "I can't answer that, Jesse. It's very possible she didn't. If she did, it didn't last long."

Jesse handed the folder back to her. Molly nodded at Tamara to go, to give Jesse time to process things in his own way. Tamara understood.

"If you need me, Jesse, I'm a phone call away," she said.

Jesse went back into his office and finished the bottle of Tullamore Dew he had bought to celebrate Healy's retirement. He hadn't been back in since Gabe Weathers drove him home that night. Jenn, Hale Hunsicker, Jed Pruitt, and Scott Kahan had all called and left messages. Many messages. Jesse ignored them all.

There was a knock on his door. He was in between bouts with himself and in the mood for a real fight, so he answered the door, hoping someone would give him an excuse to throw a punch. But it was Vinnie Morris, dressed as always in a few thousand dollars' worth of designer clothing. He had a bottle of Black Label in one hand and a large brown envelope in the other.

Vinnie nodded. "Stone."

"Morris."

"All right if I come in?"

Jesse didn't answer. He walked away from the open door and headed toward the bar in his den. Vinnie closed the door behind him and followed Jesse in, noticing the house was in disarray. Vinnie liked things smooth and orderly, neat and clean, but he understood.

"I heard you aren't doing so good," he said. "I can see for myself that's true."

Jesse ignored him. "What's that?" he asked, pointing at Morris.

"You don't recognize a bottle of Johnnie Walker Black, you're worse off than I heard."

"Stop it, Vinnie. The envelope. What's in the envelope?"

A thin smile rose at one corner of Morris's lips.

"Proof of death," Vinnie said, tossing the envelope at Jesse's feet. "Thought you might want to see how badly Peepers suffered on his way to hell. Though I gotta say, the photos don't do it justice. I woulda made a video for you, but I think you understand why I didn't."

Jesse knelt down and collected the envelope. "He's dead?"

"Never seen anybody deader or suffer more on the way to dead."

"Thanks for that. I owe you."

"No, you don't. The accounts are closed." Vinnie put the bottle down on the coffee table. "See you around, Stone."

When Jesse heard Vinnie close the door behind him, he went to open the envelope but stopped himself. He decided there was nothing in the envelope he wanted to see if it couldn't change the past. And there was nothing he'd ever seen or known that could turn that trick. Diana was gone, and Peepers, too. Nothing would undo that. Morris had said the accounts were closed, but he was wrong. There was a balance to be paid and Jesse would be paying it off for the rest of his life.

Jesse twisted off the cap and drank straight

from the bottle of Black Label Vinnie Morris had left behind. He looked at the envelope with the death photos of Peepers, shook his head, and laughed. He tossed the unopened envelope into the fireplace, threw a few logs on top of it, and put a long match to it. He sat in his recliner, drinking, watching it burn until there was nothing left — no fire, no envelope, no smoke, only ashes. He stood up and turned to the long-neglected poster of Ozzie Smith. Jesse raised the bottle and drank a giant gulp in a single swallow. After a short period of real possibility, it was back to being just the two of them: the great short-stop and the police chief. One frozen in midair, the other now just frozen.

ACKNOWLEDGMENTS

I owe a huge debt of gratitude to Chris Pepe, Ivan Held, David Hale Smith, and the Estate of Robert B. Parker. I also want to acknowledge the passing of Bob Parker's longtime agent, Helen Brann, to whom this novel is dedicated. None of this would have been possible without Mr. Parker's creation, Jesse Stone. Thanks, guys. A big shoutout to Katie Mckee.

Thanks to Ace Atkins and Tom Schreck.

As always, my deepest love and appreciation go to Rosanne, Kaitlin, and Dylan. Without them, none of this would have meaning or be worth it.

ABOUT THE AUTHOR

Reed Farrel Coleman has been called a "hard-boiled poet" by NPR's Maureen Corrigan and the "noir poet laureate" in *The Huffington Post*. He has published twenty-three novels, including nine books in the critically acclaimed Moe Prager series, and most recently, *Where It Hurts*. He is a three-time recipient of the Shamus Award for Best Detective Novel of the Year, a winner of the Barry and Anthony Awards, and is a two-time Edgar Award nominee. Coleman lives with his family on Long Island.

The employees of Thorndike Press hope you have enjoyed this Large Print book. All our Thorndike, Wheeler, and Kennebec Large Print titles are designed for easy reading, and all our books are made to last. Other Thorndike Press Large Print books are available at your library, through selected bookstores, or directly from us.

For information about titles, please call:
  (800) 223-1244

or visit our Web site at:
  http://gale.cengage.com/thorndike

To share your comments, please write:
Publisher
Thorndike Press
10 Water St., Suite 310
Waterville, ME 04901